The Silence
of the Llamas

Meet the Black Sheep Knitters

Maggie Messina, owner of the Black Sheep Knitting Shop, is a retired high school art teacher who runs her little slice of knitters' paradise with the kind of vibrant energy that leaves her friends dazzled! From novice to pro, knitters come to Maggie as much for her up-to-the-minute offerings like organic wool as for her encouragement and friendship. And Maggie's got a deft touch when it comes to unraveling mysteries, too.

Lucy Binger left Boston when her marriage ended, and found herself shifting gears to run her graphic design business from the coastal cottage she and her sister inherited. After big-city living, she now finds contentment on a front porch in tiny Plum Harbor, knitting with her closest friends.

Dana Haeger is a psychologist with a busy local practice. A stylishly polished professional with a quick wit, she slips out to Maggie's shop whenever her schedule allows—after all, knitting is the best form of therapy!

Suzanne Cavanaugh is a typical working supermom—a realtor with a million demands on her time, from coaching soccer to showing houses to attending the PTA. But she carves out a little "me" time with the Black Sheep Knitters.

Phoebe Meyers, a college gal complete with magenta highlights and nose stud, lives in the apartment above Maggie's shop. She's Maggie's indispensable helper (when she's not in class)—and part of the new generation of young knitters.

The Silence of the Llamas

Anne Canadeo

Gallery Books

New York   London   Toronto   Sydney   New Delhi

GALLERY BOOKS
A Division of Simon & Schuster, Inc.
1230 Avenue of the Americas
New York, NY 10020

Copyright © 2013 by Anne Canadeo

ISBN 978–1–62490-013-6

Manufactured in the United States of America

Good fences make good neighbors.

—ROBERT FROST

A story is told as much by silence as by speech.

—SUSAN GRIFFIN

ACKNOWLEDGMENTS

I would like to thank Paige Gaffett for the helpful information about the production of handmade yarns and exotic fibers. I can't imagine a more beautiful, or unspoiled, location for such an enterprise than Northern Light Fibers, LLC, located on Abrams Farm, Block Island, Rhode Island, where I researched this book. You can visit Northern Lights on the web at: www.northlightfibers.com to learn more about their handmade products and classes.

I'd also like to thank some good friends for donating recipes: Linda Bryce Sheldon, health coach and nutritionist, who passed along instructions for Carrot Muffins with Applesauce, and Reverend Mark Bigelow for the Perfect Pie Crust recipe. I have personally tested both and the outcomes were delicious. (Yes, all this research is tough work. But somebody has to do it.)

Chapter One

*J*ust this last stop . . . please?" Suzanne reached over the driver's seat and grabbed Lucy's shoulder, nearly causing her to veer into a field of pick-your-own pumpkins.

"Suzanne, calm down—"

"But they're gigantic. You never see pumpkins that big at the supermarket."

"We've already bought enough stuff to open our own supermarket." Dana sat beside Lucy in front and suddenly turned to look back at Suzanne—as if they were two parents, calming a child on a long car ride, Lucy thought. "You're a shopaholic on a farm stand binge today, Suzanne. One more stop and we'll definitely be enabling."

Dana's diagnosis was in jest, of course, though a PhD did qualify her to offer the opinion.

And it was true. Lucy could barely see through the Jeep's rear window. The cargo space overflowed with autumn's bounty—huge pots of mums, kale plants, and enough cornstalks to decorate every house on Suzanne's block. A pile of pumpkins, bushels of apples and vegetables, jars of apple butter, and containers of cider filled the cargo area, along with a homemade pie, balanced on Suzanne's lap.

"Thanks, Dana." Suzanne's tone was grumpy. "Joy sucker."

Lucy laughed. "Sorry, pal. She's right . . . and we're already way late."

Suzanne seemed to have forgotten that their leisurely drive through the country had a definite destination: a fiber festival at the Laughing Llama Farm.

Suzanne sat back and sighed. "Fine. We don't want to keep the llamas waiting."

"Never mind the llamas. What about Maggie? I'm surprised she didn't call yet to track us down." Dana checked her phone, then glanced at Lucy.

"She's probably too busy. Luckily."

"I hope we don't miss her spinning. Then we'll really be in trouble." Lucy couldn't tell if Dana was kidding or truly worried.

Lucy thought Maggie might wonder where they were but wouldn't really be upset if they missed her performance. They had all seen her spin dozens of times at the knitting shop she ran in the village.

Lucy, Dana, and Suzanne, along with Maggie and her assistant, Phoebe, met officially every Thursday night to stitch, chat, and unwind—either at the Black Sheep Knitting Shop, which Maggie owned, or at one of their houses. Their meeting time was a sanctuary, carved into busy schedules, a time to share their triumphs and challenges, in knitting as well as real life. Though sometimes it was hard to tell where one realm left off and the other started.

Dana had been looking out the passenger side window and suddenly turned to Lucy. "The farm should be coming up on the right, a few miles more."

Lucy had never been out to the farm before, though Dana had come out several times to see her old college friend Ellie Krueger, who had bought the property with her husband, Ben. Suzanne was familiar with the place, too, since she was in real-estate sales and the farm had been on the market a while.

Ellie and Ben had recently moved to Plum Harbor from Boston, trading in their urban lives for a new start in the idyllic countryside. They had taken over the farm in July, but the festival was their grand opening event. Dana had quickly introduced Ellie to the Black Sheep Knitting Shop and its inner circle.

Ellie had even come to a few knitting group meetings over the past few months, though starting up her business and living some distance out of town kept her from being a regular member.

Dana and Ellie had lost touch over the years but had reconnected on Facebook. When Ellie had come out to visit the previous spring, she and her husband fell in love with Plum Harbor and the farming community just beyond the village center. She and Ben had been talking about relocating to the country and starting some sort of home-based business. Ellie had run a successful public relations firm for years and recently had sold the company for a good price. She was more than ready to turn a page in her life and start a whole new chapter.

Combining Ellie's love of knitting and spinning with Ben's

entrepreneurial experience, they'd decided to look for a small farm where they could keep a llama herd and profit from the sale of the animals' coats and from Ellie's hand-spun yarns. This farm was perfectly suited to their plan, and a moneymaking apple orchard on the property made it even more attractive.

Ellie was a skilled knitter, but spinning was her true passion. She had also begun to give spinning and weaving lessons in a little extra building near the barn that she'd set up as a studio and shop. Yarns spun from exotic fibers were a booming market, sought after by discerning knitting shops and knitters. Maggie already featured Laughing Llama yarns at her shop.

Starting a llama farm had to sound like an odd choice to some people. But to dedicated knitters, like Lucy and her friends, it seemed an enviable lifestyle—being your own boss, living in such beautiful surroundings, and following your fiber bliss.

"There's a sign for the festival: 'Follow the Laughing Llama for a day of country fun.'" Lucy read aloud.

"Very cute. Ellie has a knack for marketing," Suzanne observed.

Ellie was definitely a good businesswoman, very creative and resourceful, Lucy thought. Lucy had visited a few fiber fairs since taking up knitting. Most were pleasant but low-key affairs, though this one promised to be a very lively afternoon.

Dana turned to face Suzanne. "Ellie's PR firm used to handle some big clients. Advertising the farm is a no-brainer for her. She took a full page in the *Plum Harbor Times*." Dana took a page of newspaper out from her pocket and read aloud. "'Laughing Llama Farm—Grand Opening Fiber Festival. Come out to the country for a day of family fun. Llamas, alpaca, and angora rabbits on display. Watch sheepherding, shearing, and spinning. Handmade yarns and rovings for sale in our old-fashioned Country Store. Activities for children, and much more.'" Dana finished reading and turned to Lucy. "I bet there's a crowd. Ellie rarely does things halfway. She's always been like that."

"She's got a lot going on. Do they keep all those animals?" Lucy asked.

Dana folded the newspaper and put it aside. "Only the llamas. The others are borrowed for the day."

"Phoebe must be in her glory. She might decide to leave the shop and ask Ellie for a job," Suzanne said.

Maggie's assistant, Phoebe Meyers, did love animals. But Lucy couldn't imagine her leaving the knitting shop, even for a herd of llamas. A part-time college student, Phoebe lived above the store and worked odd hours as Maggie's assistant between classes . . . and between chasing her boyfriend Josh's band around in her second, unofficial job as their road manager.

"I think she enjoys petting them but wouldn't be wild about mucking out barns," Dana replied. "She's probably just relieved that Maggie didn't ask her stay in town and keep the shop open on her own."

Lucy laughed at that scenario. "Maggie is too nice a boss to ever do that . . . and we all know Phoebe would have pouted for a month." A knot of cars up ahead suddenly slowed, and Lucy hit the brakes. "I think we made it. This looks like the line to get in."

As the Jeep crawled along, Lucy relaxed and stared out at the dark brown plowed fields, rolling meadows, and patches of woods in between. The trees were just starting to show color and shed a few leaves. Low walls built of flat gray stones bordered the road and separated properties, a typical sight in this part of New England.

The Kruegers' farm came up on the right side of the road. Lucy saw a wide, rolling meadow covered by high brown grass. A large circle of white corral fencing, several feet high, enclosed a group of camel-like creatures. Some stood grazing, while others stared blankly at the parade of passing vehicles. A shed made of wooden boards, open in front, stood behind them. One or two animals stood under the peaked roof— seeking a cool shady spot, Lucy guessed. A short distance from the corral she saw a large barn—the classic combination, bright red with white trim, like something from a picture book.

"Look . . . the llamas." Suzanne sat up in her seat. "Wow, there's a gang of them. I didn't realize the Kruegers owned so many."

The correct term was probably "herd," Lucy thought. But Lucy shared Suzanne's surprise. There were a lot of llamas out there. It probably took a lot of exotic fur to spin any profit from this enterprise. The Kruegers had made a big investment. A risky one, too, she thought, when you considered that they had come out here without any experience in country living, to hear Dana tell it.

"Ellie told me they own ten or twelve. They bought the whole herd from a couple in upstate New York who were retiring and selling their own farm," Dana explained. "How many llamas do you need to start a business selling yarn? Is a dozen enough?" Lucy asked curiously.

"Oh no, not nearly," Dana replied. "Ellie told me that it takes about three to six ounces of fiber to spin an average skein of yarn. Each llama only yields five to ten pounds of fleece when they're sheared. Which can be once a year. Or sometimes, every other. So Ellie needs to buy fiber from other sources. Other farms, and even silk and bamboo. She said she'd need a herd of two or three hundred to keep the business going otherwise. But she and Ben like having their own herd to make the place feel like a real farm. She says it's a good group, too. The llamas are well trained and very people friendly."

"And Matt says they're all healthy," Lucy added, mentioning her boyfriend, who was a veterinarian and had become another knitting circle referral for the Kruegers.

"You can train a llama? What, to do tricks?" Suzanne asked.

Lucy laughed at the idea, but Suzanne was serious.

Dana glanced at her. "I'm not sure about tricks. But they are very smart. They can come when you call their name. Or pull a cart. Or guard flocks of other animals, like sheep."

"A guard llama? Never heard of that," Lucy said.

"Ellie says some are even used for animal therapy," Dana continued.

Suzanne laughed. "You're kidding . . . right?"

"Not at all. Llamas are very calm, gentle animals. People feel peaceful and secure in their company. Though I doubt Ellie will train any in her herd for special jobs. She and Ben don't have the time right now, for one thing. But llamas do bond well with people, and Ellie seems to think of them as pets. That could also be because she and Ben aren't, well, real farmers yet," Dana admitted with a smile. "They do tend to anthropomorphize."

"I love you, Dana. But can you please speak English? Some of us in the backseat are little slow," Suzanne said politely.

"You are anything but, pal," Dana replied with a laugh. "I meant that they treat the llamas as if they were people, attributing human characteristics to their behavior. The llamas even have cute human names."

"The way Lucy acts about her dogs, you mean."

"Yes, that's it exactly." Dana nodded and glanced at Lucy.

"As if I'm the only person in this car who does that," Lucy countered. She gave Dana a look. She didn't reply but had the good grace to blush a little and stare out the window.

Everyone knew Dana had no perspective at all about her pedigreed Maine coon cat, Arabelle, that Lucy considered totally insane.

"Here we are, just in time," Lucy announced. In time to avoid an argument about the superiority of dogs over cats.

The farm's open gates came into view, decorated with blue and yellow helium balloons and a wide banner that read "Laughing Llama Farm ~ Grand Opening Fiber Festival."

They turned onto the property and followed a dirt road. A large old farmhouse appeared on the right, and Lucy slowed the car so they could get a good look at it.

"What a beauty. Looks like it was built back in the eighteen hundreds," Suzanne guessed.

Lucy had to agree. She loved old houses, and this one was a classic, a two-story eyebrow colonial with a long front porch and a row of small square windows below the roofline. It looked newly painted, the clapboard a buttery yellow color with white trim, dark green shutters, and a red door. A planter made from an old milk can stood near the front steps, displaying pink geraniums and trailing vinca vines.

Even though it was late September, some hardy perennials still bloomed in the large garden in front—black-eyed Susans, pink coneflowers, and shrub roses. The weather in Plum Harbor was mild for this time of year and the killing frost had not yet crept in, though Lucy knew that soon the cooler nights would wilt any surviving flowers and the ground would freeze hard as a rock until spring.

"Wow, the place looks great. I haven't been out here in a while. It needed a ton of work when they moved in," Dana told her friends.

"We call that 'potential' in the biz. Or 'in need of tender loving care,'" Suzanne translated. "This place did need loads of TLC, as I recall from the listing. But it has a lot of extras, too. There's an orchard back past the barn, and a sweet little cottage back there. See it?"

Now that Suzanne pointed it out, Lucy did see the cottage, painted the same color as the farmhouse. The edges of lace curtains showed in the windows, and potted plants led up the steps to the front door.

"Nothing wrong with having another stream of income while you're getting a business started," Suzanne said approvingly. "I can't wait until the kids go to college so we can rent out some of our place."

Suzanne owned a large, rambling old house in a perpetual state of renovation, and Lucy could easily see it turned into a B-and-B . . . though she knew Suzanne was only joking.

"They found the perfect tenant, too," Dana continued. "Her name is Dot. She's from Vermont and has lived on farms most of her life. They've hired her to take care of the orchard and help with the animals. Even though she's a little older, Ellie says she's a hard worker and an angel with the llamas. She helps on the farm part-time and has another job somewhere. As a home health aide, I think. They give her a break on the rent along with her pay, so it all works out."

Not far from the cottage, rows of leafy apple trees were also visible. Lucy wasn't sure how far the orchard stretched back but guessed it to be a few acres. Before she could ask Suzanne, a parking attendant caught her attention, waving her toward a field filled with cars.

Lucy turned, and they bumped along over the rutted ground until another attendant directed her into a space.

Suzanne emerged slowly from the backseat, working her way through the piles of farm stand purchases. Dana and Lucy waited for her, eager to get into the festival. They could already hear music—old-time bluegrass banjo and fiddle tunes—as appetizing aromas beckoned them forward.

They came out of the lot and stepped into the flow of fairgoers. There was a big turnout, Lucy thought, especially for this type of event, which tended to be much quieter and not quite as . . . splashy.

"It must have cost a fortune to put this together. Look at

those tents." Suzanne gazed around. "Top dollar at the rent-all places."

The tents were very pretty, Lucy thought. Peaked on top, with bright blue and yellow stripes. They reminded Lucy of fairy tale illustrations, or movies about medieval knights jousting in tournaments.

Beneath the striped covering, they stopped to visit with a cluster of fluffy-headed alpaca and, in the next pen, a group of llamas that were a bit larger and more camel-like in looks.

Another tent held cages of huge angora rabbits. "Look at that guy," Suzanne said. "He's as big as a pillow."

"He is. Couldn't you just imagine cuddling up with him?" It was the biggest rabbit Lucy had ever seen, its furry coat prized for softness.

Just beyond the animals, there were several rows of smaller white tents—the many vendors who had come to sell their wares and publicize their shops and businesses, all related somehow to spinning, knitting, and other handcrafts.

"I guess we should look for Maggie's booth," Dana said, looking around.

"Right . . . before I lose control and start shopping again," Suzanne warned them.

Lucy found a map in the pile of flyers the parking attendant had handed them. While she stood puzzling over it, Phoebe suddenly appeared. She was dressed for the country outing in a green cargo jacket, skinny jeans, and black high-tops. The purple T-shirt under Phoebe's jacket read, "Keep staring. I may do a trick."

Phoebe was just returning from a food run and her cardboard tray was heaped with items—a paper bowl of curly fries and a soft drink on one side and a yogurt, a green apple, and tea on the other. Her idea of a balanced diet—juggling her junk food with Maggie's healthy choices.

"Hey, guys. What took you so long? Did you get lost or something?"

"We made a few stops. The farm stands were hard to resist . . . for some of us." Dana glanced at Suzanne. "I hope we didn't miss Maggie's demonstration?"

"She doesn't go on for at least half an hour. We've already set up the wheel. The booth is right over here," Phoebe added, leading the way.

"I'd follow the smell of those curly fries anywhere," Suzanne murmured. "Where's the snack stand? I could go for a bite."

Lucy was tempted to remind Suzanne of the apple cider doughnuts gobbled down at the last farm stand, but she restrained herself.

"Keep it moving. We'll find some food later." Lucy gently prodded Suzanne to keep her on track, though her friend kept slowing down as the colorful displays in different booths caught her eye. It all looked very tempting, Lucy thought. Suzanne wasn't the only one eager to shop. There were handmade purses and pillows, woven rugs and fiber art, other booths with dresses and shawls, sweet-smelling soaps and lotions. Many booths offered knitting tools, unique yarns, and spinning supplies. Lucy kept reminding herself they would come back later and browse. Besides, there was only one booth where she would ever buy knitting supplies and it soon came into view.

A large oval sign with the Black Sheep Knitting Shop logo marked Maggie's spot, and Lucy pushed Suzanne a few more yards to their goal.

Maggie's booth was practically a mini version of her shop, with everything set up in an eye-catching way.

Handmade sweaters and scarves stood on stands or hung from the tent's ceiling. There were tables inside and out displaying large baskets of yarn, needles, and various knitting tools. Flyers about classes and special coupons filled other baskets near the flow of passing traffic.

Lucy also noticed Maggie's spinning wheel—a small one she used at home, not the large one she had in the shop—set up to one side of the booth, ready and waiting for its owner to make the magic happen.

Lucy had never learned to spin, though watching someone else manage it never failed to fascinate her. Maggie claimed it wasn't hard at all, but Lucy guessed it was one of those "not hard at all" activities that are only perfected with lots of time, interest, and practice, practice, practice—like playing the piano. She had never gotten very far with the instrument and felt the same fate would befall her if she invested in a spinning wheel.

Maggie was at the back of the booth, showing some customers a beautiful fringed wrap composed of a variety of stitches in a soft butternut-squash-colored yarn—a sample for one of the classes Maggie was giving at the shop in the fall called It's a Wrap!

Maggie looked up and noticed that her friends had arrived. She quickly excused herself and walked toward them.

"Sorry we're late." Dana had to practically shout to be heard above the music coming from a performance stage somewhere nearby. "You look so busy, I'll bet you didn't even miss us."

"I knew you were making a day of it. I'm sure you stopped to buy a few pumpkins and such."

"Pumpkins, yes. And a lot of 'and such,'" Lucy said drily.

"We're here for your performance," Suzanne said brightly.

"Oh, that's no big deal. You've seen my act before. Ellie asked a few of us to show how the wheel works. She's looking for more students for her classes. She's been giving free lessons on hand spinning all day and giving out these souvenir spindles. Cute, right?"

Maggie picked up a wooden spindle from the table behind her. Strands of white fiber were wrapped on one end. The flat round disk on top was imprinted with the words "Laughing Llama Farm" and bracketed on either side by the black silhouette of a llama.

Suzanne took the spindle and looked it over. "What a great idea. All I ever come up with for a giveaway is refrigerator magnets."

"I should order something like this for my shop. Very clever . . . and useful," Maggie agreed.

"Look, there's Ellie." Dana turned and waved. "I guess she has to visit all the vendors. Like a hostess at a big dinner party."

An odd way to put it, but it seemed to describe Ellie's path through the booths very aptly. Lucy saw the festival hostess work her way down the line, stopping at each tent to chat with the proprietor. When she noticed Dana, she waved and headed straight in their direction.

With her height, slim build, and glossy reddish-brown hair, Ellie would be easy to spot in any crowd. She wore a long vest knit of fuzzy putty-colored yarn and belted at the waist over jeans and high black riding-style boots. As she drew closer, Lucy recognized the vest. It was made of llama fiber from her own herd. Ellie had showed it to them once at a knitting group meeting while she was still working on it.

The homespun vest, however, did not disqualify her from looking like a cover shot on a magazine—one about high-style country living. The past few months on the farm had not dulled a certain city air, Lucy thought. Not in a bad way, but Ellie did stand out today from most of the farm's visitors.

It might have been her sleek haircut, or just her confident manner. You couldn't discount her manicure, either, Lucy noticed. Not quite the hands of a farm woman, that was for sure. But she was a talented entrepreneur. She greeted each of them with a wide smile and a warm hug.

"Thanks for coming, everyone. Nice crowd, don't you think? We've been so lucky with the weather. I knew we'd have a beautiful day. Ben was so nervous. He nearly drove me crazy."

Typically upbeat and talkative, Ellie was running in high gear. But she was the organizer, director, and hostess of the entire event. Anyone would be excited.

"Your booth looks great, Maggie." Ellie twirled around, taking in the displays. "Have you sold much today?"

"Here and there. People are mostly browsing and asking questions. It's all good publicity."

"Yes, it will be. You're such a good sport." Ellie patted Maggie's arm, then glanced at her watch. "You're not scheduled to spin for at least half an hour. The herding demonstration isn't over yet."

"With the border collies? Did I miss that, too?" Phoebe sounded thoroughly disappointed. A fry hung limply from her fingertips.

"I'm sorry, Phoebe. I did say you could see that, didn't I?" Maggie sighed. "Why don't you go right now? You can catch the rest of it."

"The end is the best part," Suzanne consoled her. "When the dogs chase those silly sheep through the chutes."

Phoebe grabbed her soda and slurped noisily as she took off. "Catch you guys later. I'll take some pictures for the shop."

"Great. . . . Can anyone take a few of me? That would be a nice touch for the bulletin board, too. In addition to the herding dogs, I mean."

"I'll take some pictures of you." Lucy smiled at Maggie's subtle sarcasm. Maggie stepped over to a display table and posed.

"The farm looks great, Ellie," Dana said sincerely. "You've done so much with the place in such a short time."

"The festival gave us a good deadline. It's amazing how far a little paint and elbow grease can go. There's still a ton of repairs to make before the winter. Ben tries to do them himself, to save money. Between you and me, he's not really that handy." She lowered her voice a bit and laughed. "But we'll get through it. Little by little."

"You have a good-sized crowd. I've been to a few of these by now. Some can be deadly boring," Dana confessed.

"Oh, yeah," Suzanne agreed. "A few sleepy sheep and a table with some scented soap."

Ellie laughed. "I know what you mean. I didn't want our debut to be anything like that. We'll probably lose money when it's all said and done. But it will be worth the publicity. There's a reporter coming out from the *Plum Harbor Times*. I hope I can catch her and get a few nice quotes in the article."

Ellie peered into the crowd as she spoke. Lucy saw her expression suddenly sour as a woman nearby waved and walked toward them. Lucy had a feeling this was not the newspaper reporter Ellie had been looking for, but someone else she had not expected to see.

In the blink of an eye, Ellie was smiling again, greeting the guest cheerfully—her professional training kicking in.

"Angelica . . . what a nice surprise. Thanks for coming." Angelica and Ellie air kissed. Then Ellie stepped back for introductions. "This is my neighbor Angelica Rossi, everyone. She owns Sweet Meadow Farm, just down the road."

Sweet Meadow? Lucy recalled passing a sign for that farm in their travels. Had they stopped there to buy something? Then she remembered. It was another organic fiber farm, one where alpaca were raised. Almost a direct competitor with Laughing Llama. What were the chances of two such enterprises opening up within five miles of each other?

Angelica Rossi must have asked herself the same question when she heard about the Kruegers and their llama herd coming to town.

Angelica, the polar opposite of Ellie in looks and style, carried a basket over her arm, partially hidden by the edge of her shawl. Lucy took a peek. She saw tiny bunches of yarn attached to business cards. Samples of Sweet Meadow Farm's products, Lucy realized. Which would be fine except that Angelica apparently had not troubled herself to rent a booth at the fair.

Ellie must have noticed, too. But generously . . . or wisely . . . or both . . . didn't make a fuss about it.

Lucy would have described Angelica as an "old hippie," though she was not that old, maybe in her mid-forties. Her wavy brown hair, threaded with gray, was amazingly long, woven in a braid that hung halfway down her back. She wore a loose peasant-style blouse, a knitted shawl, and a long denim skirt, with black lace-up boots peeking out from below the hem. Hoop earrings and a few silver bangles completed her outfit. Not a drop of makeup. Not even lip balm. Not even lip balm made from pure beeswax, Lucy guessed.

Some might have pegged Angelica as a perfect candidate for a makeover show, but the lady farmer seemed totally at ease, poised and confident. Lucy sensed that something about the owner of Sweet Meadow Farm made Ellie nervous.

Ellie quickly introduced everyone, leaving Maggie for last. "And this is Maggie Messina, from the Black Sheep Knitting Shop—"

"Oh, we know each other," Maggie interrupted. "Hello, Angelica. Nice to see you." Her tone was polite and cheerful. But Lucy could tell from a certain tension in Maggie's smile that her friend did not have warm feelings for Angelica, either.

"Your booth looks lovely. I'm not surprised, knowing your

shop." Angelica looked around at the displays. "What's this? Are you giving these away?"

Angelica picked up the spindle Maggie had left on the display table.

"Ellie is. She's giving them out as souvenirs from the fair. They have a little imprint, see?" Maggie pointed out the embellishment. "You can have that one, if you like."

"Thanks. It's very clever," she said, slipping it into her basket. "The festival is great," she added, turning back to Ellie again. "I'd love to hold an event like this at Sweet Meadow. But I know it wouldn't be half as nice."

"It's a big job. But not rocket science. I'll help if you want to try it. Let me know."

Angelica looked surprised by Ellie's offer. Lucy was, too. She wondered if Ellie was sincere. Or if she knew that her rival would never take her up on it.

An urgent beeping sound, like a cell phone, interrupted their conversation.

"Excuse me, that must be Ben . . ." Ellie took a walkie-talkie out of her vest pocket. "Hi, honey, what's up? Is Dot down there with you? I was looking for her at the animal tents and she wasn't around . . ."

While Ellie spoke with her husband, Angelica said good-bye and slipped back into the crowd, her long braid and basket swinging from side to side as she strolled away.

A few moments later, Lucy and her friends instinctively huddled around Ellie.

"That Angelica . . . she's too much," Ellie said under her breath. "She has some nerve waltzing around here all afternoon. Did you see those samples she's giving out? She should have paid for a booth, like everyone else. But I didn't call her on it. Trying to take the high road, I guess. I'm sure she's just here to spy on me, anyway. Like she's been doing since we got here."

"You know what they say," Maggie murmured. "Spying is the highest form of flattery."

"*Imitation* is the highest form," Dana corrected her. "Spying is a little . . . obsessive. You were so cordial, Ellie. It was hard to tell that she isn't a friendly competitor."

"We're new here. We can't afford to make enemies with our neighbors. I'd be happy to be on good terms with her. She raises alpaca, we raise llamas. There's a world of difference between them. But she turns it into a rivalry. And for all her Sweet Meadow sweetness, she plays pretty dirty." Ellie's expression clouded. "Oh, we act perfectly nice to each other in public. But I know for a fact she talks down our farm and spreads rumors with the other landowners and all our mutual business contacts."

"Rumors? What kind of rumors?" Dana asked curiously.

"For one thing, that alpaca fiber is superior to llamas'. Which is patently untrue. Both have their value and uses. But Angelica's a real fiber snob. Aside from that, she tells everyone that we don't know what we're doing and our llamas are not good pedigree like her herd of blue-ribbon winners. And she tells vendors that we're not spinning the pure fibers we claim, mixing in sheep's wool and other extenders. Which isn't true at all. I've never been able to catch her. But I know where all this trash talk is coming from."

"I used to carry Sweet Meadow yarn. But I don't anymore."

Maggie's quiet words caught Lucy's interest. But Maggie didn't elaborate. Now that Maggie mentioned it, Lucy did remember Sweet Meadow hand-spun products in the shop, but she hadn't noticed when the yarns had disappeared.

"She's a sharp cookie. Or thinks she is. Never mind that Mother Earth act," Ellie added. "I think there's plenty of room in the basket for everyone's boutique yarns. But Angelica is very competitive. She seems to think only one of us can survive and thrive."

"A little advice, if you don't mind," Maggie replied. "Don't get caught up in that game. Focus on your own business and the rest will take care of itself."

"My mother always told me, 'Just hoe your own row.' That seems to apply double since you're on a farm," Suzanne added.

"Maggie's right. Don't engage," Dana advised. "She'll eventually lose interest. I can almost guarantee that."

Lucy didn't have any wise words to offer. She did know that Maggie's advice came from her own experience. She'd had a fierce rival in town at one time and had let the emotions of the situation get the best of her. Unfortunately, when the rival store owner was found dead, the police looked at Maggie as the prime suspect.

"Thanks for the advice and for listening. I'll keep it all in mind." Ellie glanced at her watch. "I think it's time for your demonstration, Maggie. Do you need any help setting up?"

"Phoebe and I prepared everything a while ago. I just need my stool. It's behind the back table somewhere."

Maggie left to fetch her stool while Lucy and her friends stepped over to the spinning wheel for prime viewing spots.

Ellie stepped out into the path and called out to those passing by, "Spinning demonstration at the Black Sheep tent, starting in two minutes. Come and see some expert spinning. Maggie Messina, the owner of the Black Sheep Knitting Shop, is about to begin her demonstration in a just a few minutes . . ."

The fiddlers had stopped for a while but now started up again. Ellie had to shout to be heard over the noise but managed to pull in a large audience.

Maggie set her stool down and took her place at the back of the wheel. She briefly showed the group a handful of fur, clipped from one of Ellie's llamas, known as roving. Then she showed how the fibers were combed out and set on the spindle.

She put her feet on the pedals, explaining each step of the process, and began to work the delicate thread of fiber that slipped from the wheel.

Lucy and her friends stepped aside to give others a better view. Maggie had been right. They had all seen this performance in the shop many times before, though Lucy still found it fascinating to watch the wad of animal fur spun into a thin strand of yarn.

"So you can see here a lovely smooth strand of yarn is forming . . ." Maggie paused to show the group her handiwork.

Lucy suddenly heard a high-pitched voice shouting in the crowd, not far from Maggie's tent. At first she thought it was a child having a meltdown. But as the shouts got closer, she realized it was Phoebe and she was in trouble.

"Help . . . somebody! Please. . . . The llamas . . . out in the pasture. . . . They've been hurt. . . . Oh, it's horrible . . ."

Lucy turned to see their young friend running toward

them as fast as her high-tops would carry her. People walking on the path between the tents parted to let her through, their expressions confused and disturbed.

Phoebe's arms waved wildly in alarm, her eyeliner and mascara running down her face in tiny rivers of black tears.

"It's so awful. . . . The poor animals . . ." she sobbed, gasping for breath. Dana ran toward her, and Phoebe practically collapsed in her arms.

"Phoebe, please. Slow down. Take a few deep breaths. What happened, honey? Why are you so upset?"

"The herding show was over and I was just heading back here," Phoebe finally managed. "We all heard a loud noise . . . like firecrackers. A *pop-pop* sound? The llamas started running around like crazy in the field and making this horrible sound. I ran over to the meadow to see what was going on. They were running in all directions and . . . and a few of them are hurt. It looks like someone . . . someone . . . shot them."

"Shot at them? I can't believe it!" Ellie looked horrified. Her eyes widened with panic and disbelief.

"It wasn't a real gun," Phoebe quickly added. "It must have been a paint gun. Or something like that. The first llama that was hit was streaked with red. But the next one was blue. So it must have been paint, right? That's twisted enough, if you ask me."

"A paint gun? That's awful!" Ellie pulled out her walkie-talkie. "Ben . . . Dot . . . can anyone hear me?"

They all listened for an answer but only heard an annoying crackling sound.

"I'd better get down there . . ." Ellie stashed the walkie-talkie in her pocket and took off, headed for the pasture.

"I'm going to help her." Dana glanced at her friends.

"I'll go, too," Lucy said.

"Me, too," Suzanne agreed.

"Go ahead. I'd better stay here with Phoebe," Maggie offered.

Seeing the llamas attacked would be distressful for anyone but especially for Phoebe, Lucy thought. She loved animals and seemed to have a deep connection with four-legged creatures. Phoebe talked tough but was really a very tender soul.

As Lucy ran to catch up with her friends, she saw Maggie hand Phoebe a wad of tissues and a bottle of water, then lead her to the back of the booth. Lucy tried to catch sight of Ellie and Dana up ahead. She couldn't find them in the crowd as the flow of visitors now moved toward the parking area—seniors clutching their purchases and knitting totes, parents dragging squirming children by the hand.

The entire mood of the event had changed in an instant, as if a dark cloud had slipped over the sun.

Lucy worried about what they would find in the meadow. She hated to see animals in pain. Even though it wasn't a real gun, a paint gun was still a weapon and could cause injuries, especially when fired at close range. The llamas could have broken bones or have internal bleeding. She wondered if Ellie or Ben had called Matt yet, then decided to take the initiative. She pulled out her cell phone, and quickly hit Matt's number.

He answered on the first ring. "Hi, honey, what's up? How's the fair?"

"Not so good. Can you come out here? The llamas have been attacked. They need your help."

Chapter Two

*L*ook at them! The poor creatures! Who did this? Who could be so cruel?"

Ellie yanked the gate open and ran out in the meadow. She crouched next to a llama that knelt on its front knees, making a painful bleating sound.

The llama was splashed with red paint from its ears to its tail, and every few moments, it gave its head a hard shake, like a wet dog trying to shake off the rain. One eye was swollen shut, and Lucy felt her stomach lurch. She quickly looked away, reminding herself it was just paint, though the effect was still gruesome.

"How awful. I can hardly bear to look." Dana came to stand beside Lucy at the gate. "Quite a few look hurt. But maybe they're just stunned?"

"Maybe," Suzanne said quietly. "That one is limping. Looks like its leg was hit. Poor thing. . . . What should we do?" Suzanne's voice verged on tears. Lucy felt frustrated, too. It was like coming upon the scene of a multicar accident, with so many victims wandering about, dazed and injured.

She saw a man out in the meadow, trying to clamp a lead to one of the llamas that had been hit. He wore jeans and a yellow T-shirt that had been made up for the festival. Ellie suddenly called out, and Lucy knew it was her husband.

"Ben . . . come and help me. I think Buttercup is unconscious. . . . I can hardly hear her breathing." Ellie's llama was prostrate on the ground now, lying on its side.

"I'll be right there, Ellie. I have my hands full over here. Where's Dot?" He looked around as the animal he tended began to gag, jerking out its long neck. The sound was loud and disturbing.

"Oh, for pity's sake . . . what the . . ." Ben just managed to jump out of the way as the llama finally expelled the contents of its stomach, a mixture of partly digested hay and bright red mucus.

Internal injuries? Or just more paint? Probably the latter, Lucy thought. She'd noticed the llama licking its fur, trying to get the mess off. Lucy hoped the paint wasn't toxic—that would really be a disaster.

"I'll help Ellie. One of you help Ben," Dana suggested as she left them.

"I'll go," Lucy said. "I just called Matt. He wasn't far. He's already on his way."

Suzanne followed her out into the meadow. "Good idea. I wonder if they've called the police."

Lucy wondered about that, too. But they probably hadn't had a chance to do that yet, she thought. As Lucy jogged over to Ellie and the felled llama, another woman pulled the gate open and ran toward them. She carried a plastic bucket of water that sloshed from side to side in one hand, and held a bucket of rags in the other. She was moving surprisingly fast, considering the load and her age, Lucy thought, which was probably somewhere in her late sixties or even early seventies, judging from her white hair and short, stout body.

"Buttercup is badly hurt, Dot. Please take a look at her," Ellie called out.

Dot reached them and dropped her buckets. She was panting a bit, her round face flushed. She had pale white skin and small blue eyes, and her hair, wound in a knot at the back of her head, fell loose around her face as she bent to examine the llama.

"She looks bad. That pellet got her right in the head. Poor girl. Half an inch lower and her eye would be out."

Lucy took in a sharp breath at the description.

"It's bad enough as it is." Ellie gently stroked the llama's head, careful not to touch the red spot. "Poor Buttercup," she murmured.

The animal kept her eyes closed, breathing heavily. Then she suddenly began to shiver and jerk. Her limbs stiffened, and her eyes opened and rolled back in her head.

Ellie jumped back. "What's happening? What's wrong with her?"

"She's having a seizure from the head injury," Dot replied quietly. "We have to be calm. The more we react, the worse it will be for her. Can you give me something to put under her head?"

Ellie pulled off her vest. The old woman wadded it up and slipped it under the llama's head as a pillow.

The llama continued to jerk spasmodically, her hooves flicking and back legs kicking dust up on the ground. Dot took a position at the animal's head, out of the way of her legs.

Ellie rose to her feet and stepped back, then stood beside Lucy. "Is that it? Is that all we can do for her?"

Dot glanced up at her a moment. "That's all for now. It will pass soon. At least she's not up, wandering around. I've seen horses with focal convulsions. They try to kick out of the stall. It's better that she's on the ground," Dot said as she stroked the llama's neck. "It should be over in a little while."

"There, there. It's all right, Buttercup. We're right here with you," Dot crooned lovingly.

The llama's body went slack. Her eyes closed. For a moment, Lucy thought she had died. But the animal's chest still rose and fell with shallow breaths. Her mouth hung open, and her big tongue flopped to one side, hanging over Ellie's sweater.

"The seizure is over. She's coming around. But she might convulse again. We have to watch her." Dot came slowly to her feet.

She wasn't very tall, Lucy realized, though her assertive presence gave the impression of a taller, bigger woman. Her apple-shaped figure was covered by a large plaid flannel shirt. She wore baggy jeans underneath and dark green, knee-high rubber boots.

Ben appeared. He had taken a few llamas back to the barn and come through the gate again. "What's going on? How's Buttercup?"

"She had a seizure. But it finally stopped," Ellie reported. She looked up at her husband. Her face was pale and frightened. "How about the others? What should we do?" She looked overwhelmed. "How can we take care of them all? What about the festival? There are people out there, expecting activities, demonstrations . . ."

"The event has to be called off. Everyone has to go. This is an emergency, Ellie. Have you called the vet?"

"Me . . . ? When did I have a chance to call him?" Ellie stared at him. "You were here first. I thought you must have done that . . ."

Lucy felt awkward interrupting their marital dispute but knew she could help. "Matt told me that you have been using his practice. I called him a few minutes ago, and he's on his way over. I hope you don't mind. It just seemed like the right thing to do," she added.

"Mind? Of course not. At least someone was thinking clearly," Ellie answered. "These animals need some medical attention."

Ben nodded at Lucy but didn't say anything. He glanced back at his wife—getting a grip on his anger, Lucy guessed.

It was a very stressful situation, and they'd both lost their temper. That was understandable, Lucy thought. It didn't mean anything was wrong with their marriage.

"How long do you think it will take him to get here?" Ben asked. "Is he coming from town?"

"He should be here any minute. He was out in this area making house calls." Horse calls, actually. He had several equestrian patients. "I told him what happened and he's coming right over."

"Good. . . . I just hope none of these animals have to be . . . put down."

Ben's tone was somber.

"Ben, please. Don't even say such a thing." Ellie's response was quick and sharp. "It's just another prank. We can't let it get us all unhinged. That's just what they want to see."

Another prank? What did she mean by that? Who was trying to get them unhinged? Had the animals been harassed before? Lucy wondered.

But she didn't think it was the right moment to ask those questions. She barely knew the couple and didn't feel comfortable probing. She did wonder why the Kruegers had not mentioned calling the police. Wasn't this act just as bad as, say, someone breaking into a house? Or vandalizing a car or other valuable property?

Ellie stood near Buttercup, stroking her muzzle. The llama was back on her feet but looking dazed and weak. "What should we do with Buttercup, Dot? Do you think she can walk to the barn, or should we just wait for the doctor?"

Dot was checking other animals that had been hit, gently examining their bodies—searching for bruises and broken bones, Lucy assumed. Dot tethered a few up and started to lead them to the barn. "I think it's best to leave the injured ones here for now. I don't think we should move any of them."

Dana called out to her, "Dot, what can we do to help you?"

Dot looked over her shoulder and smiled, looking grateful for the offer. "I need to wash them. I think the paint is making them sick. You can come to the barn and help. If you don't mind getting wet and dirty."

"I can do that. I don't mind," Dana answered as she followed Dot.

"I don't mind, either," Lucy offered.

"I'll help, too. Unless you'd rather I stay out here and help you and Ben?" Suzanne asked Ellie.

"I really need someone to go back out there and call off the fair," Ellie said sadly. "Could you help me do that?"

Suzanne nodded. "Sure, no problem."

Lucy had a feeling that Suzanne would have preferred washing all the animals in Noah's Ark to being the official "fun sucker" and calling an abrupt end to the party. But this was an emergency and they all had to help.

Ellie brushed off her clothes, then picked her vest up off the ground. She seemed so sad and deflated. No wonder, Lucy thought. After all her hard work and the expense of putting on the festival, it was ending so abruptly, on such a strange, violent note.

Suzanne and Ellie walked through the gate, heading back to the tents to deliver the bad news. Lucy saw a young woman rush up to them. "Sorry to bother you. I'm Jessica Newton, with the *Plum Harbor Times*. You must be Ellie Krueger. I'm here to cover the festival."

"That's me. I'm sorry. You're a little late. The festival is . . . winding down a little earlier than scheduled," Ellie said vaguely. She was trying hard to summon up her professional persona. But Lucy could see it was a struggle.

"Oh, too bad. I got held up on another story. But looks like you have something going on out here. Someone said the llamas were shot? Is that true?"

Ellie's eyes widened with alarm. "Shot with paint. A paint gun. It was probably just a bad joke, I'm sure—"

"Yes, I see. When did this happen? Just now?"

"We're not sure. I really don't have anything to say about this situation. We'd prefer not to have it in the paper."

"Sure, I understand. Mind if I take a few pictures?" The young woman had taken out a camera and had it positioned in front of her face before Ellie could answer.

"I do mind." Ellie took a step and blocked her view. "Did you hear a word I just said? It was probably just a stupid joke. Write about the festival and the farm, the positive side of the event. That's the only story we're giving out today."

She held her hand up so the picture would be ruined, but Lucy wasn't sure that she'd succeeded. Jessica Newton seemed persistent on breaking this hot news. There wasn't much excitement in Plum Harbor. This was a real scoop, from her point of view.

"I'll cover the fair, don't worry," the reporter promised. "But you can't keep this out of the paper, Mrs. Krueger. People are already talking about it. Once the police get involved, it will be on the blotter, public record."

The police had not been called. Yet. But Ellie didn't tell that to the reporter. She drew in a deep breath.

"Look, young lady, I asked you politely not to put this in the paper. If we see an article, your publisher will hear from our attorney. Please leave. This is private property. Is that clear?"

The reporter finally seemed to pay attention and cast Ellie an admonished look. Or was faking it just to keep the peace, Lucy thought.

"Have it your way." The reporter shrugged. "If it's not me, it will be someone else. Count on it."

Ellie crossed her arms over her chest but didn't say anything. The girl turned and slowly walked away, heading back to the tents and parking lot.

Ellie had vanquished the media this time. But the reporter had been right. They might be able to keep the incident out of the newspaper for a day or so, but once they called the police it became public record. So far, however, the Kruegers hadn't mentioned calling the police. Which seemed odd to Lucy.

But she held her tongue and headed off for the barn, as she'd promised. The situation was complicated enough.

Matt arrived a short time later. Lucy saw his old red truck racing out to the meadow. He parked at the fence and jumped down, a black medical case swinging from one hand. Ellie and Ben met him at the gate and led him out into the corral, where they had kept the llamas with the worst injuries.

Lucy, Dana, and Dot had washed down about six of the llamas. The paint did not come off completely, but they managed to remove enough so that what remained wouldn't be harmful to the animals when they groomed themselves.

Or so they hoped.

Lucy rubbed one of the llamas down with a ragged towel, speaking softly to the animal as she worked. Her name was Daphne, she'd heard Dot say. "I guess Matt will know better about that paint," Lucy said, musing aloud. "I'll have to ask him."

"Ask him right now, here he is," Dana replied.

Matt walked into the barn alongside Ben and Ellie, who led the other llamas on leather leads. One had an adhesive bandage on its back leg, and Buttercup wore a bandage wrapped around her head and over one eye.

The animals looked so pathetic after their medical care, Lucy felt tearful all over again.

"Hi, honey." Matt greeted her with a kiss. Lucy tried to kiss him back but was holding a large soapy sponge.

"We've been washing down the animals," she explained.

"Yes, I heard. That was a good idea."

"Just common sense." Dot shrugged and smiled briefly at Matt, while also looking a little suspicious of him, Lucy thought. As if she valued practical knowledge of animal husbandry—like her own—over his book learning.

Lucy would match her boyfriend against any farm lady in a heartbeat. He was a terrific vet and had a first-class intellect . . . and she was very proud of him.

While most of his patients were dogs and cats, people also kept horses, goats, and other livestock as pets, especially in this area, and she had often heard Matt talk about treating them.

"What's the prognosis, Doctor?" Lucy used his official title for full effect.

"As you've already surmised, it was a paint gun. Depending on who you ask, it's hard to say how much the impact hurts. But without question it is strong enough to cause large, painful contusions, bone fractures, and eye injuries, depending on how and where a person—or, in this case, an animal—is hit," Matt explained. "Lots of people wear padding when they are out having their fake battles. And if a person gets hit in the eye, it can be very serious. You can even lose your sight. Generally, people get large welts or black-and-blues, and those contusions are quite painful."

"What about the llamas?" Ellie asked. "Is it worse for them than humans?"

"It is worse. They don't have the fleshy padding on many parts of their body that humans do. There may be permanent damage to the llama hit in the eye. One other has a cracked rib, and another was hit in the head. Her skull could be fractured." Matt spoke in a quiet, serious tone. "I can't tell for sure unless I take an X-ray. But that animal definitely has a concussion."

"You mean, Buttercup? The llama that had a convulsion?" Dana asked.

"Yes, we'll have to see how she does tonight and over the next few days."

It sounded even worse when Matt described their injuries. Lucy sighed and wrung out the soapy sponge. Who could have possibly harmed the llamas this way? And why? Except for extreme, heartless cruelty, she could think of no possible reason for a sane person to do such a thing.

Matt's cell phone sounded, and he quickly checked a text. He pocketed the phone and turned to Lucy. "I've got to run. An emergency back in the village." He knelt down and started packing his medical bag. Ellie and Ben stood by and watched him. "Have you called the police yet?" he asked. "They need to be informed. Animal abuse is a serious felony, and they need to investigate."

Ellie glanced at Ben, then back at Matt. "We'll call right away. We just didn't get a chance. With all the animals hurt and needing our help, we were totally overwhelmed."

"Sure. I understand." Matt snapped the bag shut and stood up. "Please make sure you don't forget. And you'll have to watch the llamas tonight. There could be further reactions. Someone should sleep out here, in the barn," he added. "You have the Valium and phenobarbital for Buttercup, in case she has another seizure. I'll call you tomorrow to check up. But don't hesitate to get in touch anytime if you have any questions or anything else comes up."

Matt was dedicated and generous with his time. Many vets were not available to their clients after office hours. When emergencies arose, a recording on the office phone told pet owners to go to the nearest veterinary ER. But when Matt said to call anytime, day or night, he meant it, and plenty of clients took him at his word. He and Lucy had only been living together since April, but Lucy had been jarred awake many times by crisis calls. Sometimes they were true life-or-death situations . . . sometimes not much more than a hair ball.

"Dr. McDougal, thank you so much for running over here. You've been great." Ellie reached out and shook his hand.

"Thank you, Doctor," Ben added, also shaking Matt's hand. "This must have been a little overwhelming for you, like walking onto a battlefield."

"I wouldn't go that far. But it is one of the strangest calls I've ever made."

Llamas hit by paint balls? Not covered in most veterinary medical courses, Lucy guessed.

He glanced over at Lucy, and they shared a private smile. He seemed to be reading her mind, as so often happened.

She walked over and touched his arm. "I'll walk you to your truck. What's up in town?"

"That was the Mrs. Guthrie," he told her as they left the barn. "Holly started her labor and she's already having trouble breathing. This might take a while."

Holly was a purebred English bulldog—a show dog, in fact—who suffered from the breathing problems typical of breeds with squashed-up faces. Poor Holly had been through a tough pregnancy. Lucy had heard all about it, the ups and downs of the expectant, four-footed mother-to-be. She'd been tempted to knit several sets of puppy-size booties, as a baby gift. But she'd managed to resist.

"You're jumping from one emergency to the next tonight, Doc. Good luck." She kissed him quickly as he hopped back into the truck and flung his bag on the passenger seat. "Text me when you know how many puppies Holly has," she added with a grin.

"Will do. See you at home later."

"I'll be there," Lucy promised. She watched Matt drive off the property, then headed back to the barn. She saw Maggie and Phoebe walking just ahead of her and they all walked through the big open doors at about the same time.

As they entered the barn, she heard Dot say, "I'll stay out here tonight and keep an eye on things. I'll just set up a little cot and get my radio."

"I'll stay," Ben replied. "It might not be safe."

"Oh, don't be silly," Dot scoffed at him. "Nobody's coming back with the paint gun. That was such a cowardly act. They wouldn't have the nerve to try that again. If Buttercup has another spell, you'll have to call me anyway." She sighed and hung her head. "I feel so bad about this, folks. I should have been watching them closer, with all those strangers on the property. I left them too long in the meadow. I got off the usual schedule, bringing hay and water to the animals in the viewing tents. I should have—"

"Dot, please. It's nobody's fault. We would never blame you, of all people, for this." Ellie patted her shoulder and glanced at Ben for backup.

"Ellie is right. Please don't be so hard on yourself. Someone was determined to hurt our animals today. There wasn't anything we could do about it. Why don't we all take turns tonight, a few hours each. We'll work it out later."

Dot nodded. "All right. I'm going back to my cottage. I need to change out of these dirty clothes. I think the llamas will be fine for now. Dr. McDougal gave them all sedatives."

"Go take care of yourself," Ellie urged her. "I'm ready for a glass of wine. Would anyone like to come up to the house for a few minutes? You've all been such good sports about helping out. I'd feel awful if you just ran off. Please stay and have a drink or a bite to eat with us."

Maggie was the first to reply. "That's very nice of you to offer, Ellie. I have no plans. But I can't answer for everyone."

Phoebe looked horrified. "Can't hang here . . . but thanks anyway," she added. She glanced quickly at Maggie. "Josh has a gig in Gloucester, remember? We have to pick up all the equipment and stuff in Ipswich. I should have been back to town by now."

Maggie held up her hand up like a crossing guard. "I get it. I had a feeling you'd say something like that."

It took a few minutes to sort it out, but finally Lucy's friends decided that Suzanne would take Phoebe back to town in Lucy's Jeep. Lucy and Dana would stay at the farm with Maggie, who would drive them back to the village a little later.

Lucy was glad to stay a little longer. With Matt playing doula to a bulldog, she just would have been hanging out at home, waiting for him. She was eager to hear what Ellie and Ben had to say about this strange incident and if they had any idea of who might be behind it.

She'd picked up several hints that the paint ball attack wasn't entirely a surprise, or the only time there had been some vandalism at the farm. Lucy wondered about that and hoped to get the full story. She had a feeling her friends did, too.

Chapter Three

Back at the house, the Kruegers' front parlor felt like a safe haven after the harrowing afternoon.

While Ben chose a bottle of wine from a well-stocked rack, Lucy and her friends chose seats. Lucy made herself comfortable in a big, soft armchair. Ellie had good taste and spared no expense. Lucy guessed she had bought all new furnishings to suit the antique house and left her city belongings behind with her former life. There were lace curtains and love seats covered with a floral pattern and side tables that looked suitably shabby-chic. A vintage rocker and leather armchair flanked the fireplace, and a Tiffany-style lamp shed a soft glow over all, lending the room a very cozy feeling.

Ben worked a corkscrew into a bottle of pinot noir. "I have to be honest. When I first saw those poor animals, I felt as if we were under attack. I didn't know what to expect next." He paused and pulled out the cork, which made a loud pop, reminding Lucy of the way Phoebe had described the sound of the paint ball gunshots.

"Were you the first to find them?" Maggie asked as Ben handed her a glass of wine.

"No, Dot was. The sheep-herding demonstration had just ended and I had helped Jack Gibbons get the sheep back on his trailer. We just borrowed them for the fair," he explained. "I came back up to the house to wash up and change my shirt. I smelled pretty nasty after wrangling those animals," he admitted with a laugh. "Dot called me on the walkie-talkie. I couldn't understand what she was saying. Or I thought I didn't understand her. I mean, it sounded so bizarre. I ran down to the meadow and . . . well, you all know what I saw."

Lucy thought he was about to say more, but Ellie breezed in with a platter of appetizers and set it down on the pedestal table by the love seat.

"Here's a little something to munch on. I was running around all day and didn't even eat lunch. I made the vegetable pâté myself," she added. "Tell me how you like it. I want to sell it in the store."

Lucy had not eaten lunch, either, and everything looked good. There were three kinds of cheese, a square of pâté, thin slices of apple, and slices of a dark grain baguette.

"The apples are from our orchards, of course, and the goat cheese from the farm down the way. Eden Farm, I think they call it," Ellie explained, taking a seat. "They're hippies—well, what we used to call hippies. Anyway, they make the most fabulous cheese. Live and let live, right?" She shrugged and sat down in an armchair near her husband.

"If only it were so simple, Ellie." Ben took a sip of wine and gazed at his wife. "That might be our philosophy. But all of our neighbors surely don't share it."

"Do you think one of your neighbors is behind the attack on the animals?" Maggie asked.

Ellie glanced at her husband. When he didn't answer, she said, "We really don't know. It could have been . . . anybody."

"Oh, Ellie, what's the difference? We know who it is. Justin Ridley. He's the only one who could have done this. The only one who has any reason to harass us. Who *believes* he has a reason," he corrected himself.

"We don't have any proof of that, Ben. We can't go around accusing the man. There are laws about slander."

"It's not slander if it's true," Ben countered.

Dana leaned forward and took an apple slice from the platter. "Who's Justin Ridley? Does he live nearby?"

"Right next door. The property to the east." Ellie waved her hand in that direction. "He's very eccentric. We tried to be friendly to him when we moved in. But he seemed to despise us on sight."

"The guy is crazy. Paranoid," Ben added. "Somebody told me he'd been a career military man but was tossed out with some psychological disability. He's a loner. Sort of a survivalist, I guess you'd say. He's off the grid. Drinks water from his own well, has solar and wind power rigged up all over the place. He doesn't cultivate his land at all. There are just acres and acres of weeds back there."

"I was miserable during ragweed season," Ellie cut in. "It wasn't pretty."

"Who knows what he's growing. Weeds of all kinds, for fun and profit, I bet. I can't see how he supports himself otherwise." Ben's tone was harsh, his meaning somewhat nebulous, but Lucy got the general drift. He suspected Ridley was cultivating marijuana along with the ragweed.

Was that possible? Wouldn't someone have noticed by now? she wondered. Whatever the truth of the matter, it was clear that Justin Ridley got under Ben's skin in the worst way.

"He is odd," Ellie added. "You rarely see any activity there during the day. But he roams around in the middle of the night, like a vampire or something. With these two crazy hunting dogs."

"And a loaded gun," Ben added, his voice rising on an urgent note. "He's shooting at raccoons or chipmunks or something . . . in the middle of the night."

"Chipmunks don't come out at night," Ellie gently reminded him. "They sleep, in burrows. I read about it before we moved here," she told her friends. "I wanted to know more about the local wildlife."

"Chipmunks, raccoons, what's the difference? He obviously takes pleasure in killing poor defenseless animals. That's my point. I guess we're lucky he didn't shoot our llamas with real bullets."

"Ben, please. This seems like something he'd do. But we don't know for sure."

"We didn't know for sure about the other times. But this one has Ridley's name all over it, Ellie," he insisted.

Ellie didn't answer. She looked over at the women. "There have been other incidents since we moved here," she admitted.

"Nothing nearly this violent, though." Then she sighed and sipped her wine.

"Other incidents? Like what?" Maggie leaned forward, looking concerned.

"Childish pranks," Ellie answered. "I found the mailbox stuffed with animal dung a few times. Annoying, but hardly life-threatening. And there were broken flowerpots all over the lawn in the front of the house. That happened a few times."

"That's how it started," Ben clarified. "There was more."

He offered the women more wine, but no one wanted a refill. He filled his own glass again, Lucy noticed. It might have been his third. But who was counting? Well, she was, she realized. He wasn't driving tonight. What was the difference? He was in his own home, and it had been a very stressful day.

"The barn was broken into and some tools tossed around and bent, animal feed spilled out all over the place. Everything was generally messed up. Oh, our little Country Store was trashed once in the middle of the night, too," he added. "That was a few weeks ago."

"A big mess," Ellie conceded. "A few dollars stolen out of the cash box. But it was more the breakage. Jars of jam and herbal hand lotion we sell smeared on our T-shirts. Apples all spilled out and smashed. There was a lot of yarn ruined, and they broke one of my spinning wheels." She barely looked at them as she recited these woes but tugged nervously at the fringe of a pillow that was in her lap.

"Oh, that's too bad," Maggie sympathized.

"All these things have happened since you moved in?" Dana sounded shocked. She was Ellie's friend but obviously had not been taken into the Kruegers' confidence. "Why didn't you say something?"

Ellie glanced up, then looked away. "I didn't want to worry you. We were dealing with it. I think it sounds worse when we describe it than it actually was at the time."

Lucy wondered if that were true, or if Ellie was just trying to downplay the situation, even deny it, for some reason.

"What do the police think?"

Ellie glanced at her husband. He set his mouth in a grim line but didn't say anything. "We haven't told the police," she said finally.

"You haven't? Why not?" Dana sat up, looking even more shocked by this revelation. "Hasn't your insurance company asked for a police report?"

"We haven't put in any claims. We have a high deductible, and the damage was either minimal or hard to estimate. It didn't seem worth it," Ben explained. He sighed. "I would have reported it, maybe not at first, but after a few. But . . . well, it upsets Ellie. She doesn't want the bad publicity."

"Not just that," Ellie piped up. "We're the newcomers. The outsiders. Most of the other farmers were raised in this community. Some are even living on the farms where they grew up and where their parents grew up. Say we go to the police and report these events—which, up until today, have been mostly just annoying. The police will go from farm to farm, bothering all our neighbors. They might think we were accusing them," she pointed out. "And it will be in the newspaper. You saw how that reporter acted today. She was just salivating over the sad, negative story and hadn't paid any attention to our grand opening."

Ellie sighed and sunk back against the chair. "We just want to settle in and build our business. When people hear about Laughing Llama yarns, I want them to have a positive association. Not say, 'Oh, right, that's the place with all the vandalism. The animal droppings in the mailbox, the llamas hit with paint balls.' Believe me, I know how this plays out," Ellie said emphatically. "That is not the public image or the branding we're aiming for."

Lucy glanced at her friends. Personally, she would not be worried about "branding" under such circumstances, but the Kruegers did have a big stake in the success of this farm and their fledgling business. They had more or less put all of their eggs in this basket. Or, rather, all of their hand-spun yarn.

Maggie and Dana both looked eager to say something, but Ben spoke up first.

"We've talked it through a few times, and that was our reasoning for keeping the police out of it. So far," he clarified. "I guess we have to report it now. But we do know who's behind it. There's no doubt in my mind. It's Ridley. He's off the grid and flipped his lid."

Lucy nearly laughed out loud at Ben's rhyme. But she caught herself. This situation wasn't funny at all. Actually, it sounded a little scary.

"But why does he do it? Because he's neurotic and paranoid?" Dana asked, puzzling out the situation with professional terms. "Is he fixated on this farm? Or on you two, for some reason?"

"Oh, we know the reason. It's no mystery." Ben glanced at his wife, who pursed her lips and looked away. "Ridley wanted this property in the worst way. We bid against him. He finally gave up and we won, fair and square." He glanced around the group, waving his wineglass. "I know his game. He's trying to scare us off so we'll put it up for sale and he'll have another chance to buy it. That's another reason I don't want to call the police. That would be playing into his plan. He'll think his tactics are working and we're scared. But he's wrong. He's not going to chase us out of here. Nobody is. We're not leaving. Ever."

Lucy glanced at her friends. The accusation seemed extreme. But could it be possible? If Justin Ridley was the troubled personality the Kruegers made him out to be, perhaps it was true.

"Why does he want this farm? You say that he doesn't cultivate his land or raise any livestock. What does he need it for?" Maggie sounded genuinely puzzled.

Ellie sat up and took an apple slice with cheese. "He wants to protect it, to make sure no one builds on it. He'd probably let the whole place grow over like his land, the forest primeval. He's an open spacer," she added. "I'm sorry, we forgot to tell you about that part of this situation. You know about the open space laws around here, right? The laws are about to expire, and the county has voted not to renew them. So the zoning in this farm area is about to change, big time. But there's a group around here that wants to keep the laws in place."

Lucy knew what open space laws were—legislation that protected rural communities, like the outlying area of Plum Harbor, from overdevelopment; from farmland suddenly transforming to shopping malls and condo communities or gated enclaves of mini-mansions.

But she didn't realize that the laws protecting this farming community were about to go off the books. "The laws were changed? When did that happen?"

"Oh, it's been fought over for years now," Dana replied. "A real political Ping-Pong ball. But the county finally voted to let the laws expire a few months ago, and the change will take effect at the start of next year."

"I've heard something about this, too," Maggie added. "At a meeting of small business owners. Yes, it's been a Ping-Pong ball, and it's about to be the NASCAR of real-estate brokers. I can practically hear them warming up their engines."

Dana nodded. "Good point. There will be a scramble for land out here. I'd guess a lot of people are eager to sell."

"Absolutely . . . and a lot that don't want them to," Ellie explained. "They call themselves the Friends of Farmland. They're trying to keep the laws in place just within the town limits. Justin Ridley is their ringleader," she told the others. "The town council is going to have a meeting about this soon. In a week or two, I think," she added.

"Friends of Farmland. Right. They're no friends of mine, I'll tell you that much." Ben took a long sip of his wine. "When I think of those poor llamas, the way I found them in the field today . . . who would do that to defenseless creatures? What kind of person? I don't care about their cause. That doesn't make it right." Ben's voice sounded hoarse—he was getting teary-eyed. He pulled out a tissue and dabbed his eyes. "Hypo-crites. How can they claim they want to save the environ-ment . . . and hurt poor defenseless creatures? Don't they have any heart?"

"Honey, please. Don't get yourself all upset again," Ellie crooned and patted his shoulder. "He talks tough, but I married such a sensitive man. He's just a big softy."

Lucy frowned. People did get passionate about issues like this. Though it was probably best to leave emotions out of such debates.

Ellie seemed to think it was time to reel her husband in a bit, too. She waved her hand at him. "Now, Ben, I know you're upset about the animals. But we can't take it personally. I'm sure none of those people have anything against us. They don't even know us. We love this farm. It was our dream to move here. I think once people get used to us, they'll see that we're committed to staying here. Not just dabblers."

"We researched this business for over a year before we even started to look for property or livestock," Ben told the women.

"We even lived on a farm in Ohio for two weeks taking, well, llama lessons, I guess you'd have to say," Ellie added, finally smiling a bit.

"The point is, we're committed," Ben continued. "We're not here to just flip the property to some development group once the laws expire. That's what Ridley thinks. I have a sound business plan, and we're starting off slowly and carefully, trying to build a good name for our product. Ellie's got other streams of income going to pay the bills. The little shop and her spinning classes. The apple orchard turned a nice profit this season, too. She might even do lessons online. We've got a nice website up and running," he added proudly.

"We're not dabblers or dilettantes," Ellie insisted. "Though

I guess I understand Justin Ridley's point of view. He thinks we'll get bored here. Or the business will fail and we'll sell out to developers. I'm sure he doesn't think we'll last until the end of the year."

"Has he ever said anything like that to you directly?" Dana's tone was gentle and even curious. But Lucy could see what she was getting at, trying to sort out the facts here from the hyperbole and accusations.

Ellie shrugged. "We've rarely spoken to him. We only see him once in a while. We catch sight of him walking through the woods. Or if we're in the meadow where the llamas graze, we sometimes see him on the other side of the fence, on his land."

"I've had words with him," Ben piped up. "He's said some nasty things to me. Language I wouldn't repeat to ladies. But Ellie has the gist. We're the city slickers and he's Nature Boy." Ben laughed harshly. "I work harder in one day around here than he does on his place in a month. You tell me which one of us is carrying on the great farming tradition. Which one is preserving the pristine beauty of the environment?"

Lucy saw the conflict very starkly—the urbane Kruegers, with their fine wines and vegetable pâté, clashing with their country neighbors, born and bred in this community. One neighbor, in particular.

"I can understand why you don't want to stir up trouble with your new neighbors. Or give the business bad publicity. But this attack on your livestock was more than a harmless joke." Maggie spoke in a quiet but concerned tone. "Aside from the injuries to the llamas, you may not be able to use much of the fiber on the llamas that were hit with that paint. Not until they're sheared once or twice," she added knowingly. "I have to confess, I don't understand why you and Ben are so reluctant to call the police this time. Aren't you afraid that if you don't find the person who did this, it could happen again? Maybe something even worse?"

"And it is a crime to harm livestock," Dana reminded them. "You might be putting yourself at some legal risk by not reporting it."

Dana's husband, Jack, was an attorney and had been part of local law enforcement for many years before going back to school to earn his law degree. Dana was savvy about legal matters and made a good point, Lucy thought. One she hadn't even thought of.

Ellie and Ben shared a glance. Then Ellie turned to look at Maggie. "I guess I am a little worried now. Ben and I will have to talk this over more. Weigh the pros and cons. But you're right, Maggie. This was the worst harassment so far. Whoever is behind it really raised the bar."

Ben stood up and shook his head. "Whether we tell the police or not, we're not leaving. We're not playing into their hands, running off like scared rabbits. Ridley would love that. That's just what he's hoping for."

Lucy glanced at Ben. She didn't know what to say. He clearly thought of his neighbor as the opponent, even the enemy, and this was a conflict only one could win. Was that a masculine characteristic, to think in terms of a win-or-lose contest?

"What about security? Do you have any?" Dana asked.

"We put a system in a few weeks ago. There are alarms on

the corral gates and barn. And we even put up a few surveillance cameras. But with all the people here for the festival, we decided to shut the system off for the day," Ben explained. "We usually only put it on at night anyway."

"But now we'll put it on in the daytime, too, I guess." Ellie shook her head. "We moved out of the city to get away from all that. I had some starry-eyed fantasy that we wouldn't even worry about locking doors anymore. . . poof! There goes that one." She laughed, trying to make a joke of it, but Lucy sensed she was sincerely disappointed.

Lucy imagined that the Kruegers had arrived with quite a few fantasies about country living. And that many had gone up with the same "poof" by now.

Lucy liked the Kruegers and definitely felt sympathetic about their travails here. But from what she'd heard, they had no real proof that their neighbor Justin Ridley was behind the harassment. She didn't approve of hunting and the thought of guns made her shiver, but just because he knew how to use a gun didn't mean he'd shot the llamas. The court system still operated on an "innocent until proven guilty" theory, didn't it?

She wondered what her friends thought and could hardly wait for the car ride home to exchange impressions.

Ben was yanking the cork out of another bottle of wine. "May I refill anyone's glass? This is a terrific cabernet."

"None for me, thanks. I'm driving." Maggie smiled and gently moved her glass beyond his reach. Lucy could see that she'd only taken a sip or two of the first glass he'd poured for her.

When the others declined, as well, Ben filled his own glass again and sat down.

"Would you like to stay for dinner?" Ellie offered. "I'm sure I can toss something together."

Lucy sensed that Ellie was still upset and appreciated their company. She didn't have any need to get home but didn't know about the others.

"Thank you, but I think we have to get going," Maggie answered.

Dana nodded in agreement. "I'd love to stay and visit longer, Ellie. But I'm meeting Jack for dinner in town at seven. I'll have just enough time to get there," she noted, glancing at her watch. "Maybe the four of us can get together soon. I'll call you, all right?"

"Yes, please do. That would be fun." Ellie looked a bit disappointed but forced a smile.

"Oh, and don't forget our meeting this week." Maggie stood up and gathered her things. "We'll be at the shop on Tuesday night this week. Suzanne has some sort of parents' meeting at school on Thursday. She nearly had a fit when I hinted we might meet without her," she added with a laugh.

"I'll try to make it. It would be a nice break," Ellie replied.

Everyone said good night to Ben, and Ellie walked them through the kitchen to the back door, which was closer to Maggie's car—though not by much, Lucy soon realized.

The sun had just set and the air outside had grown cooler, a crisp reminder that fall was moving in. Ellie stood at the back door in a yellow patch of light, hugging a sweater around her shoulders with one hand and waving with the other.

"Thanks again for all your help. See you soon," she called out.

Lucy and her friends waved back, their footsteps crunching

over the gravel path as they headed in the direction of the field where the cars had been parked during the fair.

"I should have brought the car around to the house, that was dumb of me," Maggie scolded herself. "It's still out in that field, where they had everyone park. Now we have a walk ahead of us."

"Oh, it's not that far." Dana took the lead with a springy step. "I could use some fresh air. I only had a glass of wine, but it was on an empty stomach."

Lucy felt the same, though she had enjoyed a few bites of apple and cheese.

"This cool air will clear your head," Maggie said. "It's a beautiful night. Very quiet out here. I can see why they like it so much."

"It is very quiet. And the landscape is lovely, day or night," Dana observed.

Lucy thought that was true. She understood the pull of this place. It really was beautiful and unspoiled.

As they walked along the dirt road that led across the property, she felt the darkness and quiet surround them. The night sky was velvety blue, dotted with tiny points of light—many more stars than were visible back in the village. The sky stretched in a wide, sheltering arc above the open farmland, the orchard and rutted fields, and clusters of trees on the other side of the meadow. Distracted by the view, Lucy stumbled and caught herself by clinging to Maggie's sweater.

"Sorry, I tripped on a root or something."

"That's all right. It is dark out here. I wish we had a flashlight. I keep one in my knitting bag. I know that sounds odd, but it comes in handy. Too bad I left it in my car," Maggie murmured.

Lucy glanced at her. "At least the moon is out. That helps."

"An autumn moon, too," Dana added. "Though it's not quite full."

The moon was bright, though veiled by wispy clouds and not all that much help once they walked beyond the light of the outdoor lamps around the farmhouse. They continued on, a bit slower, careful of their footing on the rough dirt road. All Lucy could hear were their footsteps and the rustle of the tall treetops in the breeze.

Suddenly, a long, full-throated howl broke the silence.

Maggie stopped and turned her head toward the sound. "Good heavens, what was that? Sounds like a wolf . . . or at least a coyote."

"It's a hunting dog," Lucy replied calmly.

"Even I knew that. And I'm a cat person," Dana agreed.

They heard the sound again, this time a duet and even louder. "Whatever it is, it's coming closer . . . and there are two of them." Despite Lucy's explanation, Maggie still sounded alarmed.

"Maybe it's a two-headed dog, like the one in the Greek myth, that guards the gates of hell?" Dana was trying to make a joke, Lucy guessed, but the image, along with the howling, was unnerving.

And she was not entirely correct. "That dog has three heads, Dana. Not that I want to get picky or anything," Lucy replied.

"Let's hope it's not a dog at all, then. Maybe it's just that neighbor from hell, out for his nocturnal stroll," Maggie suggested softly.

"Sounds about right, from what we've heard so far," Lucy countered.

Maggie turned her head. She was carrying a bag of yarn and clutched it to her chest. "Very funny, ladies. I hope we're still laughing a few minutes from now. I think it's almost here . . ."

The howling did sound very close now and suddenly broke into a frenzy of barking and even a few snarls. Then they heard the sound of something crashing through a nearby stand of trees and brush.

Maggie and Dana, who were in the lead, suddenly stopped in their tracks and Lucy bumped right into them.

They were far enough from the farmhouse so that their voices—even a loud shout—would not be heard. But not close enough to Maggie's car to break out into a run.

In fact, they couldn't even see the car, Lucy realized. They were now walking past a patch of woods. Lucy didn't remember passing trees, but she had been distracted when they arrived and everything looked so different now.

Maggie's car is back there somewhere, Lucy reminded herself. It has to be.

"Come on, ladies. What are we scared of?" Dana turned, looking at Maggie and Lucy. "We're all acting so silly. They're just dogs. Out for some air and exercise. Doesn't everyone let their dogs out at night?"

Before Lucy could answer, she heard a sound and turned to see a figure emerge from the nearby stand of trees. All Lucy could make out was a khaki-green barn coat and baseball cap. She stopped again and so did her friends.

"Who's that?" Maggie asked.

But before anyone could hazard a guess, a beam from a flashlight signaled a greeting. The figure walked toward them, and Lucy shielded her eyes with her hand. She couldn't see past the glaring light.

"Hey, ladies . . . where are you going?"

It was Dot. Lucy quickly recognized her voice and soon distinguished her outline. Lucy heard everyone release one huge, synchronized sigh of relief.

"We're trying to find my car," Maggie replied. "It's somewhere behind these trees, right? In the field where everyone parked today?"

"Oh my, you're way off. You got all turned around in the dark." Dot sounded amused but in a good-natured way. "The cars were parked down in that direction, just through the gate over there . . ."

She flashed her light down the road, in the direction they had come. They'd somehow missed a turn and walked right past the path that led to the field that they were looking for.

"I had a feeling we'd walked too far," Maggie said.

"Everything looks different in the dark," Dot agreed. "I'll walk you back. You need some light out here, even though the moon is fairly bright tonight," she observed, looking up at the sky.

"Apparently, not bright enough. Not for us anyway," Dana said with a laugh. "How are the llamas doing?"

"They're just fine. Resting like babies. I just looked in on them. I was taking a walk around the property, checking up on things, on my way down to the see Kruegers."

Considering what Ellie and Ben had said about their neighbor Justin Ridley's nocturnal activities, perhaps Dot was out patrolling, a one-woman security crew, in addition to her other duties. Or maybe she just took on this job out of her concern for the animals. She did seem attached to them.

With the aid of Dot's flashlight, Lucy and her friends quickly found Maggie's car and were soon on their way.

Lucy turned to see Dot standing in the empty field. She stood waving, illuminated by the silvery light.

Lucy waved back. "We were lucky Dot came along. We'd still be stumbling around out there," she said to her friends.

"It was good of her to walk us all the way to the car," Maggie said.

Dana agreed. "She certainly works hard."

"Yes, she does," Maggie agreed. "I wonder if she has any guess about who shot at the llamas today. I wonder if she agrees with the Kruegers about Justin Ridley."

"There seemed to be no doubt for Ben," Dana replied. "Though Ellie was trying to keep an open mind. You all know that I love Ellie—she and I go way back—but I do wonder if Ridley can be half as paranoid and obsessive as the picture they paint."

"Half as nuts, you mean?" Lucy asked. She had understood Dana's terms but just wanted to rattle her cage a bit.

Dana smiled. "Yes, to use more professional terms. Don't get all shrinky on me, Lucy," she teased. "What do you think Maggie?"

Maggie didn't answer at first. She stared straight ahead, steering the Subaru on the dark country road. "I think they've been under a tremendous amount of stress—leaving all their friends and connections in the city, and starting a new business. One they know little about. That's enough choppy water right there for any couple to navigate."

"And they haven't been married all that long," Dana added. "About three years, I think. They met on some Internet dating site and it was love at first e-mail."

"E-mates?" Lucy quipped.

"Something like that," Dana replied. "And before you make fun, those sites can work out for some people."

Maggie glanced at her for a moment, then looked back at the road. "And some meet a lot of insincere hucksters and even people who are married but represent themselves as single."

Her strong response got Lucy thinking and curious.

"Not that you have ever signed up on any of those sites, right?" Lucy prodded.

"Me? Of course not. That's not my style. I did take a look one night," Maggie admitted. "Just out of curiosity. . . . But the form asked too many questions. I thought it was all quite expensive . . . and annoying."

"Well, it worked for Ellie and Ben," Dana cut in. "And I agree they've been under a huge amount of stress with so many important life changes. Even without any harassment and vandalism tossed into the pot, that kind of pressure can definitely affect a person's judgment. It's only natural to look for a cause to the situation. Or someone to blame."

"A scapegoat, you mean?" Lucy asked.

"'Scapegoat' is a polite way of putting it. It sounds more like they've demonized this Justin Ridley," Maggie said frankly. "Unless . . . well, unless he's really as strange and extreme in his views as they say. Which is possible," she conceded.

"It is," Dana agreed. "I just don't understand why they haven't brought in the police. Despite their explanation."

"Me, either," Maggie said, turning at a dark, empty crossroads. "But maybe after this incident and our coaxing, they will. Personally, I'd be afraid that whoever wishes them ill will come back and do it again. Or take even more violent action."

"I feel the same, Maggie. I think we were both clear about that and voiced our concern. That's all we can do. We can't make them report it to the police. That has to be their own decision."

"Yes, I know, but . . ." Maggie's voice trailed off on a sigh.

Lucy shared their concerns but had a slightly different take. "If they don't report this to the police, I wonder if Matt has an obligation to. As a vet."

"The same as a doctor who treats a child that he or she suspects might have been abused?" Maggie asked.

"Yes, that's what I mean."

"Interesting. I never thought of that." Dana's tone was thoughtful. "I wonder if Jack knows. I'll ask when I get back."

"I'll ask Matt, too. Or maybe he's already reported it. Even if he doesn't have a legal obligation, I'm sure he feels a moral one." She knew Matt. He was not the type to let this go, to sit by and let someone harm animals without any consequences.

Maggie glanced at her. "Do you think he'll go around Ellie

and Ben? That might be a problem for them. I guess we'll see Ellie on Tuesday night, at the meeting. We can find out what happened then."

Lucy thought that was true, though she hoped that they would hear before Tuesday that Ellie and Ben had called the police and were doing all they could to get to the bottom of this disturbing situation.

Chapter Four

On Monday morning, Maggie arrived at her shop a bit early to give herself time to unload her car. A chore she wasn't looking forward to. At this time of day there were plenty of parking spaces, and she parked right in front of the knitting shop.

Maggie had opened the shop about three years ago and had been lucky to find the perfect spot: the first floor of a freestanding Victorian that had once been a house, right in the middle of Main Street.

Set back a fair space, the building had a peaked roof, a wraparound porch, and plenty of classic trim. Maggie had dressed it up with flower boxes and a border of perennials along the brick path from the sidewalk and more beds along the bottom of the porch. Whatever the season, she took care to make the shop look inviting, with eye-catching displays in the big bay window.

She'd been an art teacher for more than twenty years at

Plum Harbor High School and had found great satisfaction in that career. But soon after her husband, Bill, died, Maggie knew it was time to start a new phase of her life. Knitting was her passion, and teaching came so naturally. She had always daydreamed about opening a knitting shop—combining her talents and knowledge—and knew it was time to try.

After all this time, she never tired of getting up and going out to open her store. She still felt a little thrill each time she unlocked the door. Being a shopkeeper was much more interesting work than she'd expected. You really never knew what the day might bring.

This day was going to bring a backache, Maggie realized, if she wasn't careful about unloading her car.

Luckily, just as she tugged out the first carton, she spotted Lucy coming down Main Street, tugged along by her golden retriever, Tink, and on the other lead of her two-dog leash by Matt's dog, Walley, an aging but amazingly resilient three-legged chocolate Labrador retriever.

Lucy usually walked the dogs down to the village around this time, especially in good weather. Today Maggie was particularly happy to see her.

"There you are," Maggie greeted her friend. "I was just wondering if you were stopping by this morning."

"Wondering if I'd come in time to help you unload your car, you mean?" Lucy smiled, seeing through the fawning greeting.

"Well, that, too," Maggie admitted. "Many hands make light work, and all that."

Lucy tied the dogs to the porch railing and came down

again to help with the boxes of yarn and other supplies Maggie had used at her booth.

"I always promise myself I'm not going to bring half the store to those fairs. But I can't seem to pack light," Maggie admitted.

"I know what you mean. I have the same problem going away for a weekend."

"I hate it when my booth looks skimpy," Maggie explained. "It gives a bad impression to potential customers," Maggie continued as they returned to the car for another load. "Ellie's fair was certainly crowded enough. It was great event . . . until the end, I mean."

"Yes, too bad it ended on such a bad note."

After three loads, the car was not quite empty but Maggie's back had begun to pinch and she thought Lucy had worked hard enough for her daily cup of coffee.

"Let's leave the rest. I'll get Princess Phoebe to haul her share when she comes in. Whenever that turns out to be."

"Can't argue with that," Lucy said cheerfully.

Maggie and Lucy went inside again, and Maggie dropped a carton on the long oak worktable at the back of the shop, along with a pile of mail she'd found at the front door.

"I wonder if there's anything in the newspaper about the fair or the paint ball attack. I wonder if Ellie and Ben called the police." Lucy took at seat at the table and looked up at her.

"I was wondering about that, too. The paper is in this stack of mail. Why don't you take a look and I'll make some coffee?"

While Lucy paged through the latest edition of the *Plum Harbor Times*, Maggie slipped back into the storeroom, which had originally been a kitchen. A few fixtures and appliances were still intact, which came in handy.

She brought out two mugs of coffee and sat at the table across from her friend.

"Here's something." Lucy turned the paper around so Maggie could see the page.

A black-and-white photo showed the striped tents with a furry-headed alpaca smiling for the camera. Or looking a lot like it was smiling, Maggie thought.

Lucy read the short article aloud: "'Fiber Fest Fun,'" she began. "'It was a day of good old-fashioned family fun at Laughing Llama Farm Grand Opening Fiber Festival, held Saturday noon to five. The farm, owned by Ellen and Ben Krueger, hosted many vendors, with exhibits of spinning and other handcrafts, along with demonstrations of sheepherding and shearing . . .'" Lucy looked up. "There's more but it's just a fluff piece—no pun intended. Nothing about the attack on the llamas."

Maggie had opened a carton and began sorting skeins of yarn on the table. "I'm not sure if that's good news or bad. Good for Ellie's publicity efforts, I guess. I suppose she scared the reporter off the paint ball story. But it probably means they didn't call the police after all."

Lucy leaned back and sipped her coffee. "Maybe the Kruegers called the police yesterday. After they thought about it a little and it was too late to appear in today's paper."

"Maybe," Maggie murmured. They could have called on Sunday. But she had a feeling that they had not. "Did you hear anything more about the llamas, from Matt?"

Lucy nodded. "Matt called a few times yesterday to check their progress. I think he planned to go out to the farm this afternoon to see Buttercup. He said that, so far, they are all coming along with no setbacks."

"That's good to hear. It sounds like the patients are getting excellent care."

"The very best," Lucy agreed.

Maggie had to smile at the way Lucy beamed. She was proud of Matt and very much in love. It was sweet to see. Matt had moved into Lucy's cottage about six months ago, and the glow wasn't gone yet. A good sign, Maggie thought.

Maggie wondered if they'd get engaged soon, maybe at Christmas? But she didn't like to pry and wouldn't offer her opinion unless Lucy asked for it. Unlike their other friends.

"I did ask if he was obliged to report the incident," Lucy added. "If the Kruegers haven't already. He said he was but didn't want to put them in a difficult position. He's going to talk to them about it again today."

"That sounds reasonable." Maggie sipped her coffee.

"Look at this, an article about the open space laws." Lucy had turned the page and now folded the paper to read aloud again. "'The village trustees will meet in a special session to discuss the open space zoning laws that are due to expire throughout Essex County the first of the coming year. A proposal to keep the laws on the books within village limits, drafted by citizens' group Friends of Farmland, will be discussed in a town hall open forum meeting next Thursday night.'"

"That should be a lively one," Maggie predicted. "Every time

I need to sit through a meeting at the village hall, I practically fall asleep. I might try to catch this one, though it does conflict with knitting group night," she added. "But I don't know much about this issue, beyond Ellie and Ben's side of the story."

Lucy looked up from the newspaper. "If we take Ellie and Ben at their word, this debate will be more than lively. It could get downright ugly."

Maggie was thinking the same thing. "It would be interesting to see the personalities involved," Lucy added. "Justin Ridley will be there, don't you think? Didn't Ellie say he was the head of the Friends of Farmland?"

"'Ringleader' is the exact term she used," Maggie recalled. "Yes, I think he would be there. Unless he's even more of a recluse than the Kruegers make him out to be. What else does it say?"

Lucy looked back at the paper and continued. "'Attorneys for Friends of Farmland assert that as an incorporated village, Plum Harbor has the right to maintain the open space zoning laws within town limits, regardless of the county's change. Attorneys for the village are still studying the proposal and have not made a recommendation to the mayor and trustees.'"

"It's like states' rights or something," Maggie observed. "Not a bad thing, when you think of it. I don't know that much about the issue. But being out there on Saturday, I have to say, I wouldn't want to see that beautiful countryside looking like the turnpike up near the interstate. It does seem worth the fight to preserve it."

"I love it out there, too. I love the emptiness and peacefulness. I understand why people are passionate about the cause.

But I hate to think that Ellie and Ben are caught in the cross fire and someone really is trying to force off them off their farm because of all this. That doesn't seem fair or right to me, either."

Maggie felt the same. "When are the village trustees due to vote? Does it say?" she asked after a moment.

Lucy looked back at the paper, then shook her head. "Nothing about that here. Soon, I'd guess. Maybe once the issue is decided things will settle down and that will help Ellie and Ben."

"I hope so." Maggie had emptied the first carton and started on another.

Lucy glanced at her watch. "Whoops, look at the time. I've got to run. I didn't even get to show you my little knitting glitch." Lucy peered into her knitting tote but didn't take out her project. "That easy, breezy argyle vest I started for Matt? It's acting up again."

"That's too bad. I thought you'd take to intarsia in a snap." Maggie gave Lucy an encouraging smile. Lucy was a skillful knitter—not as advanced as some others in their group, but she hadn't been knitting as long, either. Maggie thought she was quite able but lacked confidence. She needed to break through the argyle ceiling on her own, if possible.

Lucy was not the only one to bring Maggie her knitting mishaps. Not by a long shot. Maggie sorted out just about everyone's tangles and lost stitches. It was her particular genius and calling. Her friends had started calling her the local EFT—Emergency Fiber Technician. An odd little nickname, but it fit her pretty well, she had to admit.

Lucy closed the bag and hooked it over her arm. "Oh, I'll figure it out. I'd better get Monday started."

Maggie was surprised but impressed. "It's the right thing to do, Lucy. Sorting out your own knitting problems builds character."

"Thanks for the tough love. I'll try to remember that when I'm about to throw this mess across the TV room."

"As long as you don't throw it at Matt, I think a little venting can be a good thing," Maggie advised.

Lucy waved and headed out the door. Alert to her approach, the dogs were both up on their hind legs, noses pressed against the big bay window at the front of the store.

Maggie thought Tink and Walley looked very cute, though she'd have to send Phoebe out later with some paper towels and a bottle of Windex. Lucy's canine friends had fogged up the entire lower half of the glass.

Lucy hadn't thought much about Maggie's tough love when she left the shop that morning. But that night after dinner, when she took the vest out of her knitting bag and spread it out on her lap, she suddenly regretted that she had not persuaded her knitting mentor to fix the messy spot and leave her to build character with some other, more important, life challenge.

Picking over the wayward stitches and trying to figure out where she'd gone wrong, she sighed out loud in frustration.

"What are you working on, honey?" Matt was stretched out on the couch in their small sitting room, channel surfing. The dogs were stretched out side by side on the area rug, working on chew toys.

"Building character. 'What doesn't kill us makes us stronger,'" she mumbled, quoting Friedrich Nietzsche and knowing Matt had no idea what she was talking about. She looked up at his puzzled expression. "I've messed up your vest, and Maggie wants me to figure it out for myself. She thinks it will make me a better person."

"I get it. Well, I think you're a pretty cool person right now. I don't see much room for improvement. Can't you just cut out the tangled part or something?"

Lucy had to smile at his compliment and the suggestion. "Wish I could. But, once again, knitting imitates life."

She dug the pattern out of her bag and tried to figure out where she'd gone wrong. Matt finally stopped the remote on a nature documentary about giant grizzly bears. Not Lucy's first choice. But at least it wasn't sports and he wasn't bouncing around the channels for hours, which gave her a headache.

The mighty brown bears were ambling through rushing streams and gorging on wild salmon. Matt was dozing off, one hand hanging off the couch, absently patting Walley on the head.

His cell phone rang, jarring him awake, and he pulled it from his shirt pocket. "Dr. McDougal," he answered as he abruptly sat up. "Really? That's terrible. . . . Where is the wound?"

That single word and the sharp tone of his question caught Lucy's attention. He was totally focused, listening with a somber expression to the pet owner on the other side of the line.

"Keep pressure on it. I'll be there as fast as I can."

Lucy had already dropped her knitting and waited for him to end the call. "Who was that? What's wrong?"

Matt picked up one of his jogging shoes and pulled it on without untying the laces. "The Kruegers. . . . One of the llamas was just stabbed. Dot found it out in the pasture. I have to get over there right away."

"How awful . . ." Lucy's mind spun with inferences. More violence at the Krueger farm. Who was doing this? Why? How cruel to target these poor animals . . .

She couldn't stay home alone, waiting hours for Matt to come back and tell her what had happened. She wouldn't be able to stand it.

"Can I come with you? Maybe I can help."

Lucy had never asked to go on one of his calls before. But Ellie was a friend. And she did think she could help him. If only to carry the heavy instruments he might need to examine the injured animal.

He glanced up as he tugged on his other shoe. "You can come if you want to. But it sounds bad. A lot of blood," he warned. "It won't be pretty."

Lucy jumped up and grabbed her jacket and house keys. "Don't worry, I can take it."

Lucy knew that she sounded very calm. But secretly, she only hoped that was true.

As they drove out to the farm in Matt's truck, he stared straight ahead with complete concentration on the road.

Lucy felt her anxiety building the closer they got. "This is so strange . . . and horrible. They have to call the police now, don't you think?"

Matt nodded. "I gave them a chance, but it looks like I

have to contact the police this time. I don't know what's going on over there between them and their neighbors. But I'm not going to see any more animals hurt. Not if I can help it."

Lucy nodded but didn't answer aloud. She reached across the seat and held his hand.

Once they were out in the countryside, Matt's foot was heavy on the pedal and they flew along the empty roads. Lucy hoped they wouldn't meet up with a trooper and a radar gun, hiding in a cruiser behind the trees somewhere. Maybe the police gave a pass to veterinarians on emergency calls?

They arrived at the Laughing Llama Farm about forty minutes later, and Matt only slowed down a little as he drove the truck through the gate and straight out to the meadow where the llamas were corralled.

Darkness had settled across the landscape, but out in the field they saw a cluster of flashlights and a large camping lamp. Lucy could make out the shadowy figures of Dot, Ellie, and Ben gathered around a llama stretched out on the ground. Dot knelt beside the animal, wearing yellow rubber gloves and pressing a folded towel to the llama's shoulder. A blood-soaked towel, Lucy realized as they drew closer.

In the darkness she could see a dark pool beside the animal and Dot's gloved hands covered in blood, as well.

Matt ran straight to the llama, clutching his medical bag. Lucy followed.

"Matt . . . thank God you're here. She's fading. We can hardly hear her breathing anymore . . ." Ellie sounded nearly hysterical. Ben stood beside her and touched her shoulder.

The animal seemed in distress, breathing heavily. Dot

was near the llama's head, petting her body and making soft sounds. She looked distressed, too, her face tear-stained.

Matt knelt down and quickly examined the llama. He lifted the towel to check the wound, which was in the animal's shoulder, just below its long neck. Then he put it back again. "You need to put more pressure on this wound, Dot. It's in a tough spot. We can't make a tourniquet."

Dot nodded, her expression bleak. Lucy watched her lean forward and press down with both hands on the blood-soaked towel.

Matt quickly peered into the llama's eyes, which were almost closed, and then listened to its heartbeat with his stethoscope. He already had gloves on, somehow, though Lucy had not noticed when he'd managed to do that.

He flipped open his bag and pulled out instruments. "We have to stop the bleeding. She's lost a lot of blood and there's no time and no way to give her a transfusion. I can't give her any tranquilizer—her heartbeat is too slow. We have to hold her down while I close this up. . . . Someone hold that light up for me. Right here, above her head . . ."

Ellie grabbed the camp light and held it where Matt said.

"The rest of you get down here and help hold her." He turned to Dot, Ben, and Lucy and showed them where to grab on to the animal. "She's very weak. She won't put up much of a fight," he predicted, pulling out what looked like a plastic clamp from the bag. "The cut is deep. Looks like it hit an artery. I'm going to try to clamp it and stop the blood flow . . ."

He pushed the towel aside and began working on the wound. Lucy turned her head away. Matt had been right—it was difficult to watch. She focused on her task, holding down the llama's right foreleg, which jerked back and forth a bit. But the poor thing was quite weak, and Lucy was able to hold the leg steady.

Matt worked on the wound for a few minutes. Lucy couldn't tell if he was making any progress, though he did begin putting in stitches.

Suddenly the llama made a horrid, gasping sound. It shivered all over, and pink foam bubbled up at its mouth.

Ellie screamed and dropped the light. "What's that? What's happening to her?"

Ben looked up at her but didn't say anything. He looked stunned, Lucy thought, his eyes about to spill over with tears as he stared back down at the animal. Matt had taken out a syringe but didn't use it.

The llama went rigid, its eyelids flickering wildly for a moment. Then it shuddered again and its body went limp. The llama stared up at them with a sightless gaze.

Lucy knew instinctively it had died.

Matt felt its neck for a pulse, then closed the llama's eyes with his hand. He sat back on his heels and looked up at Ellie and Ben. "I'm sorry. . . . I did all I could. I clamped that artery. But she'd lost too much blood. . . . I'm sorry," he said again. "She's gone."

"Gone? You mean she's dead?" Ellie sounded shocked. Her mouth hung open a moment, and her eyes widened in a horrified stare. "That's horrible! I can't believe it. It was just a cut on her shoulder. How could that be?"

Matt stood up and tugged off his gloves. "The wound was

short but deep. The blade hit an artery. By the time I closed it off, it was too late."

"Oh . . . I'm sorry. I didn't mean to blame you. It's not your fault," Ellie apologized. She turned back to the llama and reached down to touch her head. "Poor Daphne . . . she was my very favorite . . ."

Ellie's voice trailed off on a loud sob as she started crying. Ben comforted her, turning her face in to his broad shoulder.

"Why is this happening to us, Ben?" Lucy heard her say. "Why?"

Ben didn't answer at first, just stroked her back and hair.

He looked at Matt. "I still don't understand. It was just her shoulder. How could she have died from that?"

Matt nodded. "Yes, I know. It didn't look serious. But it was."

Lucy was amazed at his patience. He explained again how the cut had severed an artery, which caused severe blood loss. That, combined with the time it had taken him to reach the farm, had left her with only a slim chance of survival.

Dot let out a long sigh, then a quiet sob. She sniffed hard and wiped the back of her hand across her eyes. "Poor thing. . . . It just isn't right. She was such a sweetheart. The sweetest in the herd. Who would do a thing like that to poor little Daphne? I don't understand. I don't get it at all."

She looked over at Ellie and Ben, tears squeezing out the corners of her small blue eyes and down her chapped cheeks. Ellie stepped over and patted Dot's broad back.

Matt stood up. Lucy's heart hurt for him; he looked so sad and defeated. She knew that he lost patients from time to time and had to put many animals down. That was just part of his practice. But she knew it hurt him to see an animal die, especially this way, from a violent, unnatural cause.

"I'm sorry," he said again. "You can have an autopsy performed to find out the exact cause of death."

"We will have her autopsied," Ben answered in a low tone, edged with anger. "We'll need that for court. When the police arrest Justin Ridley."

Ellie turned to him. "We need to call the police, Ben. This time, we really have to."

"Don't worry. I'll call right now." Ben took out his phone and dialed 911. Lucy heard him talking to the dispatcher, explaining the situation. While it wasn't a true emergency, Lucy guessed that uniformed officers, or even detectives, would be sent out to make a report and examine the area. She wondered if they could find any clues at all in the dark.

She did recall that there were security cameras set up around the property. She wondered if any had captured the stabbing incident. The police wouldn't have to look too far to catch the guilty party if the cameras had done their job, she reflected.

Matt was talking quietly with Dot. Lucy walked over and stood beside him.

"We've been keeping the herd in the barn at night," Dot was explaining to Matt, "ever since Saturday. I had led most of them back and put them in their stalls. Only Daphne was left. I saw her at the very edge of the pasture, by the road, and decided to come back for her. It had gotten dark, and I could hardly see without my light. When I came back out, she was gone. I thought maybe she had bust loose somehow. Taken a leap over the fence. But she was a good girl. Never a jumper. So that didn't make sense."

Dot sighed, looking sad again, recalling the llama's sweet disposition. "I flashed the light around, calling her name. Then I heard her bleating and found her. She'd fallen to her knees, the blood streaming out of her side. . . . It was . . . horrible." Dot shook her head, overcome now with emotion. She wiped her hand across her mouth and sighed. "I started screaming and Ellie came out. We tried our best to stop the bleeding. We didn't know what else to do."

Matt reached out and touched her arm. "You did all you could, Dot. That was a mortal blow. Short of a transfusion, there was nothing anyone could do to save her."

Dot sighed and nodded. "At least I was with her at the end, talking to her, stroking her head. I think that calmed her a little."

"I'm sure it did," Matt said knowingly.

Dot had removed her large rubber gloves, but the front of her clothes—a flannel shirt and jeans—were covered with blood. She seemed unmindful of the mess. She was in shock, Lucy realized, but still holding herself together. She was a hardy one, that was for sure.

Ben and Ellie had been talking privately after he finished his call to the police. As they walked over together, Ellie held Ben's arm and wiped her eyes with a clump of tissues.

"The police will want to talk to you, Dot," Ben said. "And with you, too, Matt," he added.

"We can stay. It's not a problem," Matt replied.

Ben nodded. "I guess they could catch up with you in town tomorrow, but it's probably best to just get this over with."

"Were you out here with Dot when she found Daphne?" Matt asked him.

"No, I was on my way home from town. Ellie was in the house, starting dinner. Right, honey?" He turned to her and she nodded.

"I was at the sink, and I heard Dot scream. I grabbed a light and ran out as fast as I could. After I saw what happened, I called Ben on my cell phone. Dot and I didn't know what to do. Well, she had some idea. But I was . . . horrified. I'm afraid I wasn't much help."

Lucy could imagine the panicked scene. A replay of Saturday's event . . . only this time with real blood instead of paint.

"Luckily, I wasn't far," Ben added. "I told Ellie to call you and drove straight out to the pasture."

Dot had walked back to the barn and now returned. Lucy could see that she'd changed into a clean sweatshirt and khaki pants rolled up at the cuff to accommodate her short legs. She carried a large blue tarp and spread it carefully over Daphne, as if tucking a beloved child into bed.

"I think we should keep her covered so the animals that are out at night won't bother her."

Matt crouched down and helped her secure the covering. "Good idea. An agent from the county's animal control department will come tomorrow to collect the body. They'll do the autopsy and send me the information."

Ben crossed his arms over his chest. "I know it's necessary, but we all know what happened. Ridley snuck over here, when he knew Dot was back in the barn. He must have been waiting, watching from somewhere in the woods, on his side of the property. When he saw his chance, he came over and stabbed Daphne. Plain and simple."

Ellie didn't respond; she took a long deep breath and glanced at Dot. Dot came to her feet and looked down at the ground. Lucy thought that perhaps Ben's explanation made her feel guilty. As if she'd neglected the animals or failed to protect them. Again.

Ellie took a step closer and put her arm around Dot's shoulder. "Dot . . . it's not your fault. This was senseless, crazy cruelty. I'm glad you didn't see the person who did this. You could have been hurt, too."

"That's right," Ben agreed. "I'm glad you weren't out here. Who knows what could have happened. Believe me, the police will say the same thing."

He'd no sooner mentioned the police than Lucy saw the blue flashing lights of a cruiser out on the road, rolling past the pasture fence. The car pulled through the gate, passed the house, and drove up the dirt road to the pasture.

A uniformed officer got out of the passenger side. His blue hat topped a tan, weathered face and a fringe of sandy, grayish hair. A bit of paunch hung over his leather belt. A younger officer, with the wide shoulders of a weight lifter, got out of the driver's side.

Ben walked over to meet them at the pasture gate. Lucy could see he was explaining what had happened. The older officer asked all the questions and took notes on a small pad. A short time later, they walked over to Daphne's body, covered by the tarp.

"I'm Officer Hanson," the older policeman said, looking

around the group. "This is my partner, Officer Stahl." He looked down at the blue heap on the ground. "This is the animal?" he asked Ben.

Ben nodded. "We thought it was best to cover the body. It can't be removed until tomorrow."

Officer Hanson leaned over and pulled off the covering, then squatted down to look at the wound. "Looks like she was sliced with a knife. A fast, clean cut." He shook his head and stood up. "Who found her?"

"I did, Officer." Dot stepped forward. She explained again how she had been in the barn, with the other llamas, and returned to get Daphne. Then realized the llama was hurt.

"Did you see or hear anything unusual while you were in the barn, or while coming outside again?"

"I don't think so." She paused and stared down at the ground a moment. "I did hear the dogs over at the neighbor's house fussing and barking." Dot pointed to Ridley's property. "By the time I came out here, they'd stopped."

"Of course they were barking," Ben cut in abruptly. "They're tied up in his yard, and he passed by and they wanted to go with him. But he was on a solo mission. He didn't need his dogs to hunt down poor Daphne . . ."

"Sir?" Officer Hanson turned to Ben. He seemed confused but interested in Ben's rambling. "You're talking about your neighbor now?"

"Yes, our neighbor Justin Ridley. That's his property, right over there." Ben pointed to Ridley's land. "He could have easily come over here, stabbed Daphne, and gone back through those trees without anyone seeing him."

The police officer made notes. Then he looked over at the low stone wall that marked the property line and the thick trees just beyond the Kruegers' side. There was a fence around the portion of the pasture where the llamas grazed. It was not high, just a corral height, easy to scale coming and going, Lucy thought.

"Want me to go take a look around over there?" Officer Stahl offered. "I might find something."

"All right, but don't disturb anything," Hanson told him.

As the younger officer trotted off with a flashlight, Officer Hanson turned back to Ben. Lucy thought it was too dark to find much evidence, but maybe the dried grass and ground were soft enough for someone to have left a trail of entry and retreat.

Officer Hanson turned back to Ben. "Go on, Mr. Krueger. Any idea why your neighbor would do something like this?"

"He hates us. He wants to scare us off this farm. He's been harassing us since we moved in, back in July."

The officer looked at Ben quizzically. "Harassing you? How?"

Ben recounted the incidents, including the paint ball attack on Saturday. "We should have called the police after that. We thought about it. We just weren't sure what to do. We believed it would stop. We're new here. We don't want to cause trouble with our neighbors . . ."

"Slow down a minute. These incidents have been going on for weeks and you haven't reported them?"

"We should have. I can see that now," Ben said with regret. "But we didn't want to make a big drama out it. We're just starting a business out here. We didn't want a lot of bad publicity."

Ellie bowed her head. Lucy could see she felt contrite now, even foolish.

The police officer stared at them both a long moment, then checked his pad again. "I need to ask you a few more questions for my report. Then I'm going to call this in. Detectives from the county will come out to follow up. Might be later tonight or even tomorrow. It's hard to say." He glanced down at Daphne again. "Don't disturb anything in this field. Keep the other animals out of here until the property has been examined for evidence. We're going to secure the area with tape."

"Do you have to?" Ellie sounded upset. "I mean, people will be able to see that from the road. Is it really necessary?"

"This is a crime, ma'am. A felony. Whoever did this could get up to five years in jail."

"They deserve fifty," Ben said loudly.

Officer Hanson didn't reply. He flipped his pad closed and stuck it in his back pocket. "I hate to see animals hurt. I hear llamas can be pretty good pets. Gentle creatures."

"Oh, yes, they are. She was very dear. We're going to miss her," Ellie said quietly. She dabbed her eyes again.

The younger officer returned—looking eager to report, Lucy noticed. "There are some scuff marks on the fence. They show up pretty well on the white paint. And some footprints nearby. Over there, the side of the corral facing the woods." He pointed with his light.

Officer Hanson didn't seem surprised. "Okay, show me." He left the group and headed across the pasture with his partner.

As the two officers walked away, Lucy noticed Ben looked

suddenly alert. She followed his gaze and noticed a tall, thin figure at the edge of the woods—a man in a military-style camouflage jacket and a black baseball cap pulled down over his brow. He stood still and straight, blending in with the trees and brush.

Lucy blinked, wondering if she was just imagining him there. She wondered how long he'd been watching them. She would never have noticed if it hadn't been for the sudden change in Ben's body language.

Lucy stepped closer to Matt. "That must be Justin Ridley," she whispered. She touched his shoulder and showed him where to look.

"Just stay right here." Matt gripped her arm and drew her closer. "Don't go near them."

Ben had already started marching across the pasture, the beam of his flashlight fixed on Ridley, like a spotlight on a black stage.

Ridley didn't flinch. He barely moved. Only lifted his chin a notch higher, staring straight into the light.

"Returned to the scene of the crime, did you?" Ben shouted as he marched toward his nemesis. "There he is. That's the guy." He pointed at Ridley as he called to the police officers, who were now on the side of the corral facing the road.

Lucy saw Officer Hanson turn. His gaze darted between the two men.

"Come on out here, you coward," Ben shouted at Ridley. "Come on. The police want to talk to you. You're not getting away with this, you cold-blooded killer."

Ben was now only a few yards from the stone wall but still

behind the corral fence, inside the pasture. Ridley stood on the other side of the wall but took a few steps out of the shadows.

Lucy could now see that something was tucked under his arm. A hunting rifle, she realized. Her breath caught in her throat.

"You're crazy, Krueger. I have no idea what you're talking about," Ridley called back.

"You lie, Ridley. You're a black-hearted liar," Ben shouted.

Officer Hanson and his partner were now running along the outside of the corral—trying to end the argument before it went any further, Lucy imagined.

"Matt . . . this is getting scary," she whispered.

"I know. . . . These guys aren't fooling around. They really hate each other, and Ben has a temper," he added quietly.

"And Ridley has a gun," Lucy whispered back. "A really bad combination . . ."

"Don't blame me if your damn llama died. I'm not surprised," Ridley taunted Ben. "You don't know the back end of an animal from its front. It's a wonder they all don't die on you."

"You crazy, paranoid freak . . . get out of my sight. Before I choke you with my bare hands . . ." Ben started climbing over the corral. Officer Stahl rushed to the other side and pushed him back.

Officer Hanson ran in Ridley's direction. "All right, that's enough," the police officer ordered. "We don't want any more problems here tonight. Break it up. Or you'll both ride back to the station with me."

Justin Ridley didn't move. "I'm on my own property, Officer. Any law against that?"

Officer Hanson ignored his question. "There was an incident here tonight. I need to talk to you, Mr. Ridley."

"No problem," Ridley replied in his low, flat voice. "That man and his wife, they're the problem," he shouted theatrically. "Just sitting on that property until they can cash in. They won't give a damn about those animals after that . . ."

Officer Hanson walked even closer to Ridley, then stepped over the stone wall. They talked for a few minutes more. No one could hear what they were saying.

Officer Stahl finally persuaded Ben to turn his back on Ridley and walk to the other side of the pasture. By now, Ellie and Dot were waiting for him at the corral gate, along with Lucy and Matt. He walked by everyone and glanced at Ellie.

"Ben . . . what in the world were you doing out there? Do you want to get killed, too?"

"I'm sorry, Ellie. I saw him and just lost my head." He let out a long breath and glanced over at Officer Stahl. "I'm sorry, Officer. Thanks for breaking it up."

"You've got to stay away from your neighbor, Mr. Krueger. Let the police handle this now," the young man advised.

Officer Hanson walked toward them. "Stahl is right. You're lucky we were here. This situation is going to be investigated, Mr. Krueger. It will take some time, but we'll figure out who killed your livestock. Just let us do our job and stay out of Mr. Ridley's way. I just warned him, and now I'm warning you," he said firmly.

Ben nodded, looking embarrassed and contrite. "I understand, Officer. I'm sorry. I was just so upset about Daphne. . . . I won't go near the guy. I promise. If I see him, I'll go back inside."

Officer Hanson gave him a look. Lucy wasn't sure if he believed Ben, but he didn't belabor his point. "All right, everyone clear out of here. We need to seal off the area."

Officer Stahl had already returned from the squad car with a roll of orange crime scene tape and begun the task. Officer Hanson took down Matt and Lucy's contact information.

"The detectives assigned to this case might have more questions for you," he told them.

"That's fine. They can call anytime," Matt replied. Matt and Lucy said good night to the Kruegers and Dot and then headed back to the village.

Lucy looked out the window as they drove back down the dirt road that cut across the farm and led to the main road. Darkness shrouded the landscape. The large lanterns and policemen's flashlights eerily illuminated the scene. The canvas-covered mound, the tarp covering Daphne's body, could still be seen clearly on the ground, in the center of the pasture. The orange crime scene tape now circled around the corral and cordoned off a swath of the pasture, between the corral and the woods on Ridley's side of the property.

"You must feel bad," Lucy said as the truck bounced down the dirt road and past the barn. She reached over and rested her hand on Matt's shoulder.

"I do. The wound was in an odd place. It was almost as if someone had tried to just slash her, thinking she'd bleed but it wouldn't be really dangerous. I mean, if you were a real hunter—like they say Justin Ridley is—you would stab an animal in a truly critical place. Across the throat or in the heart. Or even the gut. But this cut was just across the shoulder.

Not really going for the kill," he explained. "Maybe the knife slipped and it just went too deep. Deeper than the attacker intended? But once the blade severed the artery, there was no way to save her." He turned to Lucy, looking sad and pale. "I've rarely seen an animal maliciously and fatally injured like that. There's something very wrong with anyone who could do that. I hope that person ends up in jail a long time. But they hardly ever do. Usually, they just get off with a fine."

Matt's voice was strained with anger and frustration. Lucy shared his outrage and disgust. But his observations also made good sense. Did Ridley actually attack Daphne, as the Kruegers believed? Or had it been someone else? Someone who lacked real hunting skills. And intended to just injure her but accidentally dealt a mortal blow?

Whatever the truth was about Daphne's death, Ridley was definitely a scary guy. There was no question in Lucy's mind about that.

Chapter Five

*a*s Matt got ready to leave for his office the next morning, Lucy could tell he was still thinking about the horrific scene at the Kruegers' farm last night. They both were.

Lucy sipped her first mug of coffee, staring out at the small yard behind the cottage.

Low gray clouds filled the sky, and a light rain fell. Gusts of wind blew handfuls of wet, dappled leaves to the ground, covering the garden and lawn behind the cottage.

Lucy wondered if Matt would have to go out to the farm again today, when the animal control unit collected the llama's body. She imagined a dismal scene—the wet, muddy pasture; rain splashing the blue tarp and probably washing away most of the evidence the detectives might find in the field today.

She turned when he came in the kitchen but didn't ask him about it. Just watched as he poured a pile of bran flakes in a bowl and filled his travel mug with coffee.

"I have my knitting group tonight." He crunched down on

his cereal, standing up, staring into space. She wondered if he'd even heard her.

"I remember. I'm going to work late and catch up on some paperwork," he said between spoonfuls of cereal. "Guess it's just me and the dogs . . . and some takeout. We'll carry on bravely without you for a few hours," he added in a mock-serious tone.

He smiled down at Tink and Walley, who sat side by side under the kitchen table. They answered with looks of adoration and beat their tails on the floor.

Lucy laughed. "I'm sure you'll all be fine. Do you have to go back to the Kruegers' farm today?"

"Gee, I hope not." He looked somber for a moment and placed his empty bowl in the sink, then turned to her, his expression relaxed. "Thanks for coming with me last night. It was a pretty nasty scene. You really hung in there."

His warm words pleased her. But she made light of her part. "You don't have to thank me. I didn't help much."

He stood in front of her and put his hands on her shoulders. "You always help me. Just by being there. And being . . . Lucy." He gave her a hug and kissed her good-bye. Heading out the door, he added, "Get cracking on that vest, slacker. That was supposed to be my birthday present."

That was true. Matt's birthday was back in September. She was only a month off, so far. He might get it for Christmas at this rate, she calculated, but didn't tell him that.

Once Matt left, she took care of her morning chores, skipping a dog walk into town due to the rain and a deadline on her current project, the graphic design of a children's book about farm animals. Thankfully, there were no llamas grazing on these pages. Just the usual collection of chickens, cows, and a horse or two. Once she got into her office, she felt distracted again, thinking of the sad twilight scene at the Kruegers' place, a different story entirely.

Lucy knew her friends would be mad if she didn't toss them at least a scrap of news before the meeting. She dashed off a group note just to put it out of her mind and get on with her day.

Dear All:

You'll probably hear this from Ellie, or it might even be in the newspaper today. There was another strange event at the Kruegers' farm last night. A violent one too. One of the llamas was stabbed, at about dusk. They called Matt, but by the time we got there it was too late. The Kruegers called the police. Finally. Maybe they'll get to the bottom of it. If Ellie comes tonight, she'll tell us more.

See you later—xo Lucy

P.S. to Maggie: I still have very weak character . . . and a very big tangle in my argyle project. Just warning you.

The weather had cleared by the time Lucy arrived in the village that night. Patches of night sky and a nearly full moon could be seen behind the branches of tall trees along Main Street. Lucy parked her Jeep across from the shop and spotted Dana's and Suzanne's cars parked nearby. Ellie's car was not there, she noticed, and Lucy wondered if she was coming.

"Last but not least, as usual." Maggie greeted her from the back of the shop as she walked in. Her friends were assembled around the long oak worktable, with their knitting projects out and glasses of wine at hand.

"What did you bring for dessert?" Maggie asked curiously as Lucy shrugged out of her knitted wrap.

"It was my turn? You're kidding . . . right?"

Maggie bit her lower lip. Suzanne put her knitting down and groaned.

Phoebe rolled her eyes and let out a moan. "Really?"

She managed to drag the word out to at least five syllables, Lucy noticed.

Dana was the only one who didn't miss a beat in her stitching. She peered over her reading glasses, looking amused. "I have a few dried-fruit-and-nut bars in the car in my gym bag, if that helps. Gluten-free," she noted.

"Yum-my. Let me at 'em." Suzanne stuck out her tongue.

Lucy laughed then, too. "Of course I didn't forget. I was just teasing. I can see now you'd probably banish me."

"Not forever. Just a month or two. To teach you a lesson." Suzanne collected herself and focused on her knitting again.

"You ought to be banished a little while for terrifying us. Some joke." Phoebe set a stack of dishes on the sideboard alongside a pile of flatware rolled in linen napkins.

"I think the sentence depends on what she brought us." Maggie walked in from the storeroom, following her assistant with a large covered pot. As she placed it on the sideboard next to the dishes, an appetizing aroma wafted in Lucy's direction. She was curious to see what was for dinner.

"Carrot muffins with cream cheese frosting." Lucy glanced

around to gauge her friends' reactions. "I used carrots I bought on Saturday at a farm stand."

"You are absolved," Maggie announced regally. "Just put them somewhere safe and we'll start on dinner."

Lucy put the muffins away, then settled into her place at the worktable.

She took out her knitting and glanced at Maggie. "Is Ellie coming tonight?"

"She'd planned on it, but she just called a few minutes ago. She and Ben are still upset over the incident last night and were dealing with the police again today. She's feeling drained and didn't want to leave Ben alone."

Dana looked up from her project, a long striped scarf. "This probably isn't the last of it, either, if the police are investigating now."

"Finally," Suzanne said. "Too bad a poor llama had to get slaughtered before they called the police in."

"Ellie regrets that now. She can see that they should have called sooner. I don't have much experience with llamas. But I hear they can be very nice pets. Very sweet and playful," Maggie said as she looked over her stitches. "That makes it a little worse, don't you think? I mean, they had a real connection to the animal. Like a pet dog or something."

"That's true, Maggie. Emotional bonds with animals are very strong. Animals love us unconditionally, even when we don't deserve it. And Ellie and Ben are not such experienced farmers yet that they're used to losing livestock," Dana noted.

"That's what Matt said, too," Lucy recalled from their conversation at home last night.

Maggie looked over at her. "Tell us what happened, Lucy. Ellie didn't really go into the details, and I didn't want to press her. One of the llamas was stabbed, out in the pasture?"

Suzanne had taken a skein of red yarn from her bag and was rolling it into a ball. She was making a sweater for her fourteen-year-old daughter, Alexis, who was very particular about her appearance these days. Suzanne predicted the teenager would probably not even wear the sweater when it was finished, even though she had personally selected the pattern and yarn.

"Did it die right away?" Suzanne asked quietly.

"It bled to death. Matt tried to save her, but by the time we got there it was too late. The stab wound was in the shoulder and shouldn't have been life-threatening. But he said it was deep and severed an artery. There's going to be an autopsy," Lucy added.

"Animals are autopsied? I didn't know that." Suzanne looked up in surprise.

"It's done by the county's animal control center," Lucy explained as she pulled the dreaded argyle project out of her bag. "They test wild animals, like raccoons, for diseases. Pet owners can request autopsies, too, if a dog or a cat dies unexpectedly or for some suspicious reason. The officer who came to the farm last night said it's a felony to maliciously harm livestock. Whoever did it could go to a jail for a few years."

"They should be locked up forever. It's like killing a person. Almost worse, when you think how defenseless that poor llama was." Phoebe looked angry, and her eyes were glossy, as if she was about to cry.

Dana took a pack of tissues from her bag and handed them

over. "I'm glad to hear Ellie and Ben finally called the police. It's about time. They reported all the incidents, I'm assuming?"

"Yes, they did. A detective was coming by today to interview them and search the property for evidence. Did Ellie mention anything about that to you, Maggie?" Lucy asked.

"She did. Guess who was assigned the case? Our old friend Detective Walsh." Maggie sounded as if the name left a bad taste in her mouth.

With good reason, Lucy knew. They all remembered Detective Walsh. He'd led the investigation of the murder of Amanda Goran, a knitting shop owner in their town who had been found dead in her store, her head bashed in by a hat block. It had all happened a little over a year ago now.

With no solid evidence at all, Detective Walsh had fixed his sights on Maggie as his prime suspect and relentlessly dogged her. Of course, she was totally innocent.

Luckily, Maggie's knitting group friends had done some sleuthing of their own and discovered the real culprit. But Maggie still shuddered just thinking of those dark days and at the very mention of the bumbling, narrow-sighted lawman.

"It makes sense in one way. He's so incompetent; maybe he's been demoted to murder cases of farm animals. He didn't do too well with humans." Suzanne was alternating between her knitting and bites of her dinner—a tasty mix of shrimp, broccoli, and mushrooms served over brown rice. "This is yummy, by the way," she added, pointing her fork down at her plate.

"Thank you," Maggie replied. "And by the way, you're probably right. Law enforcement is a tight-knit bunch. He's too young to retire, and I guess they can't fire him outright."

"So they've sort of sent him out to pasture?" Lucy knew the quip was corny, but she couldn't resist.

Phoebe held her head and groaned. "That was bad, Lucy. If you do that again, we might have to kick you out tonight anyway."

"Go ahead. But the muffins go with me, kiddo," Lucy teased her back.

"I thought it was cute," Suzanne countered. "'Out to pasture.' Says it all to me."

"Case assignment is just the luck of the draw. Detectives are assigned cases as the calls come in," Dana said knowingly. "Of course, there is some favoritism by department heads," she added.

"My hope that the police will find the menace who's been harassing Ellie and Ben was significantly reduced when I heard Walsh's name," Maggie confided. "I didn't tell Ellie that, of course."

"This could be a slam-dunk case, even for Detective Walsh, if Ellie and Ben are right. Ben even got into a shouting match with Ridley while we were there. He must have seen the police cars and wondered what was going on. He was standing in the woods at the property line," Lucy explained, "just watching everything. With a gun tucked under his arm. It was really . . . creepy."

Phoebe cringed. "Ugh. . . . Sounds like a slasher movie."

"He had a gun? You're kidding, right?" Suzanne dropped a needle in her lap and looked down to find it.

Dana looked up from her work, too. "Maybe he was out hunting. Ellie and Ben said he did that at night a lot."

"Hunting poor defenseless llamas, sounds like to me," Suzanne countered. "So they were yelling at each other?"

Lucy nodded. She was trying to untangle the strands of yarn in her project, but it was starting to look even worse.

"It got pretty nasty. Luckily the police were still there and broke it up," Lucy reported. "Ridley does think that Ellie and Ben bought the farm to flip it over to investors when the open space laws expire. He said they were just sitting on the land to make a profit and flung a few other choice insults in the same vein at them."

"Do you know if the police found any evidence in the pasture today?" Dana asked Maggie. "Did Ellie mention anything?"

"Ellie said they found some marks on the fence that were probably footprints of someone climbing over. And a track of footprints coming from the woods," Maggie replied.

"We heard about the marks on the fence last night," Lucy said.

"They may have found other physical evidence, too, that they didn't tell her about," Dana added.

"I'm sure Detective Walsh has talked to Ridley," Suzanne said. "That's only logical."

Maggie glanced over at Lucy's sweater vest and silently winced, then waved her hand in a "give it here" gesture. Lucy quickly handed it over.

"Thanks, Maggie," she practically whispered.

"Don't thank me yet," Maggie nearly shouted back. She peered down at the mess through her reading glasses. Lucy sensed the prognosis was not good.

Dana turned her knitting over and examined the stitches. She was making a scarf for her stepson, Tyler, who was in his second year of college. She and Jack also had a son named Dylan, who was still in high school. They were all going to visit Tyler next weekend to watch his team in a lacrosse tournament, and the scarf's stripes were his team colors.

"It seems pretty simple to me," Suzanne said. "Ridley does hate them, just like they said, and he can get on their property any time he wants to."

"That's true," Dana conceded. "But these situations are seldom as simple as they seem. It could be Ridley. Or it could be someone else, entirely unknown to Ellie and Ben. And their reasons for doing this unknown to the Kruegers, as well."

"Come to think of it, what about Angelica Rossi?" Suzanne asked. "Ellie talks about Angelica as a fairly hostile rival, even though Angelica acts like a big sweetie pie in public. Ellie said she smears Laughing Llama Farm every chance she gets. She probably wants them to clear out, too. I think her motives are even stronger than Ridley's."

Maggie looked up from Lucy's vest a moment. "I thought of Angelica, too. She doesn't look it, but she's a hard-nosed businesswoman. I used to carry her yarns, but she told me that she was going to start distributing only to shops that carried Sweet Meadow exclusively as their organic line. I wouldn't agree, so that was that. No more Sweet Meadow yarns for me."

"She does sound like a tough cookie. But is she capable of doing all that nasty business with the paint gun at the fair? She did disappear into the crowd after we spoke to her at your booth," Suzanne recalled. "I guess she could have managed that trick."

"All right . . . but killing a llama with her bare hands?" Lucy asked doubtfully.

"Good point, Lucy," Phoebe cut in. "She'd have to be a real pioneer woman. Not just dress like one."

"That is a good point." Dana paused in her work and took another ball of yarn from her tote bag. "Stabbing a knife into an animal's hide and muscle requires a certain amount of physical strength. Even a really fit woman, like Angelica, would have trouble. . . . But that still doesn't mean it's Ridley."

"He does have means, motive, and opportunity, Dana," Maggie pointed out.

Phoebe shook her head from side to side, the little mannerism she had when she got excited about something she wanted to say. "Yeah . . . but just because you have a weird neighbor doesn't mean he's out to get you. Look at Boo Radley in *To Kill a Mockingbird*. He turned out to be a pretty cool guy."

Phoebe had been studying the novel in a literature class. She'd been very moved by the book, and everything these days seemed to have some connection to the story. In this case, the comparison was not that far-fetched, Lucy thought.

"Very true, Phoebe. I always loved that book. I should read it again." Lucy glanced over Maggie's shoulder, trying to see where she had gone so terribly wrong.

Suzanne put her knitting down and sighed. "Oh, I loved that movie. Gregory Peck as Atticus Finch? He was so smart and quiet and strong. The way he just faced down that rabid dog and all that. . . . He was really yummy," Suzanne said decidedly.

"He was," Maggie agreed. "That was the only novel Harper Lee ever published, isn't that too bad?"

"At least she wrote one great one. Justin Ridley does have a lot in common with Boo Radley," Dana said thoughtfully. "Ellie and Ben say he only comes out of his house at night."

"Come on, that has to be an exaggeration. He's not a vampire. They just don't see him during the daytime," Suzanne guessed.

"Maybe," Dana conceded. "But he could be agoraphobic or suffer from some variation of that condition," she pointed out.

"If he has as psychological block about leaving his house in the daylight, I wonder how he managed to stab the llama," Lucy asked. "It wasn't quite dark out when they called us, though it was by the time we arrived. But poor Daphne had been attacked well before that."

Dana shrugged. "It's impossible to say since we don't know him. I'm just giving Ellie and Ben the benefit of the doubt."

Dana was usually the most objective and dispassionate of all her friends and the most clear-sighted when trying to understand a complicated personality. Lucy wasn't surprised, however, that she accepted Ellie's impressions of Justin Ridley without question. Dana knew Ellie best, since their college days, and obviously respected her judgment.

"I'll tell you something else about Justin Ridley." Suzanne sat back and put her knitting aside. "There was some buzz the other day in the office about the open space laws and the meeting coming up at the village hall. The Friends of Farmland are organizing a big protest. And we all know that Ridley is their head farmer. Even though he doesn't actually grow anything," she added. "Whatever. . . . My point is, he must have some social skills. He can't be that much of a nut job and be able lead a big group like that, right?"

Lucy looked to Dana for some comment, but she didn't say anything, just calmly continued knitting.

"It wouldn't be the first time an unhinged fanatic attracted a following," Maggie replied drily. "In fact, that seems to be a standard requirement for the job. The leader of just about every revolution in history was a social misfit of some kind."

"If you want to make an omelet you must be willing to break some eggs," Phoebe piped up. Everyone looked over at her.

"That was pretty *random*," Lucy noted.

"Lenin said that, sitting in a boxcar outside of Paris. Just before he returned to Russia to start their revolution," Phoebe explained.

"File under passionate fanatics," Lucy noted.

"Passionate or not, if the police discover that Ridley is responsible for the ill deeds at the farm, it will reflect very badly on the open space cause and his group," Maggie pointed out.

"That's true, Maggie. He would be risking the reputation of his group," Suzanne said.

"And their moral authority," Phoebe added.

"True," Dana agreed. "But someone like Ridley might also feel he's invincible in some way, or too clever for the police to catch. It does sound as if he's fixated on Ellie and Ben, and when people are that obsessed, they lose all perspective. And they convince themselves that the means justify the end."

"Even killing a poor defenseless llama," Phoebe said quietly.

"Even taking a human life." Dana's tone was grave, and a sudden hush fell over the room. "Not that I think it will ever come to that," she added quickly.

"Don't even say it," Suzanne scolded her.

"That's my point. I didn't," Dana defended herself. "Not really . . ."

Maggie suddenly looked up from Lucy's project. Had she made any progress with the big glob of yarn in the middle of the vest? Lucy couldn't tell. "Ladies . . . I think it's time for Lucy's muffins and for us to talk about something else. Something a little more cheerful?"

Lucy retrieved the dessert, which she'd brought in a plastic container. She set out the muffins carefully on a white china platter Maggie had brought in from the storeroom.

"Those look super-scrumptious. You totally outdid yourself, Lucy." Suzanne sat up in her seat and stuck the red sweater in her tote bag. She practically rubbed her hands together in glee, giving the muffins her full attention, Lucy noticed.

Lucy passed Suzanne the platter first, and she carefully chose her treat. "Thank you, Lucy," she said politely right before she took a huge bite.

"Awesome muffins, Lucy. Really." Phoebe took hers next, carefully peeled back the paper, and sniffed the icing before she took a bite, reminding Lucy of a little cat. A cute cat she might even like.

Even Dana, who often passed up sweets without seeming tempted, did not let the muffins pass by without choosing one. "Well, it is some comfort to know that there are fresh vegetables in here."

"Some," Lucy agreed. "And I did use low-fat cream cheese."

"Oh . . . in that case, I'll have another. They're not that big," Suzanne noticed. She slowly peeled back the paper and cut the muffin in half with her fork. "I don't know if this is a more cheerful subject or not, but the worst dieting months of the year are moving in, ladies. Like a huge tsunami of calories. From that pile of Halloween candy haunting me every night through November, to Christmas parties all over town and New Year's Day brunch. If I didn't have extra pairs of tummy-control jeans on hand, I'd only be coming out of the house at night, too. "

"I can't believe Christmas decorations are in some of the stores already. We haven't even hit Halloween yet," Lucy said.

"The marketing machine really rushes our lives along. You have to stand your ground," Dana advised. "I just want to focus on fall and be here now. I'm not ready to think about the holidays yet."

"I'm totally with you on that, Dana," Maggie agreed. "But we have to think ahead knitting-wise. I'm starting a few classes this week with holiday gift projects."

"I'm ahead of the curve on this one, Maggie," Phoebe promised. "I had this idea of how to do something nice for people. To get with the Christmas spirit and all that stuff? And I got this really cool project idea for us," Phoebe said eagerly. She had quickly devoured her muffin and spoke while licking the icing off her fingertips.

"Yes . . . go on. We're all eager to hear it, Phoebe." Maggie's schoolteacher tone kicked in, gently coaxing Phoebe to get to the point.

"I was going to make, like, a huge pile of socks—all different, amazing kinds—and sell them at school, in the student union and the bookstore and stuff. Then I was going to donate all the money to a charity."

"What a nice idea. That's great, Phoebe." Suzanne smiled at her and sounded sincerely impressed.

"But wait . . . I have an even better spin on it. You guys can be knitting philanthropists, too."

"Knitting philanthropist? It has a nice ring," Maggie murmured.

"I've always wanted to be a philanthropist of some kind." Lucy smiled at the terminology.

"Well, what if we all knit up a bunch of really nice, but fast stuff? Like mittens and scarves and headbands and maybe little purses?" Phoebe asked them.

"Okay, go on," Maggie coaxed. "We knit fast, small projects. Then what?"

"We sell this stuff all over the place. In this shop and around town. Like maybe Edie would put a basket on the counter at the Schooner. Or down at the Book Review? And we get a lot of money, and we help a family like in a third world country start . . . *a llama farm.*" She paused and looked around the table at her friends, her dark eyes wide and bright. "Wouldn't that be like totally awesome?"

Phoebe was so excited she practically jumped out of her seat. Her friends glanced around at one another. No one said a word for a long moment.

Maggie was the first to speak. "I like the part about raising money with little projects we knit and sell. But how can we buy a llama herd for a family in some distant country? We can't just pack them up and FedEx them somewhere."

"Funny, Mag. You're kidding, right? That's the easiest part. Wait . . . I'll show you . . ." She reached under the table and leafed through her big leather knapsack, then pulled out a dark red pamphlet with the photo of sheep on the front. "Heifer International—ever hear of it?"

Phoebe held out the pamphlet and passed it around. Dana was the first to take it in hand. "Oh, sure, I get this once in a while. It's a great organization. They help people around the world lift themselves out of poverty with small-scale businesses that improve the economy of the entire community."

"You can buy, like, two baby chicks or a sheep . . . or an ox. Or an entire ark, see?" Phoebe showed them the pictures. "The llamas are in the back. Aren't they cute? They're only a hundred and fifty dollars each. I think that's a pretty good deal, don't you? I thought we could raise enough money to buy two or three?"

"Let me see." Maggie took the pamphlet and scanned the pages with interest. "I've seen this catalog before, too. But I never had a brainstorm like that one, Phoebe. I think that's an excellent goal for our group. I'm sure we can sell some items here, and some other shops in town will take them, too. I'll ask around."

"I'd love to take part. As long you don't ask me to make anything that's argyle," Lucy warned. "I'll start right now."

"Me, too," Suzanne agreed, then turned to smile at Lucy. "Are you really going to abandon Matt's vest?"

"Not abandon it . . . just put it aside awhile. This is a good cause. He'll understand." Lucy knew he would understand, but she was also secretly relieved to take a break from the vest. It had shaken her knitting confidence. Some fast, simple projects were the perfect way to get her mojo back.

"I want to start tonight, too. In fact, I'll donate this scarf,"

Dana said, looking down at the project, which was almost complete except for a few binding rows and some fringe on the ends. "Tyler will make a fuss when I give it to him. But I know he'll just stuff it in a drawer somewhere and hardly ever wear it. I'll figure out something else he might like better."

"I'm so glad you guys like my idea. I'm totally psyched," Phoebe bounced in her seat.

"I'm psyched, too," Maggie echoed in her dignified tone. "Totally," she added. "I think this is a very worthwhile project that will help us feel good about the holidays and keep us focused on the real meaning of the holidays."

"No matter how commercial and crazy the weeks ahead will become," Suzanne added. "I'll see if the real-estate office will put a basket of our projects out somewhere, too."

"Matt will put some in his office. Maybe I'll do some dog sweaters or booties?" Lucy thought she had a real brainstorm there. Although her significant other might feel slighted when he noticed she'd put aside his special vest for a quickie dog poncho.

"This is shaping up. I'm happy to donate all the yarn," Maggie offered in a grand tone. "As long as you pick from the box in the storeroom with my excess inventory."

There were many perks to hanging out in a knitting shop, including a fairly steady flow of free yarn. Maggie was never stingy—though she did tend to push yarns with odd colors and textures that hadn't sold well, Lucy knew.

The friends glanced at one another—thinking the same, she guessed. Dana was hiding a little smile, Lucy noticed. "I'm happy to buy my supplies, Maggie. We don't want to put you out of business."

The others all quickly agreed.

Maggie sat back and grinned at them. "Oh, bother, I thought I could unload some of those odd ducks back there. I'll have to save them for a sidewalk sale. You all see through me so easily."

"Sorry, but yeah. We do," Phoebe agreed with a quick nod.

They cleared away the remaining muffins—which were few, Lucy noticed—and wiped off the table. Maggie found some easy, quick patterns on her laptop that she thought would make good projects and printed them out.

Suzanne was good with numbers and worked out the math. "If we want to buy three llamas, we need four hundred and fifty bucks. So if we make about forty-five items and sell them for ten dollars each, we'll definitely have enough."

"Forty-five items? That's nine items each. Is that too much knitting?" Maggie looked around, checking everyone's reaction.

"Not if it's little things you can make in a night or two. Like a one-skein scarf with big needles. Or a headband," Lucy suggested. She was the queen of extra-large needles. She knew what she was talking about.

"We can sell nicer things for more," Phoebe pointed out. "People will spend at least fifteen dollars on some really nice socks, for instance."

"Or a very long scarf," Dana added, stretching out her donated project.

"Very true. I think we shouldn't even worry about the math," Maggie told her friends. "Somehow, when you set out to do good, the universe conspires to help you along, and the math has a way of working out. Ever notice?"

Lucy had noticed that. As if some force for good gets in your corner.

"That's true, Maggie," Dana agreed. "Too bad Ellie isn't here tonight. I know she'll want to help. Especially since the goal is a gift of llamas. Maybe she would sell our items in the shop on her farm. I bet she'll do some great publicity events and decorating there during the holidays."

Lucy also thought Ellie would like this idea and would probably think of a million ways to attract visitors to her farm in the coming months. Lucy could practically see the farm decked out for Christmas, the llamas with garlands around their necks or dressed up in some sort of cute reindeer gear, complete with red-and-green halters and jingle bells.

But the holidays seemed a very long way off when she thought about the Laughing Llama Farm. There was so much trouble there. She felt as if a dark cloud hovered above the place now, casting everything in malevolent shadows.

The image of the wounded llama flailing on the ground in a puddle of her own blood stuck in Lucy's mind. If these frightening events continued, what would happen at the farm by the end of the year . . . or even by the end of the month?

Lucy didn't even want to imagine it.

Chapter Six

Maggie was sorry that Ellie had missed the meeting. She called her on Wednesday morning and told her about the holiday project the knitting group had decided on.

"And we're going to use the money we raise to buy about three llamas to donate to families who will use the animals to start their own little businesses. Microeconomies . . . and all that. It's all in the Heifer International pamphlet. I can show it to you."

"I love that idea. Of course, I'll help. I can sell some of the items in my shop."

"We were hoping you'd say that." Ellie hadn't been part of their knitting circle very long, but it didn't feel that way to Maggie. She'd always felt that Ellie was very much in tune with the group and added a certain, special energy.

"I'm a little tied down to the farm this week. Dot is needed at her other job. So Ben and I are in charge of the animals. I should be able to get into the village Saturday morning, after I do my chores. I can pick up the patterns then."

"If you come around ten or so, Dana and Suzanne might be here. They usually drop in on Saturday morning around that time."

Maggie thought that was a good plan. Dana and Suzanne often stopped in on Saturdays morning. Lucy did, too, sometimes. Even though they all said they were terribly busy and didn't have time to hang around, they managed to gab and fit in a fair amount of knitting on those visits.

Maggie got to the shop a little later than usual on Saturday. She put on a pot of coffee, straightened the stock, and set out supplies on the worktable for her first class.

She also found the packet that she planned to give Ellie of fast and easy patterns for their fund-raising project and put it on the front counter.

Her friends were a creative bunch. Even though they were working from the same patterns, she was sure the items would all be attractive and diverse, embellished with the unique style of each knitter.

The phone rang. Maggie could tell from the caller ID that it was Ellie.

"Hi, Ellie. I just got your patterns together. I'm teaching a lesson from eleven to twelve, but—"

"Maggie . . . something terrible happened . . ." Maggie drew a breath. Ellie sounded as if she was in shock. On the brink of hysteria. "I couldn't reach Dana," Ellie's shaky voice continued. "She's not picking up her cell."

"She's still in her yoga class." Maggie glanced at her watch. "It should be over any minute now."

"I just need to tell someone . . ." Ellie paused. Maggie heard her draw in a deep, ragged breath.

"What is it? Was another llama killed?"

"No, not a llama . . . Justin Ridley." Ellie could hardly speak now. Ridley's name was emitted on a gasp.

Maggie stood in stone-cold silence, not knowing what to say. "Justin Ridley? That is awful. How did he die? Was it an accident?"

For some reason, all Maggie could picture was Ridley tramping around the woods in the dark, with his dogs and big gun, and tripping over a stone or root and shooting himself.

"No, not an accident. Just the opposite. Someone killed him. He was stabbed . . . in the throat . . . with . . . with a spindle. We heard his dogs barking and barking. Howling really loud. You know the way they do? It wasn't even light out yet," Ellie continued. "We let it go for a while. Sometimes we hear them at night, acting up, if Ridley's roaming around. Finally Ben went out to check. Even though the police told him to stay away from Ridley. He saw the dogs loose on our property, just past the big tree in the meadow. When he got closer, he saw Ridley on the ground. He didn't even realize he was dead. The dogs were guarding his body and they wouldn't let Ben get by. Of course we called the police immediately. They caught the dogs somehow and rolled Ridley over. Then we all saw it, the spindle in his throat and all the blood . . . and . . . we knew."

Maggie didn't know what to say. The story was horrific and unbelievable. What a ghastly scene.

"How sad. . . . What's happening now? Are the police still at your farm?"

"Yes, they've been here and at Ridley's place for hours. A huge swarm of them. Detective Walsh is back. They're searching every inch of our land and the woods . . . and Ridley's property, too."

Ellie gave a long, loud sigh. When she spoke, her tone was a mixture of tears and angry frustration. "Oh, Maggie, why is this happening to us? We just wanted to move out to the country, to live in peace and quiet. A simple life, close to nature. So far there's been nothing simple or peaceful about it."

"I'm so sorry, Ellie. I'll bet the police are asking you and Ben a lot of questions."

"Endlessly. But they haven't asked us to go down to the police station or anything like that. So far, I mean," she added in a hushed tone.

Maggie guessed that there were some law officers in the house in range of hearing her conversation. Or maybe Ben was near and she didn't want him to overhear her.

"I wish I could help you in some way. Would you like me to come out there? Keep you and Ben company?"

Maggie wasn't sure how that would help, but she meant it sincerely. Saturday was prime time at the shop, but she was willing to leave Phoebe in charge if it would help Ellie. She knew the Kruegers didn't have any family in the area, and Ellie did sound in need of some support.

Maybe Dana would go. She wasn't working today, Maggie remembered.

"Oh, thank you. That's kind of you to offer. We'll be fine. There's nothing you can do. I just hope the police finish their business soon and leave us alone."

"I hope so, too, Ellie," Maggie said sincerely, though she expected just the opposite. A dead body had been found on their property. The victim was their neighbor and her husband's avowed enemy. Maggie expected that the police would not be leaving the Kruegers alone any time soon at all.

Maggie hung up feeling anxious and wanted to share this story with her friends. She picked up her cell phone and started to send Dana a text. Dana didn't like to be interrupted at yoga and most likely had her phone off, but Maggie thought she'd give it a try. At least she'd see the note as soon as class was over.

Maggie was slow at typing out texts. She could barely read the tiny keyboard and knew she was the only person on the planet who spelled out complete words and was mindful about punctuation.

She had barely punched in the opening words—"Dana, I have something important to tell you"—when the shop door flew open and Dana stood staring at her, still dressed in her sleek exercise outfit.

"Maggie . . . you'll never believe it. Justin Ridley was murdered. It happened late last night. His body was found on Ellie's farm. Jack just called me."

Dana had dashed in the store and run straight to the counter. She was breathing a little heavily, and Maggie guessed that she'd jogged all the way from her car.

Maggie nodded. "I just heard about it. Ellie called. She was supposed to stop by this morning to get the patterns for our project. She told me the whole story . . . or at least what they know so far."

"Poor Ellie. I have to call her. Maybe I should just go there, see if I could help in some way."

"She didn't want me to come, but you're her closest friend in town. She might appreciate your company now."

Maggie knew that Dana was a calm, steady presence in an emergency, and knew how the law worked, too. It would be good for Ellie and Ben to have her help right now.

Dana was already dialing Ellie's number. She stood listening for a moment, and then Maggie heard her leave a message. "Ellie, it's Dana. I just heard the bad news. I want to come out and help you and Ben. Give me a call when you can."

She ended the call and looked back at Maggie. "I really want to help her, but I don't want to intrude."

"I know what you mean. It's a fine line." Maggie nodded and came out from behind the counter. Two women had entered the shop and were looking through a basket of angora yarn marked "New Arrivals." They were regulars, and Maggie greeted them with a quick smile before turning back to Dana.

She'd settled on the love seat in the alcove near the front of the store and sipped from her water bottle. "What did Ellie tell you? I think Jack only got the highlights of the story."

Maggie quickly recounted the conversation. "She said she couldn't wait until the police left. As if that will be last of it for them." Maggie shook her head. "It's no secret that Ben despised Ridley and even threatened him the night the llama was killed. With police officers as witnesses, no less. He'll be the first suspect Detective Walsh hones in on," Maggie predicted. "We are talking about an investigator who does not look much further than his own nose," she reminded Dana. "I just hope Ridley had disputes with a few other neighbors."

Dana seemed calmer about that question. "Sounds as if Mr. Ridley was a classic antisocial personality and not winning any popularity contests around here. The Kruegers can't be the only ones who had words with him. I'd guess lots of his neighbors want to sell their land to the highest bidder come January and are annoyed at his interference with the open space issue."

Maggie had considered that, as well, but it did feel better to hear Dana say it out loud.

But before Maggie could reply, Suzanne breezed into the shop, her big leather tote over one arm, a large takeout coffee drink in the other. Dressed in a Saturday sales outfit—a long black belted sweater, black dress pants, and a hot pink blouse—the attractive brunette looked very professional and very Suzanne.

"I never get one of these big special coffee drinks in the morning, but I really needed a little treat today. I pulled this open house in the Marshes. A total falling-down wreck . . . listed at top dollar. Why make it easy for the real-estate people?" She shook her head and set down her bag, the coffee, and a little white paper bag that Maggie suspected held some other well-deserved treat. "Now I have to sit there all morning. Total graveyard shift, I'm sure. But at least I'll get some knitting done . . ."

Before she could say more, Maggie spoke up. "We have some news from Ellie's farm. There was more trouble there last night."

Suzanne put her cup down. "Really? What happened?"

"Somebody killed Justin Ridley," Dana answered. "The body was found on Ellie and Ben's property."

"Oh, no . . . that's awful. How did he die?"

"Stabbed in the throat, with a spindle," Maggie explained.

"Just like Ellie's llama. Wasn't Daphne stabbed, too?"

"That's right." Dana nodded. "A strange coincidence. Or maybe he was killed that way on purpose," she quickly added.

"Where were Ellie and Ben?" Suzanne turned to Maggie, her expression a mixture of shock and curiosity.

"Asleep in bed. It happened sometime in the middle of the night. A few hours before dawn, Ellie said. Ridley's dogs woke them up, barking and howling. Ben found the dogs guarding the body, out in the pasture somewhere."

"He must have been out hunting. Just like the Kruegers said he always did. And someone . . . got him," Suzanne added.

"Yes, but now that you mention it, I wonder why he didn't defend himself. They said he always carried a gun." Maggie looked at Dana, wondering if she knew any more about that question.

"Jack didn't say one way or the other if the police found a hunting rifle nearby. I'll have to ask him later," Dana replied.

"So nobody heard an argument or anything? Where was Dot? She lives in that little cottage. That's even closer to the meadow," Suzanne recalled.

"Dot wasn't home. She was at her other job. She's a home health aide and often stays over with her patient," Dana explained.

"Ellie mentioned that to me, too," Maggie added.

Suzanne was picking small bites from a muffin in the paper bag, chewing thoughtfully. "I wonder how the killer got close enough to stab him. I mean, if the dogs were so protective of him dead, imagine how they felt when he was alive."

"What is in that coffee drink? You are really on your game today." Dana's tone was admiring.

"Thanks . . . too bad I'm not showing some really hot property. What a waste of a good groove."

"It's hard to get everything working together, isn't it?" Maggie sympathized. "I'm sure your groove won't go to waste entirely," she added. "But getting back to Ridley, that is an excellent point. It suggests it was someone who knew the dogs, doesn't it?"

"Or knew how to get around them," Dana added. "Maybe the police will find some solid physical evidence that answers these questions. I think this investigation is going to be complicated. And Justin Ridley was a real cipher, to hear Ellie and Ben tell it. Who knows what an investigation will turn up about him."

Maggie agreed. You learned a lot about a person once they passed on. Sometimes acts of kindness and altruism they'd kept anonymous. Sometimes the psychic wounds, shady dealing, or unsanctioned relationships they had struggled to hide from the world—and even struggled to deny within themselves. Urges and acts that contradicted their own cherished self-image and reputation.

So much came bubbling to the surface during a murder investigation. Maggie had learned that lesson. It was only a little over a year ago that their good friend Gloria Sterling had died, found drowned in her swimming pool. Maggie and her friends believed they had known Gloria well. But after Gloria's death, Maggie wondered if she'd ever known her at all. Gloria had secrets. And Justin Ridley probably did, too; Maggie had little doubt.

"Oh, darn . . . look at the time. I've got to run." Suzanne hopped up from her seat and gathered her belongings, sweeping out as quickly as she'd come in. As she stepped out the shop door, she turned and called back to them, "Keep me posted. I'm going to ask the real-estate gurus if they think Ridley's passing will impact the big debate in town."

"It could be a game changer," Dana agreed. "That's another angle the investigation should consider."

"Should consider," Maggie echoed. "Will consider?" She sighed. "No comment."

Dana rose and grabbed her water bottle. "I'm going home to grab a shower. So I'll be ready if Ellie calls. I don't want to go out there uninvited. They may need their privacy right now, or just be too busy with the police. I guess I'll wait to hear from her."

"Good idea. She might want you there, but maybe they are too overwhelmed right now."

Just as her friends left, two customers entered the store. Maggie greeted them and answered their questions about a felting project one of the women had started in a class at the shop. It hadn't gone very well, Maggie noticed. The customer had been aiming for a tote bag and wound up with a coin purse. As usual, Maggie tried to make the best of the situation and tactfully showed her where she'd gone wrong.

As the day went on, a steady stream of customers commanded her attention and Maggie's thoughts turned away from Justin Ridley's murder. But just as she was closing up, she found an e-mail from Dana, sent from her iPhone.

Maggie—Finally reached Ellie. The police did ask Ben to go down to the station today. As a formality, they say. But she's very upset. I'm going out to the farm tomorrow, around noon. Are you busy? Want to take a ride with me? Dana

Maggie replied with a quick note:

I have no plans and would love to come. I'll bring Ellie her patterns and some yarn, and we can both bring her some comfort and encouragement.—M.

Much needed comfort and encouragement, Maggie reflected. The police weren't wasting any time. Formality or not, they were looking hard at Ben Krueger as a suspect. Or "a person of interest," as law officials called it.

That was the first step. The Kruegers had to be careful now that Ben did not travel any further down this sorry path.

Ellie had invited them for lunch, and Dana picked up Maggie at noon the next day. Maggie had been looking forward to a ride into the country, though the actual visit at the farm did not promise to be relaxing. Anything but, she expected.

The weather was just the opposite of the temperate Indian summer day they'd all enjoyed at the festival only a week before. A low, gray sky stretched above the open fields that streamed past, and dark clouds were a backdrop to flocks of geese, practicing for the long flight south.

As Maggie got out of Dana's Volvo and grabbed her purse

and knitting tote from the backseat, a damp, chilling breeze cut through her thick sweater and fluffy brown wrap.

Dana had parked in the circle in front of the farmhouse. She'd brought a few things to cheer Ellie up, a box of pastries from a fancy bakery and a bunch of flowers. It might have been a purely social call, Maggie thought, except for the subject they'd be most likely to discuss.

"Lucy wanted to come, too," Dana said as they headed for the front door, "but she has a deadline on a project and has to stay in and work all day."

"It's just as well. Ellie and Ben might feel invaded if too many of us descend on them."

Ellie greeted them warmly and led them inside. "Thanks for coming out. It's so good to see friendly faces."

They followed her into the dining room, where the table was set with a floral-patterned cloth and old-fashioned-looking china.

"What beautiful dishes, Ellie. They go perfectly with the house," Maggie noticed.

"I bought these dishes at a tag sale when we'd just started looking at property around here. I think this is the first time I've used them for entertaining. I thought we would have made more connections out here by now. I imagined lots of new friends. Dinner parties. That sort of thing." She sighed and headed to the kitchen. "It hasn't turned out like that at all, has it?"

Maggie and Dana exchanged a glance. They followed her into the big country kitchen. "You have the knitting group," Dana reminded her. "That's a start, right?"

Ellie turned from the counter, where she was tossing a

green salad. She touched Dana's arm. "That's a lot. Really. I didn't mean to sound as if I don't treasure your friendship. Believe me. I do."

They were all silent for a moment. Maggie felt as if Ellie had slipped away into her private thoughts and concerns.

"Can we help you with something? Carry things out?"

"Oh, yes . . . please. There's a basket with rolls and a platter of cheese on the sideboard. I have some grilled chicken in the oven."

The lunch was quickly set out. It looked delicious, and Maggie felt suddenly hungry. She noticed that the table was only set for three and wondered about Ben.

Dana was bold enough to ask. "How is Ben doing? Isn't he having lunch with us?"

Ellie filled their glasses with sparkling water and then her own. "He said it sounded like a girls' thing. He felt a little awkward. He's still upset after yesterday. He took a ride to Newburyport. There's a movie house up there that shows classic films. I think he said he was going to see *Arsenic and Old Lace.*"

"That's a good one. With Cary Grant when he was very young," Maggie said, though she couldn't remember the plot.

"Yes, that's the one. Ben is a bit of a film buff. That's one thing he misses up here. That and good Thai or Indian food."

Ellie laughed, and her friends did, too. But Maggie thought it sounded a bit forced.

"Newburyport isn't that far. That town has everything Ben likes," Dana pointed out. "It was probably a good idea for him to go up there and unwind."

"That's exactly what I thought," Ellie agreed.

While they enjoyed Ellie's well-prepared meal, Maggie took out the patterns and yarn she'd brought. They talked about their plans for the knitting charity project and other random topics, carefully avoiding the Ridley murder.

But once the dishes were cleared away and Ellie brought in coffee and dessert, the conversation turned back to Justin Ridley and Ben's experience at the hands of local law enforcement.

"They kept saying it was just a formality. But it really was an ordeal," Ellie admitted. "No wonder Ben needs to zone out at the movies today. I don't think I've ever been inside a police station before. Maybe once, just in the entranceway for some reason. Ben was taken back to some office. I wasn't allowed to go with him. I had to sit in a waiting area outside."

"Did you call an attorney?" Dana's voice was quiet, but Maggie sensed her intense concern.

Ellie just shook her head and stared down at the table. "Everything was happening so fast. The police just said they wanted to ask more questions. We didn't think . . ." She suddenly lifted her head. "Ben didn't need a lawyer. He didn't hurt Justin Ridley. He never went near him."

"I know." Dana reached across the table and touched Ellie's hand. "I just wish you'd called me. I know he had nothing to do with Ridley's death, but he should have a lawyer anyway. Just so the police don't step all over his rights." Dana was concerned, and she sounded like it.

"Dana's right," Maggie quietly chimed in. "I was in the same situation. I doubt I'd be sitting here, having this lovely lunch, if I hadn't taken that advice."

Ellie didn't answer at first. "All right. I'll have Ben call Jack tomorrow and get a recommendation, whether we need it or not. I still hope yesterday was the end of it."

Dana took a sip of coffee. "What happened at the police station? Besides the questioning. Did they ask for Ben's fingerprints or a DNA sample?"

Maggie could see Ellie was reluctant to answer. Finally she nodded. "Yes, they did. They kept saying it was just so they could eliminate Ben from the investigation. Ben found the body, and even the police had seen him argue with Ridley. Ben just did what they said. He knows he's innocent and just wanted to get out of there. I was upset at first," she admitted, "but later I thought, well, maybe this is a good thing. If they find fingerprints or other evidence, they'll see he's not a match. They'll have to accept that he wasn't involved."

"Good point. Detective Walsh could be onto a new lead right now," Maggie said sincerely.

Dana, who was always more objective and dispassionate in her thinking, didn't let it go at that. "Did they say they'd found fingerprints on the spindle?"

"I'm not sure. They didn't tell Ben if they did," Ellie replied.

Dana's expression was serious. "It doesn't necessarily mean that they didn't. It could be that they're having trouble lifting off a clean image. Or they're just not ready to disclose that information. I'll ask Jack to find out for you. Do you know what type of spindle it was?" she continued. "Did it have any yarn or fiber on it?"

Ellie looked upset by this question. Maggie was sorry Dana had pressed. But she was wondering about that, too.

"The police told Ben it was the same type of spindle I gave out at the festival. I must have given away at least a hundred of them. Maybe more. Anybody who came to the fair could have one and could have killed Ridley. We told the police that," she added quickly. "But I kept getting the feeling that they still connected the spindle with us, with me and Ben."

With Ben, she really meant. Maggie just nodded.

She hadn't even addressed the other question, about fiber on the murder weapon. A good one, Maggie thought. A piece of physical evidence like that could say a lot.

Suddenly Ellie bowed her head and covered her face with her hands. "I know Ben has a bad temper sometimes. He's very emotional. But he could never do anything like this. Never in a million years."

She was quietly crying, and Dana leaned over and laid a hand on her back.

"Ellie, please don't cry. I'm sorry for all the questions. I'm just concerned. I know what you're saying is true. I don't believe Ben did this, either."

"Oh, it isn't that. . . . You didn't ask anything worse than Detective Walsh did yesterday. That's for sure." Ellie lifted her head and wiped her eyes with a tissue. "And I do know you're trying to help. But it's even worse than you think." She sighed and took a deep breath. "The police asked where Ben was at the time of the murder. He said he was with me the entire night and only got up when the dogs woke us. That must have been about . . . half past four, or even five o'clock," she added.

"But he wasn't with you?" Maggie leaned forward in her seat. Ellie was talking so quietly now she could hardly hear her.

"No . . . not the whole night. But once we called the police, we knew they'd ask us that. So we agreed to stick to that story. It's just . . . less complicated."

"Less complicated than what? Where was he . . . exactly?" Dana asked.

"Ben has trouble sleeping through the night from time to time. We thought moving to the country would help. All the fresh air and exercise?" She shook her head, as if baffled now by her own naïveté. "It did help at first, but there are still stresses here. Maybe even more, in some ways."

Dana looked as if she wanted to ask more questions, but restrained herself. "Go on, Ellie. We're listening," she said simply. "He doesn't sleep well some nights."

"He starts off fine, snoring away," Ellie continued. "Then he wakes up and worries and gets so agitated, he has to get up, walk around. He usually goes into his office awhile. He'll tinker with our website or take care of the orders. Or go over our finances. That rarely helps to put him back to sleep," she added with a sigh.

"He worries about your business," Maggie clarified.

"Night and day," Ellie answered in a sad tone. "I feel so responsible. I was the one who pushed to come out here. He would have been happy to put the money we got from selling my PR firm in some easy, no-fuss investment—an apartment building or a fast food franchise. But I wanted the farm and the fiber business, and he wanted to make me happy."

Ellie sighed. "We have a good business plan. It all works out on paper. But we've had to draw down on some savings that we'd promised not to touch. The harassment on the farm only added to the stress and his anxiety. No wonder the poor man can't sleep. That's not a crime," she added.

"I understand," Dana said simply. "Most people experience insomnia at some point or another. I think about eighteen million are actually diagnosed and get help for it. . . . Medication, or behavior modification therapy."

"Oh, Ben would never take pills . . . and he's not big on therapists, either. No offense," Ellie quickly added.

"So he gets up and works. Sounds like what I'd do," Maggie said sympathetically.

"If he was on the computer, there'll be a record of e-mails and online activity on the hard drive," Dana reminded her.

"Yes, I know that. I even told him. But he was all shaken up after finding Ridley's body out there. We both were. We weren't thinking clearly. He wasn't sure when he was online and when he was just going over our bookkeeping. We had no idea when Ridley was attacked, either. He didn't want to take a chance. It was simpler if I just backed him up and said we were in bed and he never got up until the dogs woke us."

Simpler, yes . . . but couldn't Ben have left the house and come back while Ellie was fast asleep? Maggie quickly caught herself. She didn't want to go there. Though she knew the police had already found that hole in his alibi.

Maggie decided to change the subject. "I'm just curious, what happened to Ridley's dogs? Where did the police take them?"

"To a shelter, I think. I'm not sure. I felt bad about it," Ellie admitted. "But I certainly won't miss hearing that howling at all hours. I'll never forget the way they sounded the night Ridley was killed."

Maggie could only imagine. Dogs were so devoted. They must be so confused now. Waiting for him to come and take them home again.

"What about the llamas? Did you hear them that night, too?" Dana asked.

"The llamas? Do they make sounds?" This was news to Maggie. The llamas looked so solemn and wise. Above making sounds of any kind. They reminded her of the ever-silent Sphinx, though she wasn't sure why. Maybe it was their exotic origin and flat, bold stare.

"Oh, yes, the llamas can be pretty vocal. When they feel like it. But mostly it's a humming sound," Ellie explained. "There are snorts and growls, too. If they get annoyed with something. Like being sprayed down with the hose. And there's a sound called orgling. It's a gurgling sound males make during breeding season. They do have a cry," she added, "when they feel threatened or sense danger and want to warn the herd."

"I'd heard that they make noises, but I didn't realize they were so varied. Did you hear them that night? Were they frightened of anything?" Dana asked.

Ellie shook her head. "No . . . we didn't hear a thing. Just the dogs barking."

Before anyone could say more, they all heard the back door open and slam. Ben called out from the mudroom, "Ellie? I'm home."

"We're in here, Ben," Ellie called back. "Come and say hello to Dana and Maggie."

While Ellie turned and watched the doorway for her

husband, Dana and Maggie exchanged a quick glance. Here was their cue to go, Maggie thought. She sensed Dana felt the same.

"Hello, everyone. Nice to see you." Ben nodded and smiled as he walked in. He bent to give Ellie a kiss on the cheek, then stood beside her chair.

"How was the movie, as good as you remember?" Ellie asked him.

"It was great. Better than ever. Cary Grant was brilliant. I had a good laugh."

"I know I've seen it, I just can't remember the story," Maggie mused aloud.

"Very funny. Cary Grant has these two old aunts who are killing off their boarders—out of good intentions, actually—and burying them in the basement. You should catch it if you have a chance. I'm not sure how long it will be there." Ben put his hands in his pockets. His wide smile looked forced, Maggie thought.

He knew they'd been talking about Ridley's murder and talking about him, too, and he felt self-conscious. It was only natural. She would feel the same under the circumstances.

"That sounds like fun. Jack and I should go. We love old movies. Well, I think we ought to hit the road, don't you, Maggie? Even Jack will be done playing golf by now," Dana joked.

"Yes, I do. Thank you for lunch, Ellie. You didn't have to go to so much trouble for us. Everything was lovely. You'll have to come to my house next time."

Maggie felt that she needed to say the usual things expected of a luncheon guest. Even though the reason for their visit had not been the usual kind at all.

Ellie walked them to the front door and gave them each

a hug good-bye. "It was nothing. Thanks for coming. And for listening," she added in a quieter voice. "I'll have Ben call Jack tomorrow and get a referral," she promised Dana.

Dana touched her shoulder a moment and nodded. "Will we see you this week at the knitting group meeting?"

"I'm going to try my best," Ellie promised. "It's hard to make plans right now."

Maggie knew that meant she wanted to come but just wasn't sure what the days ahead would bring. Fair enough. Who would have ever expected to find a dead body on her property one Saturday morning? The body of her husband's worst enemy, no less.

After something like that happens, anyone would be wary of planning ahead.

Chapter Seven

*L*ucy had beat Maggie to the shop on Monday morning. Maggie found her sitting on the porch with her dogs, one on either side. They all were panting away, as if they'd just run a marathon—Lucy included, Maggie noticed.

Leashes were tied to the rail and a portable dog bowl sat between the dogs in a small puddle. Lucy sat sipping some human water from a plastic bottle.

Maggie smiled as she walked up the path. "Did they drag you out of bed like a sled team, or is this an early knitting emergency?"

Lucy came to her feet as Maggie unlocked the door. She wore a huge fleece pullover that Maggie suspected was Matt's and black running tights.

"New exercise routine. Living with Matt is definitely putting on relationship pounds."

Maggie tipped her head. "You look fine to me. But isn't that why they call them love handles?"

"I can fit into my favorite jeans and still love him. I'm going to jog into town with the dogs every day. It's not as easy as it looks."

"I would never say that routine looks easy. How do you keep them from stopping and sniffing every other minute? And how does Walley keep up?"

"I haven't quite mastered the first challenge yet. Walley keeps up fine. You'd be amazed. Dogs don't think like humans. He doesn't feel sorry for himself or realize that anything's wrong with him."

The victim of a hit-and-run, Walley had been left for dead on the side of the road until a good Samaritan brought him to Matt's clinic. The big-hearted Lab survived but lost a leg and the sight in one eye. Matt didn't have the heart to send him to a shelter and just adopted him.

"We could all take a page from that book." Maggie stepped into the shop, and Lucy followed.

"How did Dara's soccer tournament go?" Maggie was tempted to tease Lucy about almost being a soccer stepmom, but she gallantly held her tongue.

"It was so cute. She plays goalie. She looks awesome with all her gear her on. Like a character in *Peanuts*. I have some pictures on my phone. I'll show you later."

Even more tempted to tease, Maggie forced herself to squelch the impulse. "Did her team win anything?"

"Not really. But it was one of those meets where every kid gets a little trophy just for showing up."

"I'm not sure how I feel about that approach," Maggie said as she turned on the coffeemaker.

"I think it's a good thing at that age. They all battle pretty fiercely out there. You'd be surprised. Didn't somebody say ninety percent of life is just showing up?"

"Woody Allen. And he does have a point," Maggie conceded. More than ninety percent of her business was just showing up at the shop every day. That was for sure.

"How are Ellie and Ben? Did they talk about Justin Ridley a lot?" Lucy was sitting at the oak table, and Maggie brought her a mug of coffee. Very strong and hot, with nothing in it. Just the way her friend liked it.

"We saw Ben for a minute as we were leaving. We mainly spoke to Ellie. Which was just as well. This situation has shaken her to the core. She needed to vent about a lot of things she wouldn't have talked about if Ben had been there."

Maggie quickly filled Lucy in on the way Ben had been questioned by the police. She also passed on Ellie's admission that Ben suffered from bouts of insomnia and hadn't been asleep in bed when the dogs woke them, as they'd told the police.

"I don't think they did the right thing, misleading the police like that. But it probably won't matter in the long run," Maggie added. "Ellie said he was working in his home office but not in her sight, and they were panicked and not thinking clearly after finding Ridley's body."

Lucy sipped her coffee. She didn't answer right away. Maggie sensed she agreed that the Kruegers had made a mistake lying to the police in their statement. These things always have a way of coming out.

Lucy glanced at her. "What has Jack heard from his police friends? Does Detective Walsh really consider Ben a suspect? Or is he just trying to eliminate him from the possibilities?"

"Jack hasn't heard anything yet, one way or the other. But he was going to make some calls today. I'm interested to see what the newspaper has to say. Maybe they have some information on other leads the police are following."

Maggie had dumped a pile of mail in the middle of the table and now sifted through to find the newspaper. The *Plum Harbor Times* did not print an edition on Sunday, so the Monday issue in hand was the first to report on Ridley's death.

"Front page, above the fold." Maggie held up the paper a moment to show Lucy the big headline. "'Local Farmer and Activist Found Dead.' He wasn't actually a farmer, come to think about it. But I guess that fit better than 'landowner.' Let's see, what does it say . . . ?" She scanned the story quickly, peering down through her reading glasses. "'The body of Justin Ridley was found by Ben Krueger early Saturday morning on the Laughing Llama Farm, a neighboring property to that of the victim . . .'"

"Ellie won't like that part," Lucy noted. "That's what I call really bad publicity."

"You're right. She won't. But it's a fact, no getting around it. What else? We know most of this already," Maggie noted as she scanned the page. "I won't read it all aloud. Oh, this part is good: 'Ridley apparently bled to death after being stabbed in the neck with a wooden spindle. A preliminary autopsy showed that the spindle struck both the trachea and an artery in the throat and the victim suffocated on his own blood.'"

Maggie paused and swallowed. "Gruesome." She shook her head and took a sip of coffee. "I was wondering how a person could die from being stabbed with a spindle. I imagine Ridley was fairly fit."

"He did look fit," Lucy recollected, "though I only saw him from far away. I was thinking the same thing. A spindle would be painful and do some damage. But it would be unlikely to kill you."

"Unless someone stuck it right in your heart. Or some other critical spot," Maggie countered.

"I guess it was just a lucky shot. Or an unlucky one, depending on how you look at it," Lucy remarked. "Maybe the person who attacked him wasn't trying to kill him. Maybe they were just defending themselves?"

"Good point. I wonder if the police thought of that." Maggie had put the paper down, and Lucy leaned over to get a better look.

"Look at these pictures," Lucy said.

Maggie had hardly noticed but took a closer look now. Two photographs of Ridley were printed side by side. One appeared to have been taken recently, during a demonstration by the Friends of Farmland—Maggie could tell from the banner in the background. Ridley was standing at a podium, speaking.

Dark, deep-set eyes stared out from his angular face. He had a long nose and a droopy mustache and thin cheeks shadowed by a few days' growth of beard. A soiled bandanna was tied around his forehead. A denim shirt and hunting vest added to his survivor-man style.

"He's pretty much the way I pictured him. An outlaw type. Or maybe a folk singer," Lucy decided.

"Or a folk hero," Maggie mused. "Oh . . . look at that one, in his military uniform. So young and fresh-faced. He was very handsome back then, wasn't he?"

"Before . . . and after, you mean," Lucy replied. "How old was he? Does it say?"

"Let's see . . . sixty-two. He looked older, but it's hard to tell under that beard. It says underneath that army photo that he was drafted in 1968 and served in the military for four years. Discharged with a disability."

"Physical . . . or psychological?"

"Doesn't say," Maggie replied, her eyes still on the article. "After the service, he enrolled at the University of Massachusetts Amherst and studied philosophy and political science. But he dropped out after three years, just a few credits short of earning his degree. He was married for a year and divorced."

"Intelligent," Lucy remarked. "But undermined himself. Self-destructive? Dana says he had all the earmarks of post-traumatic stress syndrome."

"Possibly. He came to Plum Harbor about thirty-five years ago," Maggie continued, "and always lived on that land next to the Kruegers, though he didn't own it at first. Just rented the house on the property. The reporter mentions his activities with the Friends of Farmland. He was the founder and co-chair," Maggie noted. She suddenly turned and looked at Lucy. "Guess who the other 'co' is."

Lucy sighed. "I hate when you do that. I can't guess. Who?"

"Angelica Rossi." Maggie shook her head. "That was a no-brainer, Lucy. I'm surprised at you."

Lucy rolled her eyes. "Interesting. Go on. Is that it?"

"Nope. . . . 'Continued on page B32.' I have to find the page. . . . Oh, here we are." She paused a moment. "Nothing more about FOF. It says that he's survived by a daughter,

Janine Ridley of Portland, Oregon." Maggie looked up. "I wonder if she'll come to claim the body and settle the estate."

Lucy looked surprised by the question. "Don't you think most people would come, under the circumstances?"

"I do. But you never know. He was clearly a difficult, solitary man and may have had a poor relationship with his daughter."

"That's possible. But even so, she would still come to settle the estate. To sell the farm and all that," Lucy replied.

Maggie thought that was likely, too. She had turned the paper to the back pages to read the end of the article and now glanced down at the advertisements printed in the right-hand column. Listings for the local movie houses, mostly.

One for the Newburyport Cinema Arts Center caught her eye. The 1940s classic *Gaslight* was listed with show times. Maggie clearly recalled the story—set in the late nineteenth century, a scheming husband convinces his naive wife that she's going crazy by secretly adjusting the light fixtures. A slim concept, but somehow, with Ingrid Bergman in the starring role, it worked.

It looked like the film had been the only feature playing there on the weekend, as part of an Ingrid Bergman film festival. *Arsenic and Old Lace* was not listed there, she noticed. Or at any other theater.

"That's funny," she mumbled.

"Something else in the article?" Lucy asked.

Maggie looked up and shook her head. "No. Just a misprint. Doesn't matter."

"I wonder what kind of relationship they had."

Maggie looked up at Lucy, confused for a moment.

"Janine Ridley and her father. I wonder if they got along or if he'd alienated her, too."

Maggie wondered about that, also. "Good question. Maybe we'll find out."

The little brass bell on the front door sounded. Two women walked in carrying knitting totes. They stood at the front of the store and shyly waved at Maggie.

"Good morning, ladies," Maggie called out. "Just take a seat in the front. I'll be with you in a minute."

She quickly stood, closed the paper, and gathered up her mail. "It's showtime," she said quietly to Lucy. "A Is for Afghan. A beginner class. They're so sweet and sincere at this stage," she added, as if talking about kindergarteners.

Lucy picked up her coffee mug and grinned. "I'm sure you're very positive and encouraging with them."

Maggie shrugged. "We all have to start knitting somewhere. Ninety percent is just showing up for the class."

Lucy laughed and headed out to get her dogs and walk home.

Maggie headed for the alcove just to the left of the shop's entrance, where a love seat and several armchairs were set up around a low marble-topped table. She liked using this space for small groups, instead of the worktable at the back of the store. It was more relaxed and intimate, more like sitting in someone's parlor than being in an official class.

She also had a good view of the whole shop from this spot—who was coming in and out—and could quickly tell if Phoebe was floundering and needed help covering the customers. Her lifeguard post, she secretly called it.

Toward the end of the day, Maggie was back in the cozy spot, teaching another class to a small group, this one about knitting for newborns. Her students were expectant mothers, aunts, and grandmas, all eager to master Bibs, Booties, and Beyond. The class was almost over when she spotted a customer near the counter who seemed to be waiting for assistance.

Phoebe was in back helping an elderly customer pick out buttons for a child's sweater. The process promised to go on for a while. Phoebe did exhibit admirable patience with seniors, Maggie had to grant her that. Maybe because the girl's mind often worked in the same wandering way.

Maggie excused herself from the class and headed for the unattended patron. "May I help you with something?"

The woman turned to face her. Something about her looked familiar. Maggie guessed she'd been in the shop before.

"I'm trying to match this blue merino, or find something that will complement it." She handed Maggie a small ball of yarn. "I don't have enough left for the sleeves and thought I could do them in another color."

Maggie put on her reading glasses and examined the blue yarn. "If you have the label from the skein, I should be able to order it."

"How long would that take?" the customer asked.

"Oh, a week or so. It's hard to say. It depends where we find it." Maggie knew she sounded vague, but that was really the truth of the matter.

"I don't think that works out for me. I don't live around here. I'm visiting from out of town. I have a lot of downtime in the evenings. That's why I brought my knitting along. It was stupid of me to leave the rest of the yarn at home. I was in a rush and not thinking."

Maggie looked at the young woman again and nodded sympathetically. She spoke quickly and sounded a bit anxious. She still looked familiar, out-of-towner or not.

"Knitting is my favorite way to fill the downtime in life. But that's probably obvious. . . . Are you here on business?" Maggie asked, trying for a friendly, not-too-nosy tone.

"Not really. My father lived around here. He died over the weekend. Justin Ridley. You've probably heard about what happened to him. It was in all the local papers and on TV the other night." Her voice trailed off, softer now. She met Maggie's eye a moment, then looked away.

That was it. Of course. She was Ridley's daughter, Janine. The same deep-set eyes and thin face. The same dark hair and tall, thin build—though the family genes expressed themselves much more attractively in a feminine version, Maggie thought. A slim brunette, she was in her mid-thirties, Maggie guessed. Her thick hair was blunt cut, curling around her face, softening the angular features so reminiscent of her father.

"Yes, I heard that news. I'm sorry for your loss," Maggie said sincerely.

"Thank you. I didn't see him much. But I'll miss him." She looked tired, Maggie thought. Or maybe that was just jet lag . . . combined with sadness over her father's death? And dealing with the police all day. Maggie could only guess where she'd been today and what she'd done before finding her way to the knitting shop.

She looked straight at Maggie. "Did you know my father? Did you ever meet him?"

Maggie shook her head. "No, we never met. But I do know the couple who live on the farm next door to his, the Kruegers. Ben Krueger was the man who found your father's body," she added, though she expected that Janine Ridley would recognize the name.

Janine Ridley's expression changed quickly. "Oh . . . right. The police told me they'd questioned that man about the murder. He's a friend of yours?" She looked at Maggie oddly.

Maggie acted as if she hadn't noticed. "Oh, I doubt Ben was involved. In fact, I'm sure he wasn't. I know he didn't get along with your father. But neighbors often have grievances. I'm sure the police questioned him because they can't rule anything out at this stage."

Janine didn't answer. She did seem to pull back and sort of close up, looking distrustful. Having second thoughts about patronizing a shop that harbored sympathies for Ben Krueger, Maggie guessed.

"I can check the storeroom for some yarn that might work for you. Would you like me to look?" Maggie asked politely.

Janine Ridley thought about it a moment, then nodded and handed over the ball of yarn she had in hand. "All right. I'll wait."

She either wanted that yarn badly or was much more composed and even-tempered than her father. Maybe a bit of both, Maggie reasoned.

Maggie went back to the storeroom. By the time she had found a few possibilities and returned to the front of the store, the students from Bibs, Booties, and Beyond had left and the button-selecting senior was gone, too. Phoebe sighed as if cleaning out the Aegean stables as she sorted piles of buttons into their correct drawers again.

Maggie headed for Janine Ridley, who was sitting up front near the bay window and had taken out her knitting project.

Maggie stood next to her chair with a basket of yarn. "I found a few merino possibilities. I have a lot of stock in all these colors, too."

"Thanks. Let me see what you have." Janine Ridley looked over the selection of yarn Maggie had brought out for her. She held each up in turn against the blue section of the sweater she was working on, trying to choose a good complement.

"Will there be a memorial service? The newspaper article this morning didn't mention anything," Maggie noted.

"I would have held one for him, but he didn't want anything like that. He asked to be cremated and have his ashes scattered on a certain favorite spot on his land. I have to wait for the police to release his body."

"Yes, of course. That could take a few days." Maggie nodded sympathetically. She didn't think it was legal to scatter ashes anywhere you pleased, though she suspected that in trying to honor the requests of deceased loved ones, people did many odd things with cremated remains. Hadn't Suzanne once said she wanted her ashes to be tossed on George Clooney?

Janine Ridley's voice distracted Maggie from her rambling thoughts. ". . . I know my father rubbed a few people in town the wrong way, and scared people, too, roaming around at night with his gun and his dogs," Janine said frankly. "But he had friends. Many people in this town accepted that he was different. And respected him, too."

Maggie nodded. "Yes, I'm sure that's true."

It was true, she thought. Despite what the Kruegers thought of him.

"He wasn't a bad person," Janine insisted. "He was very sincere about saving the farmland out where he lived. The landscape out there gave him great comfort after he left the army."

"I'm sure a lot of people would have come to a memorial to pay their respects," Maggie said, feeling that this was what the young woman was driving at.

Janine glanced at her and nodded, then looked back at the basket of yarns again. She rejected a few of the skeins and put them aside.

Maggie watched her a moment, then said, "The newspaper said that you live in Portland. Did you grow up there?"

"Yes, I did. My parents divorced when I was six months old. It was a very bitter breakup. My mother got full custody and took me to the West Coast. She had family there. I didn't meet my father until I was in high school. That was pretty difficult," she admitted. "When I was a teenager, I thought he was such an oddball. But as I got older, I came to appreciate him. He wasn't like other people. I'm very angry about the way he died. But in a way, I'm not surprised."

Maggie's eyes widened at that admission. "Why do you say that? Did he ever tell you that he'd been threatened by anyone around here?"

"No . . . he never said that. But he was so different. He didn't fit in, and he didn't even want to. People lash out at

things they don't understand. And at people they don't understand. It's out of fear, mainly. I see it all the time."

Maggie found this turn in the conversation surprising. She
sat in the chair across from Janine. "You do? How is that? . . .
If you don't mind me asking."

"I don't mind. I'm a school counselor. I specialize in children who've been bullied."

Something about that made sense to Maggie. Janine Ridley seemed intelligent and self-aware. She could easily see her
working with misfit children.

She was also as open and forthcoming as her father had been
closed and antisocial. Maybe it was her West Coast upbringing
or her background as a therapist. Or maybe the atmosphere of
the shop and the relaxing knitting break had helped her open up.

Maggie wondered if she was asking too many questions
now and would offend the young woman by seeming too nosy.
But Janine Ridley was alone in town, handling a very heavy
situation, and she did seem to want to talk to somebody.

"I guess you have a lot to do, sorting out your father's affairs, settling his estate."

"Not really. He was very organized that way. The last time
I visited him here, he told me everything I need to know.
There's a good lawyer in town handling his will." Janine sighed
and put aside two more of the skeins. "I can't go into his house
yet. The police are still looking for clues. I wouldn't stay there
anyway. But I am worried about his dogs. He had two beautiful hunting dogs, Thelma and Louise."

"Those were the names of his dogs, Thelma and Louise?"
Maggie couldn't quite believe it. From all she'd heard, she'd

never once imagined Justin Ridley as the type to pick amusing pet names.

Janine glanced at her and guessed what she was thinking. "Oh, he didn't name the dogs. The names were on the papers when he bought them. He'd never heard of the movie, and when I tried to explain it, he wasn't very interested. He didn't care much about popular culture. Didn't even own a TV set." Janine smiled, remembering, and Maggie wasn't surprised to hear that. "He never mentioned it, but I think he would have wanted me to take care of them," Janine continued. "Find them homes or something. The police said they were left at a shelter. I felt bad about that. I'm going to look for them tomorrow. But I don't know what to do after that. I can't keep them with me. I'm staying at a B-and-B in the village. Do you know a place where I can board the dogs for a while? Someplace nice. Where the dogs will be treated well?"

Maggie didn't have to consider the question very long. "There's a good vet in town who might board them for you and help find homes. The office is just down Main Street, Harbor Animal Hospital. The vet's name is Matt McDougal. Tell him I recommended him to you."

Of course, she'd alert Lucy about this situation, too.

"Thanks." Janine nodded. She seemed relieved. "I'll go talk to him tomorrow. That's one thing I can do for my father. The only other thing I can do is stay here until the police catch his killer. I think I owe him that much."

Maggie didn't know what to say. It could take a long time to close this investigation. From what she'd heard so far, the police had barely scratched the surface.

Janine held out the skein she'd finally selected for Maggie

to see. "I like this blue-gray color. I think it will work well for the sleeves. And maybe a border."

"Good choice. Let's see. . . . Looks like you'll need four skeins altogether. I'll get three more from the back."

A short time later, Maggie had packed up the purchase. Janine took the bag and thanked her.

"If you have any other knitting needs, or want to start another project while you're in town, you know where to come," Maggie said as she was leaving.

"Thanks, but I hope I'm not here that long. I think the police will figure this out very quickly."

She sounded confident of that. Maggie wondered if Janine had learned today that the investigation had made some new progress.

But she didn't feel bold enough to ask her that.

"I hope the police do figure this out quickly," Maggie said sincerely. A quick resolution would help everyone involved— Janine Ridley and Ben and Ellie.

Of course, as soon as the shop door closed, Maggie could hardly wait to share the news that she'd just had a long chat with Janine Ridley.

But even Phoebe had disappeared up to her apartment. Maggie decided to send a quick e-mail to everyone before she closed up and headed home.

Dear Friends,

You'll never guess who just left the shop. Janine Ridley—daughter and sole surviving relative of the deceased, in case you didn't read the paper today. She's come to town to settle his estate and turns out she knits. She greatly resembles her father. But very talkative and forthcoming. Didn't take after him that way. It was interesting to see him through her eyes. That's all I'll say for now. It's been a long day and I need to head home ... and work on my own knitting.

XO Maggie

Maggie was still cleaning up and closing out the register when the replies started flying back.

Phoebe's note didn't even have a salutation:

Boo Radley's daughter was here!? Why didn't you tell me?! I never get the good customers ... P

The next was from Lucy, replying to all:

Guess this answers our questions, Maggie. ie: If they got along and if she'd come to town. But now I have a lot more questions. Will try to stop by before the Thursday night meeting if I can. It's at Dana's this week, right? (Please warn me ASAP if it's my turn ...)

xo—L.

Dana replied to all as well:

Want to hear more about Janine Ridley, too. What luck that she's a knitter. But we're all separated by just six degrees. (Knitters by a stitch or two?) Yes, Lucy, it's my turn. But can we meet tomorrow night, instead of Thursday? I don't want to miss the meeting at village hall, about the open space laws. Sorry to change the plan at the last minute. Let me know what you all think.

xo Dana

A few more negotiating notes flew among them, and Maggie and her friends agreed to meet at Dana's house on Tuesday night.

It had seemed like a good solution for all, but when Tuesday rolled around, the timing was a little tight for Maggie. She taught a class that ended at seven. She had to hurry her students out of the shop a few minutes early, then raced over to Dana's house.

Phoebe had to be at school, so she wasn't coming at all. Ellie had been included in the second round of e-mails, but Maggie didn't see her SUV in the driveway. Maggie wasn't surprised. She imagined that all the stress of the investigation had been very tiring for Ellie and she probably didn't have the energy to come into town at night.

She hadn't been in touch with Ellie since the visit on Sunday and wondered if the police investigation had officially eliminated Ben yet. From what Janine Ridley had said, it didn't seem so.

The front door of Dana's house was open, and Maggie called out a greeting as she walked in. "Hello? It's just me."

"We're in here," Dana called back from the living room, just off the entrance hall.

Maggie knew her way by now to the spot where her friends were assembled.

Dana's taste was sleek and clutter-free—Zen-inspired, Maggie always thought—but comfortable, nonetheless. The group sat on the leather sectional in front of the fireplace and a dramatic black granite mantel that was topped by a few pieces of exotic-looking pottery. A tapestry Dana and Jack had found somewhere in South America hung on the wall above.

Maggie was glad to see a large fire shimmering in the hearth. She took a seat nearby and felt warmed by the flames, the greetings of her good friends, and a sip of red wine from the glass Dana handed down to her.

A large slate-topped table, set between the couches, was covered with appetizing dishes. Italian . . . Maggie's favorite. A dish of mozzarella balls mixed with basil vinaigrette dressing, and another that held fat, juicy olives. There was also a platter of crostini—crusty bread slices topped with chopped tomato, herbs, bits of red onion, and grated cheese. They looked yummy and smelled as if they'd just come from the oven.

Maggie leaned forward and filled her small plate. "Sorry I'm late. I tried to rush the class along, but they all had their little knitting dramas tonight, if you know what I mean."

"Don't think, just knit. That's what you used to tell us," Lucy reminded her.

Lucy, Suzanne, and Dana had met in a class at Maggie's shop years ago, though it was hard to believe that now. It felt as if they'd all known one another forever.

"Did I say that? How wise of me." Maggie savored a bite of the fresh mozzarella.

"Yes, you did. I still say that to myself when I'm in a jam," Suzanne admitted. "Sometimes, I'm not even knitting."

"Well, that's what I'll have to tell this group. They're all too . . . left-brained or something. They have too many questions."

Dana had stepped into the kitchen to get more wine, but now she took her place on the couch next to Lucy. "Speaking of knitters and questions, I want to hear more about Janine Ridley. What's she like? How did you know it was her? How long is she staying in town? You hardly said anything in the e-mail."

"Let's see, what didn't I tell you?" Maggie paused and thought about it a moment. "She came in the shop at the end of the day. Something about her looked familiar, but I couldn't figure it out. Then she told me that she was visiting from out of town because her father had just died. She asked me if I'd known him. I told her I hadn't, but that I did know the Kruegers."

"What did she say to that?" Lucy asked curiously.

"She knows that the police questioned him and I got the impression that either the police have given her the impression that they strongly suspect Ben, or she hopes that her father's killer can be found that easily. She seems quite even-tempered and calm. But she said she was very angry at the way her father died. And she's determined to stay in town until the police find the person who did it."

"That might take a long time," Dana said knowingly.

"I know. But it wasn't the sort of thing you can say to the child of a man who's just been murdered."

"Of course not," Dana agreed. "How long did you talk to her?"

"We spoke for a while. She's a very thoughtful and reasonable young woman. Pretty much the opposite of her father. At least, the way we've heard him described."

"Maybe the gene for being a nutty, paranoid recluse skips a generation," Lucy offered.

"Possibly. Though she didn't see her father in the same extreme light. She wasn't blind to his eccentricities, either." Maggie paused and took a bite of the crostini. "I think she might be a little lonely and just needed to chat with someone. She's dealing with a lot. Not just coming across the country to bury a parent who she hardly knew but one who has been murdered," Maggie pointed out.

"That's very true, Maggie." Dana nodded. "And you're a good listener," she added.

"I try to be . . . when I'm not asking too many questions," she admitted. "She didn't seem to mind my curiosity. She was picking out some extra yarn in order to finish a sweater, and she took her time deciding. She was very straightforward. Told me the whole family history. Seems her parents divorced before her first birthday and her mother took her to the West Coast. She didn't meet her father until she was in high school."

"How awful. That's not right. No matter how crazy he was." Suzanne shook her head.

"Oh, she knew he was eccentric. She had no illusions about that. 'An oddball,' she called him," Maggie added. "But she spoke very well of him. How he was devoted to protecting the land around here and how living out there had healed him after his military career. She understood and respected him. And loved him."

"That's nice to hear. At least he had a child who loved him. I know he had his dark side. But he always sounded so lonely. I felt so sad for him," Suzanne said.

Dana nibbled on an olive. "People are complicated. No one is all good or all bad."

"Ellie and Ben might argue with you about that," Maggie said as she helped herself to the last crostini. "Where is Ellie? I thought she said she was coming tonight."

Dana rose and picked up some empty dishes. "I thought so, too. I just texted her a few minutes ago, and she hasn't answered. I hope nothing else awful is going on out there."

Dana cleared off the appetizers and brought in the main

course, a huge bowl of pasta mixed with vegetables and topped with basil and fresh grated cheese. The garlicky smell alone made Maggie's mouth water. She had thought she was full from the appetizers, but suddenly felt hungry again.

"That looks so good, Dana. I've been running almost every morning. I guess I can go for it," Lucy said.

"It's whole-wheat pasta. That helps, right? All the vegetables are fresh, from our ride out to the country Sunday." Dana glanced over at Maggie.

"I bought vegetables, too. But I haven't cooked anything as delicious as this. Not yet, anyway," Maggie added, tasting a forkful.

The pasta primavera tasted as good as it looked, and they all enjoyed the dish in silence for a few moments, savoring bites between sips of red wine.

The doorbell rang, and Dana rose to answer it, dabbing her mouth with a napkin on the way. "That must be Ellie. Just in time."

A few moments later Maggie heard Ellie's voice in the foyer, confirming Dana's guess. But something didn't sound right. Their exchange, too distant to make out word for word, had a distinct note of urgency and emotion.

Everyone noticed it and stopped eating. They sat up, listening.

"Is that Ellie?" Lucy asked quietly. "Sounds like something's wrong."

They all listened a moment or two more.

"She's crying," Suzanne whispered. "That can't be good."

Maggie agreed but didn't have to say it out loud. It didn't bode well at all.

Chapter Eight

Everything is getting so complicated. I don't know what we did wrong. Ben found Ridley's body in the field. Is that a crime? Why can't the police start looking for the person who actually did this and leave us alone?"

Ellie sat beside Dana, sipping a glass of wine. Dana had served her some pasta, but she didn't seem to notice it. She was crying, and it was hard to understand every word. But Maggie didn't have the heart to interrupt and ask questions.

"Start from the beginning, Ellie." Dana's tone was calm and comforting. "The police were in touch since we saw you Sunday, is that right?"

Ellie nodded, her expression bleak. "On Monday, they called and asked Ben to come down to the station for more questions. We called the attorney Jack recommended," she added, turning to Dana, "and he met us there. We told him the whole story, and he advised us to revise our statements—to tell Detective Walsh that Ben was not asleep the entire night," she clarified. "Ben told them he never left the house, and I totally believe him."

"How did Detective Walsh react?" Maggie asked.

"He acted as if he suspected we'd been hiding something all along. It made us feel very guilty . . . and then I had to stop myself and think, What are we feeling so guilty about? We didn't do anything wrong. Once you get involved with the police, they can twist around everything you say. You get confused. You start to question your own memories of what happened."

Maggie knew that was true. That type of interrogation was so stressful, and Ellie did look as if the stress of this whole situation was getting to her. She looked tired and overwhelmed. Her appearance was not nearly as polished and put-together as usual, either.

She and Ben had been dealing with a lot these last few days—actually, ever since they'd moved onto the farm. Nothing had gone smoothly for them. That didn't seem fair, either.

"I'm sure the police were not happy to hear you lied on the statements. But coming forward about that was the right thing to do." Dana's tone was encouraging. "The activity on the computer will show that he was in the house during the time frame of the murder. That will be that. He'll alibi out."

"I'm not so sure about that. And neither is Ben," Ellie said bleakly. "We had to hand over our computer and give the police access to our phone records and all that . . . but our attorney seems concerned."

Ellie started crying again. She dabbed her eyes with a napkin. "Ben says it won't prove anything. So what if they see e-mails or visits to our website? That could have been me, or anyone, on the computer. It's not like he had a teleconference for hours in the middle of the night. That would be the only way to really prove he was in the house all that time."

"You have a good point," Dana agreed. "But it shows something. Even though it's not airtight. What about the security cameras? Were the cameras on that night?"

Ellie nodded. "They were on. The police took the CDs with the video from that night right away. Ben and I looked at the backup files, but we didn't see anything unusual."

Ellie sat back and sighed. "Why do we have to prove anything? What happened to innocent until proven guilty? Why do we need to go to all this trouble? It's an invasion of our privacy. Ben didn't do anything. He said this would never happen in the city, and I think he's right. He thinks the police out here are just country bumpkins who can't get out of their own way long enough to figure out who really did this. So they're fixating on him."

Maggie sympathized. Her own experience with the police in town had been much the same. But she didn't want to fuel Ellie's anxiety.

"What does your attorney think?" Maggie asked.

Ellie glanced at her and sighed. "He asked if there were any blocks of time that might be unaccounted for. Ben doesn't really remember. He wasn't on the computer the whole time. He went downstairs to make a snack. He dozed off awhile watching TV. It might have been the same time that Ridley was killed. The police haven't told us specifically when that happened. Why would they?" Ellie sighed again and shook her head.

"Have they told you anything they've found out so far?" Lucy asked gently.

"Only that the spindle used to stab Ridley came from our

farm. It was one of the souvenirs we made up for the festival. I thought it was such a clever publicity gimmick. Now it's being used to frame my husband for murder."

Her eyes had filled with tears again, and she covered her face with her hands, shaking with sobs.

Dana leaned over and rested a comforting hand on Ellie's back. "I know it looks bad but, you said it yourself, you gave out dozens of those spindles. Anyone at the festival could have taken one and used it to kill Ridley. That fact alone makes any case against Ben very weak."

Ellie sat up and took a deep breath. They waited for her to calm herself. "Yes, I know. We thought of that. But I'm starting to think it was better when we lied. At least that covered the whole night, including the time Ridley was killed. I know it sounds terrible, but I would have stuck to that story for Ben. And a wife doesn't have to testify against her husband in court," she reminded them.

Ellie sounded desperate. But who could blame her? She and Ben were in a bind. Nobody said a word. Maggie felt so sorry for Ellie and wished that there were some way to help her. She sensed that her friends felt the same.

"The police are focusing on Ben more and more every day. And now that Ridley's daughter's in town, it's going to get even worse," Ellie added.

"I spoke to Janine Ridley today. She came into the knitting shop." Maggie looked over at Ellie.

Ellie sat up, suddenly alert. "Really? Did she mention us?"

"Not at first. I told her that I knew you and Ben, and that I didn't believe he had anything to do with her father's death," she added quickly.

"But she thinks so. I just know it. She'll be pestering the police every minute to arrest him."

"Ellie, it doesn't work like that. Detectives are trained to ignore emotional relatives," Dana assured her.

Suzanne had been quietly eating her pasta and now put her empty dish aside. "Follow the money. That's what the police have to do. That's how they can find the person who killed Ridley."

Everyone looked at her. "What money?" Lucy asked.

"You're kidding me, right? Don't you hear that sound?" Suzanne cocked her head, listening. "Flapping wings high above? The development vultures circling, looking for prey. Property owners ready to sign on the dotted line. Once that open space zoning is off the books around here, they'll swoop down for the kill. There's huge money in this debate, ladies." Suzanne took out her knitting and began to work—one of the fast and easy hat patterns, Maggie noticed. "Justin Ridley was definitely gumming up the works. A lot of people are secretly—and not so secretly—happy that he's out of the way."

"So you think his killer was connected to this zoning issue? Someone who wants the open space laws to expire and is willing to take another life to ensure that?"

"Yes, I do." Suzanne stretched out a length of yarn and began stitching. "Someone who has a lot to gain and didn't want Ridley and his group screwing up their payday. Maybe someone who has some bad history with him already?"

"But what about the rest of the Friends of Farmland? Eliminating Ridley doesn't stop them. It might even energize their efforts," Lucy pointed out.

"It could work either way, I think," Dana said. "Sometimes

when a group like that loses its leader, it does fall apart. But Suzanne has a point. It could have been someone who had issues with him in the past for other reasons. This was just the last straw."

Maggie sat in silence a moment, recalling her meeting with Janine Ridley.

"His daughter said she wasn't surprised that he was killed. Isn't that an odd thing to say? When I asked her why, she said it was because he was so different and some people react to that with fear and want to lash out."

"This all sounds very likely to me." Ellie's voice sounded stronger and steadier than it had all evening, Maggie noticed. "People will do a lot of things when money is at stake. Even at the risk of turning Ridley into some sort of martyr."

"Well, maybe he was," Lucy said simply. "Not all martyrs were really nice guys—or women—you'd like to hang out with."

"Saint or curmudgeon, this line of reasoning definitely lets Ben off the hook," Maggie asserted. "What about your other neighbors, Ellie? Do you know of anyone who's eager to sell their property if the laws expire? Maybe someone who also had issues with Ridley? Let's try to follow the money and see where we go."

Maggie sent a playful glance Suzanne's way.

Ellie sat thinking a moment. "Good question. I'm not really sure. We don't know all the other landowners around us very well. There's a vineyard directly behind our orchard. Red Hawk Winery. They have a very good business going, so I don't think they're ready to sell. But there's a farmer on the other side, Walter Kranowski. He grows potatoes and some vegetables. Cabbage and kale, I think. I heard his wife died a few years ago and he's getting ready to retire."

"Or has some grown kids who are saying, 'Hey, Dad, you're sitting on a gold mine here. Let's cash in these potatoes for some lettuce,'" Suzanne chimed in.

"Suzanne? That was a really bad one." Lucy had also taken out her knitting. A scarf was starting to take shape on big needles, another charity fund-raising project.

Dana glanced at Suzanne, too, but didn't comment on the pun. "How did he feel about Ridley and the Friends of Farmland? Do you know?"

"We haven't spoken to him much. But one time we were chatting and Ridley's name came up. It was clear that Mr. Kranowski didn't like Ridley and also thought the man was an oddball," Ellie explained. "He also made a few nasty remarks about the Friends of Farmland," she added.

"Don't you think the police questioned him and know all this?" Maggie asked the others.

"They took statements from all the property owners in the area after the murder. That's routine procedure. But Kranowski isn't in the crosshairs, the way they've focused on Ben." Dana knew these things from her conversations with her husband. "He either alibied out, or they didn't think his grievances against Ridley were the type to inspire homicide."

"I wouldn't cross Farmer Kranowski off the list yet just because our local police force has," Maggie said. "Anyone else you can think of, Ellie?"

"There are the hippie organic farmers farther down the road, just past Kranowski's place. They mainly raise goats and make cheese. They're definitely Friends of Farmland. But I think they're pretty harmless. Angelica Rossi's farm, Sweet Meadow, is over in that direction, too. We know what side of the question she's on."

"Yes, well . . . I still wouldn't cross her off. She always seems nice enough. Very professional. But there's something about her I don't trust," Maggie said bluntly.

"Me, either," Ellie agreed. "But I have even more reason. I've told you about the rumors she spreads about our products. She'll say anything. She doesn't have any ethics or conscience at all. Not when it comes to business. Maybe she tells herself all's fair in love, war, and business."

"She was close to Ridley, too," Dana pointed out. "They ran the group together. It is statistically true that most murder victims are killed by someone familiar. Someone they have a close relationship with."

"I saw her come and go a few times from Ridley's property," Ellie recalled. "I wondered at the time if she was just using him to spy on my farm."

"Did they have a romance or something going on?" Suzanne's thoughts predictably turned in that direction, Maggie knew. But this time the question was pertinent.

Ellie shrugged. "I don't know."

"You never know. It could very well be," Suzanne said to the others. "Which would make Angelica even more likely to be the killer . . . if you ask me."

"I'm not sure if they were in that kind of partnership," Maggie said. "But I do know there's nothing like a common enemy to draw people together. Maybe they were working together to harass you and Ben?" Maggie said to Ellie.

"Yes, I wondered that myself. I even told that to the police," Ellie added. "Not that it made any difference in their thinking."

"Let's just skip over why Angelica may have done it," Suzanne suggested. "*Could* she have done it? She had easy access to Ridley and certainly knows how to handle a spindle," Suzanne pointed out. "And we all saw her take one of the spindles from the festival. Which was, by the way, already coated with fiber from Ellie's llamas and would have been an ideal weapon to frame Ellie or Ben."

"That's very true. Have the police questioned her?" Maggie asked Ellie.

"I don't know. I guess we can get our lawyer to find out."

Dana had also taken out her knitting. She was adding fringe to the striped scarf, which was otherwise completed. She looked up, energized by this line of reasoning. "Even if no one saw her around his farm at the time of the murder, she was one of his few friends. She could have come and gone without anyone knowing. Even his dogs knew her and wouldn't have made a fuss."

"Good point, Dana. We might be on to something." Lucy turned to Maggie. "We know she has a tough side. Maggie saw it when Angelica pressed her to drop all the other organic yarns and carry her products exclusively."

"But you refused her?" Ellie asked.

Maggie realized that Ellie had not been at the shop the night she related that story. "That's right. I think Sweet Meadow is a very high-quality yarn. But I like to carry a wide selection and give everyone a chance. I'm not going to be told by anyone what I can and cannot sell. Some shops did take her deal. It was sweet," she conceded. "But I didn't like her yarn *that* much."

"That's our girl. Nobody's going to push Maggie around," Suzanne said proudly.

"Not at this stage in my life," Maggie said with certainty. "Certainly not Angelica Rossi."

"I wouldn't doubt that she and Ridley were scheming together to get us off the farm. They both had their reasons for wanting us out," Ellie said quietly.

"They could have been close but had some sort of falling-out," Dana speculated. "It certainly would be to her advantage to try to frame you or Ben."

"There you go. We're not following the money now. But we are following the fiber. It's almost the same thing," Suzanne pointed out.

"In this case, it is," Ellie agreed. "It's all so confusing." She paused and took in a long breath. Then she looked around at the circle of friends. "It's fine to speculate like this. It does give me hope. But if the police aren't thinking this way and looking into any of these possibilities, what good is it for me and Ben?"

Maggie and her friends exchanged glances. It wouldn't be the first time they'd stepped in and helped the police solve a crime. Not that local enforcement ever welcomed their assistance. Quite the opposite. In fact, they'd been warned several times to mind their own business.

But the welfare of a friend—especially a knitting friend—was always their business. How could they not offer to help Ellie and Ben if it was within their powers?

"I have a good idea." Suzanne sat up, her knitting in her lap. "Why don't we all go to the town council meeting Thursday night? I bet most of the players in this game will be there.

Angelica Rossi, definitely. And probably Walter Kranowski. We can just sit and observe and try to figure out who's really hot to unload their property. Or had bad blood with Ridley."

"I planned on going anyway, out of curiosity. But now I have a real theory to work on. Reading body language and all that fun stuff." Dana seemed excited about the prospect of putting her skills to use.

"I'm going to research the properties around your farm, Ellie, and do a few rough appraisals," Suzanne told her. "Then we can match up the landowners with their likely payouts."

"Great idea, Suzanne," Maggie noted. "That will definitely give us a better picture of what's at stake."

"I think hearing what everyone has to say at the meeting should help, too," Lucy said.

Maggie felt the same. "The meeting could be very enlightening."

Maggie believed that was true. For Ellie and Ben's sake, she hoped so even more.

She knew that the knitting group was getting involved again in police business, and if they went any further, they'd soon be hearing from Detective Walsh or some other police officer involved in the investigation.

But knitters had to do what knitters had to do. They couldn't sit idly by and watch poor Ben get railroaded into an arrest for a crime he did not commit.

Maggie closed her shop at half past six on Thursday night, leaving herself plenty of time to get to the village hall for the meeting, which started at seven. The building was so close, she left her car at her shop and took off with her purse and her knitting bag tucked under her arm. It was a pleasant night—perfect sweater weather—and she needed a walk after being cooped up in the shop all day.

But her peaceful mood was soon disturbed by the energy and activity in the village center. Every parking spot along Main Street was filled, and the public lot across from the town hall was filled up, too. Main Street was usually fairly empty at this time of day, but now the sidewalks were full, with streams of people headed to the village hall, coming from all directions. Some looked very serious, wearing business suits and carrying briefcases or stacks of file folders. Others looked like her own friends and neighbors, interested citizens who had come out after dinner. All with the same destination in mind.

Out in front of the building, a group in matching green T-shirts stood in a circle, holding signs and chanting a slogan.

The Friends of Farmland were staging a demonstration. She paused to read the slogans on their signs—"No Farms, No Food" and "Save Some Green Spaces for Our Children." One or two had blown up photographs of Justin Ridley: "Our Friend Justin. RIP. He Stood Strong for the Land."

Maggie felt a chill. They were making him a martyr for their cause, just as Ellie had predicted. Did they really believe Ridley had lost his life because of this debate? Or was that just a convenient slogan for the meeting? It was awful to think they would exploit his brutal death to shore up their argument. A cynical thought, but not out of the question.

A young woman offered Maggie a flyer as she passed by. Maggie smiled briefly and tucked it in her purse.

She'd been on her feet all day but quickly abandoned all

hope of a comfortable seat when she saw the throng in the village hall lobby. She elbowed her way through the crowd, looking for her friends. Many people seemed in no rush to get into the hearing room and stood in little huddles, consulting quietly with one another.

Suzanne was right. A lot of people took this issue very seriously. All around her, she heard a hushed discussion of business matters. There was money to be made, as Suzanne had pointed out, and high stakes always made the game dangerous.

Maggie worked her way to the door of the hearing room and peered inside.

The large room held rows of seats, more than Maggie had ever seen set up there. But they were just about all filled. The Friends of Farmland had a big presence in here, too, with more green T-shirts filling up several rows in the back of the room. No signs, she noticed. They must have been told to leave those outside.

Angelica Rossi sat with the group but looked so deep in thought she may as well have been by herself. She sat on the aisle, her head bowed as she read through a sheaf of typed pages in a folder.

There was a long table in the front of the room, set with water pitchers, microphones, and the name plates of the mayor, three trustees, and the town clerk.

Maggie was looking around for her friends again when she heard her phone buzz with a text. She quickly opened a message from Suzanne:

We're down on the right, toward the front. Saved you a seat.

Maggie looked up and spotted Suzanne on the right side of the room, waving at her. Lucy and Dana were there, too. They had all come with their knitting and were busily stitching away. Maggie headed down the aisle and quickly squeezed in next to them.

It was Thursday night, their usual meeting night, and they were all conditioned by now: It actually felt odd not to be knitting at this hour. Especially when they were gathered together like this. Maggie took out her own knitting and set her bag on the floor. "This is a hot ticket. Who grabbed these seats?"

Suzanne shrugged. "An old mommy trick from attending so many school plays and band concerts. I was in the building this afternoon to check the property lines on one of my listings. So I slipped in here, draped an old raincoat over four chairs, and hoped for the best."

"Good thinking," Maggie commended her. "Look, here comes the mayor and trustees. It must be starting."

The village officials filed in and took their seats. Maggie didn't know them all by name. One trustee was a woman in her mid-fifties; the other two were men, one fairly young, his late thirties, and the other in his sixties, she'd guess. She did recognize the mayor, Lillian Swabish, who was also in her early sixties and had formerly been a partner in a prominent law firm in town.

Mayor Swabish called the meeting to order and announced the agenda. Only one item: the discussion of a motion to keep the open space zoning laws in force within village limits.

"If anyone would like to speak about this issue, please sign in and form a line at the podium."

There was considerable movement in the room. Maggie held her knitting needles steady a moment. She practically felt the wooden floor vibrate.

Many spoke in favor of going along with the county and letting the laws expire. They spoke about community vitality, increasing the supply of housing to welcome new families into the area.

"There's a lot of talk against these laws expiring, on the grounds of nature and ecology. But villages and towns have ecology, too," one speaker pointed out. "We have to grow or die. That's just the way it is. Do we want to promote a healthy, thriving community? Or end up stagnant? Or even a ghost town?"

"There is such a thing as controlled, planned growth," another citizen insisted. Increased tax revenue is necessary to keep the town running as costs increase, he pointed out, and there were many benefits to allowing more housing and controlled commercial development in the area.

"Think of the jobs. Think of the boost to our town's economy. Think of the vacant stores on Main Street. Are we crazy? What's the problem here?"

The "pro" side sounded pretty persuasive, Maggie had to admit. Much more than she had expected.

Suzanne leaned over and whispered in her ear, "Pretty smooth, right? I'd guess those speakers are either eager to sell or actually in the pocket of the development companies. They could make acid reflux sound like a really fun hobby."

Maggie laughed quietly but didn't reply. She didn't want to miss anything.

A few other residents stepped up and spoke in favor of the

open space laws expiring. They all looked genuine and seemed sincere, Maggie thought. Their main point was that Plum Harbor should be governed by the same laws that applied to the rest of the county and not isolate itself.

". . . And the silent majority in our village shouldn't be pushed around by a very vocal minority," one woman stated bluntly. She glanced over at the rows of green T-shirts.

A chorus of loud boos rose in reply from the Friends of Farmland, drowning out whatever else the woman had to say.

The Friends hardly seemed to be the minority, Maggie thought, if their showing in the hearing room was any indication.

Some others in the front row shouted back: "Go back to where you came from, you bunch of trouble makers. What do you know?"

The mayor clacked her gavel. "Simmer down. Or I'll end this meeting and clear the room."

Maggie hoped it wouldn't come to that. This was just getting interesting. She felt a sharp elbow in her side. Suzanne leaned closer and whispered in her ear, "Look who's up next. The siren of Sweet Meadow."

Maggie glanced back at the podium. Angelica Rossi was next, that's who.

All eyes were on her as she approached the microphone in slow, measured steps. She wore her long denim skirt again, with a Friends of Farmland T-shirt attractively cinched around her waist with a wide leather belt. Her long hair was parted in the middle, as usual, and clipped at the back of her neck, and large, dangling earrings were an arty touch.

She looked very serious and sincere, Maggie thought. It

was hard to reconcile the woman who stood before her with the theories they'd spun on Tuesday night—scenarios that paired Angelica with Ridley, scheming together to drive Ellie and Ben off their farm. Or their speculation that Angelica was Ridley's killer, driven to it by some passionate argument or falling-out.

But people can show one face to the world and be far different in their private, secret lives. Angelica seemed capable of that. She presented well with excellent social skills. But Maggie guessed she was secretly seething . . . and scheming.

"My name is Angelica Rossi. I live on Sweet Meadow Farm, on County Road Twenty-three," she began, identifying herself for the record. "I'm here to speak as a property owner, as a farmer, and as the co-chair of the Friends of Farmland. As you all know, just days ago, we lost our founder, Justin Ridley. He was a brave man who believed in this cause with his whole heart and soul, and who fought bravely for it. Our group mourns his passing, and we are sure the community at large shares our sorrow and our sympathy for his daughter, Janine."

She glanced over to the far side of the room, where Maggie had already spotted Janine Ridley sitting alone.

Angelica easily had the crowd in her hand, Maggie noticed, and the rest of her statement was predictably dramatic—mixing a lecture on the environment and a plea to town residents to put aside their greed and think of their children and grandchildren and even their great-grandchildren, winding it all up with a well-known Native American proverb.

"As the Native Americans believe, 'We do not inherit the

Earth from our ancestors; we borrow it from our children.'" She paused and solemnly bowed her head. The room was silent, Maggie noticed, with only the sound of papers rustling.

Then Angelica looked up again. She spared a small smile for the trustees and Mayor Swabish. "Thank you for the opportunity to speak in defense of the innocent parties involved that can't speak for themselves—the birds, the wildlife, the woods and wild places. The wide blue sky and abundant fields."

The Friends of Farmland stood and applauded, calling out her name and cheering loudly.

"All right . . . calm down." The mayor, who was not a tall woman, jumped up out of her chair to shout into her microphone. "No demonstrations back there, or you'll all be escorted out."

The Friends of Farmland seemed satisfied and quickly settled down again. Though there were hugs and smiles all around for Angelica when she returned to their ranks.

"She's good," Dana whispered to Suzanne.

"Oh, baby . . . real good," Suzanne agreed.

"I'm on her side of the question," Lucy whispered back. "But why do I find her so annoying?"

Maggie felt the same. It was a curious thing.

After Angelica, a long line of citizens stood waiting to speak their piece. But the Joan of Arc of the farm set had definitely been the high point. It was almost nine by the time everyone had had their say. The mayor leaned toward her microphone and addressed the audience that was left.

"These comments and concerns will be taken into careful consideration. A vote on this issue will go on the agenda for the next trustee meeting, which will be held in approximately four weeks, date to be determined."

Then she struck her gavel to the table and the meeting was adjourned.

"They're not going to vote on this for four weeks? I can't believe that." Lucy stood up and stuffed her knitting into her tote bag. "It's like sitting through a two-hour movie and the projector breaks down before the film is over."

"Annoying, right?" Suzanne stood up and stretched, though space was limited. "I had a feeling that would happen. These zoning situations move so slowly. It's like watching grass grow. It's only fair to let everyone in town have their say. But there's a lot that goes on behind the scenes, believe me."

That sounded very likely to Maggie. There were always people in a small town who wielded big influence.

It was difficult to work their way out of the meeting room and lobby, but they eventually emerged on to the street. Maggie took a few deep breaths. The room had been stuffy, and the chilly night air roused her.

"That was pretty entertaining. As good as most reality shows," Suzanne remarked.

"I'm glad I went. I didn't know much about this issue," Dana said. "But I don't think I know any better now if this debate connects to Justin Ridley's death . . ."

"And to the question of who killed him and why," Lucy finished for her.

"I know what you mean. It was sort of a bust that way," Suzanne agreed. "The neighbor we were looking for, that potato farmer . . ."

"Walter Kranowski?" Lucy filled in.

"Right. Either he didn't come or didn't get up to have his say," Suzanne noted.

Dana quickly turned to her. "Maybe his silence is saying something. Maybe he purposely avoided this public shouting match because he doesn't want to draw attention to himself. Or his fractious relationship with Ridley."

"Good point, Dana. We know Mr. Kranowski feels strongly about this issue and has a strong personality. Yet he hasn't come to town to make his opinion known. His absence might be meaningful," Lucy suggested.

Maggie thought that was a good observation. The mystery of Justin Ridley's death was complicated. She suspected that there was more to this story. Much more.

"As for the rest, when the sauce boils down, you see what you've got left," Maggie told her friends. "My grandmother used to say that. She was usually right, too."

"This pot has just started to simmer," Dana observed. "I think it has a ways to go."

Chapter Nine

The pot was still simmering on Saturday morning when Maggie opened her shop. Lucy arrived a few minutes later and dumped a colorful pile of knitted items on the counter.

"Look how many projects I've finished for our fund-raiser. Awesome, right?"

Maggie looked over the bounty: two frizzle scarves in multicolor yarn, a blue headband embossed with white snowflakes, a pair of black fingerless gloves, and a baby bib.

"Lovely. I'll add these to the basket. We've already sold a few things this week," she reported.

"I wish I could knit this fast all the time. I knit better when it's for a cause."

Maggie glanced at her and smiled. "Keeping Matt warm isn't a compelling enough cause for you?"

"Of course it is. But I have other ways of solving that problem." Lucy smiled and changed the subject. "I'm going get some coffee and raid that reject yarn box."

"Knock yourself out," Maggie murmured. Lucy had already taken some extreme skeins from the box but had used them very creatively, Maggie thought. She hated to waste yarn and would be happy to see that box completely empty by the end of this project.

Lucy soon returned, the yarn box in one hand and a coffee mug in the other.

"By the way, Janine Ridley followed up on your recommendation and took her father's dogs over to Matt. They're boarding at the animal hospital for now. He's going to find a good home for them or get them into a rescue group."

Maggie nodded, attaching price tags to Lucy's handmade items. "I knew he'd come through for her . . . and for Thelma and Louise. I wonder if she'll come back to the shop. I did see her at the town meeting. Sitting by herself."

"She must have been curious to hear the debate since her father was so involved. I have a feeling you haven't seen the last of her, Maggie."

"I think you're right. I have the same feeling."

She watched Lucy dig through the skeins in the box and finally hold up a rather hideous fluorescent-orange acrylic.

"What were you thinking?" Lucy stared at her.

Maggie did a double take. "I never ordered that. I swear on my— It must have come by mistake in some shipment, and I never returned it. Give me some credit."

Lucy laughed. "Everything is good for something."

Maggie gave her a quizzical look. She couldn't imagine what Lucy would make with that. "A glow-in-the-dark toilet paper cover?"

"Good idea. But I'd have to crochet for that one. I was

thinking a dog-size jogging vest. I'll stick some glow-in-the-dark tape on the edges, for night visibility."

"Good idea. Dogs are sweet but don't have very demanding taste in outerwear. Not like cats," Maggie added, just to get Lucy going.

Before Lucy could answer, another voice did.

"Hi, everybody. . . . Wait till you hear where I'm going this morning. I'm so brilliant sometimes, I can't stand myself." Suzanne breezed into the shop, dressed for her workday in a sleek leather blazer, espresso-brown, with matching wool pants and a creamy white turtleneck. She'd looped a long scarf around her neck, a golden-yellow color—perfect for finishing off an Amelia Earhart sort of look, Maggie thought.

Suzanne sighed and dropped her leather tote bag on a chair. "Here's the scoop: I just made an appointment to visit Walter Kranowski and work up a listing on his property. Pretty sharp, right?"

Maggie and Lucy stared at her in shock. Maggie was the first to speak. "How in the world did you manage that?"

"Part luck, part smarts. Part fabulous personality. My usual winning combination." Suzanne quickly explained how she'd done some research on the potato farm right before the town hall meeting. But then Kranowski never showed up.

"I had a few printouts about the farm around the house and Kevin reminded me that he'd done some work for the old man, about two years ago. He put a new roof on the barn or something. So that gave me at least a toe in the door," she continued, talking now at top Suzanne speed, which was almost faster than Maggie could hear.

"I called Mr. Kranowski and said I'd heard he was interested in listing his property soon, and he knew my husband, and blah blah blah, and it all worked out." Suzanne waved her hand and took a sip of coffee, leaving them to imagine the rest.

"She makes light of it, but the secret is in her blah-blahs," Lucy remarked to Maggie.

"To be sure. It's a gift. And I mean that in a good way," Maggie hurried to add.

"Thanks. I'll take that as a compliment. I have an appointment to see him in . . . one hour," she said, checking the time on her phone. "Just stopped in for a little victory lap. And to see if there's anything you guys think I should ask?"

"Hmm. Let me see. 'Did you stab Justin Ridley with a wooden spindle?' Or is that too direct? Even for you?" Lucy teased her.

"It would be refreshing. I doubt the police have asked him that yet," Maggie noted.

Suzanne rose and picked up her bag. "Want to tag along, Lucy? I think this is a two-woman job. Besides, you can keep me on track. I might get distracted with the real-estate stuff and forget all about Ridley. I would die for this listing." Her dark eyes gleamed with a barracuda-like enthusiasm.

"Okay, I'll go. But can I pass as a real-estate lady?" Lucy looked down at herself, doubting it. She didn't have the dogs with her today and was dressed for shopping in a khaki utility jacket over jeans and a black T-shirt.

"I'll just tell him you're in training," Suzanne decided. "And we'll give you some jungle red lipstick and big, fashiony earrings in the car."

Maggie nearly laughed out loud at Lucy's expression.

"Um . . . okay," Lucy said slowly. "Really?"

"I'm kidding, silly. But I do have some badges from an open house, and you can carry a clipboard or something."

"I can go with that." Lucy collected the yarn she wanted, and the two women were soon on their way.

"Good luck," Maggie called out. "Report in soon so I don't worry. Don't do anything dumb."

The potato farmer could be dangerous, she realized suddenly.

They either didn't hear her or just didn't answer.

Suzanne had a heavy foot on the gas pedal. But Lucy knew she usually drove that way and this morning she was particularly excited to get out to Kranowski's farm. They flew along the country roads in Suzanne's huge vehicle, which was part truck and part school bus. Lucy was starting to have second thoughts about her impulsive agreement to come along.

But the idea of Suzanne venturing out here alone, to chat up a man who was known to have a bad temper and may have even attacked Justin Ridley, didn't sit well with Lucy, either.

She'd done the right thing, Lucy decided, glancing over at the driver.

"Here's the turn onto Crooked Hill Road. We're almost there. The lipstick is in the little outside pocket of my purse. Help yourself," Suzanne added.

Lucy gave her a look. She didn't even own a real lipstick. Her beauty efforts stalled out at an all-purpose cover-up stick and a tube of lip gloss. "I'll have to pass. Sorry. Do you want me to wait in the car?"

"Just testing you. I thought if you went for it, I'd sneak a photo and post it on Facebook."

"Suzanne . . . you're truly evil."

"Yeah, I know. It's the kids. They're a terrible influence on me." She looked contrite for a moment, but the mood passed quickly. "Hey . . . isn't that Ridley's place?"

Suzanne nearly slammed on the brakes to slow down in time. She pointed to the property on the right side of the road that was just coming into view.

Lucy saw a few wisps of crime scene tape dangling from the fence posts and front door. The house was fairly close to the road but surrounded by tall trees and brush. All she could see were fragments of dark brown cedar shake shingles and a white compact car in the driveway.

They coasted by, peering through the trees.

"There's a car in the drive," Suzanne noted. "I wonder who's visiting. It looks like the police are done searching for evidence."

"It could be Janine Ridley. That seems to be the kind of car you'd rent at the airport," Lucy added.

"You're probably right. I wonder if she's planning on putting the place up for sale."

"You should call on her next, Suzanne. You could have a real monopoly out here. Though I don't remember any farms in the board game. They should have tossed a few in, don't you think? Planting those little green houses and red plastic hotels would have meant something."

"Definitely. That was a real oversight."

The Kruegers' farm came into view next. Lucy saw the cheerful wooden sign as they passed the entrance and farmhouse. She gazed back at the orchard and noticed someone working among the apple trees, digging into the rich earth and lifting shovelfuls into a wheelbarrow.

"There's Dot," she remarked, recognizing the older woman. "She works hard."

"I can't believe it. And at her age. She must be in her late sixties, don't you think?"

"I would say so," Lucy agreed. She thought Dot might even be a bit older. "Ellie says she's had a hard life. It shows."

Lucy's heart went out to Ellie's farm helper, still doing such heavy, physical work. But Dot seemed to thrive on it.

"I thought the apple season ended weeks ago. What's she doing out there?" Suzanne asked.

"The picking season is over. But trees need attention practically year-round."

Suzanne gave the road her full attention and picked up speed again. "There's a ton of real work on that farm. Don't kid yourself. I'm not sure Ellie and Ben realized what they were getting into. As much as they researched the business, I think they took over the farm with some idealistic notion of how it would be. Ellie even jokes that Ben isn't very handy, and that's got to be a problem, right?"

Lucy didn't feel comfortable speculating about Ellie and Ben's relationship. But she did agree on that point. "Let's just say, it's not a good thing."

They soon arrived at Walter Kranowski's property. Suzanne pulled onto a dirt road and drove down to a gray farmhouse with peeling green shutters and a porch that sagged under an assortment of miscellaneous junk.

The single word that came to Lucy's mind to describe the house was misshapen. Boxy, added-on sections branched out in all directions, with no rhyme or reason. Certainly no architectural knowledge had been applied here. It was hard to figure out where the original structure began and what parts were extensions. Finally, she just gave up.

Suzanne stared at the house a moment. "On a scale of one to ten, I'd give this one a negative five on curb appeal."

Lucy was ready to go, but Suzanne took a moment to get her binder in order and then found two plastic badges that said "Prestige Properties" for them to wear.

"I feel a little guilty putting this on," Lucy admitted as she stuck the badge to her jacket.

"The badge or the lipstick. Take your pick." Suzanne waved the tube of jungle-fever red in Lucy's direction. She'd already freshened up her own sultry smile.

Lucy quickly opted for the badge.

"Let me just make a few notes before we ring the doorbell. It's easier to do that now than when we leave. They're always watching out the window," Suzanne explained as they got out of the car. "Let's see, what do we have here?"

Lucy followed her gaze around the front yard, where there were a few tall elm trees, a toppled bird bath, and a lawn ornament of a Victorian lady holding a lantern who just happened to be missing her head.

"Nice touch." Suzanne rolled her large brown eyes.

They walked behind the house, where Lucy saw a lopsided cedar picnic table and a clothesline that stretched from the back door to a tree. Behind that was a big gray barn with some farm machinery parked nearby—a tractor and tilling equipment and some other big vehicles she couldn't identify.

"The barn is the best feature so far. My husband does nice work," Suzanne said proudly.

Lucy would have said the land itself was the best feature. But she didn't want to quibble with Suzanne and she was sure that point was understood.

Kranowski's fields stretched out behind the barn like large rolling blankets, the dark earth plowed into neat rows, the green tops of the potato plants stretching almost as far as you could see.

"Wow, he's got a lot of land, doesn't he? It must be worth a fortune," Lucy guessed.

"It will be, if the open space laws are allowed to expire. Personally, even though my inner real-estate lady is saying, 'Cha-ching!' the *real* me would feel awful about seeing those fields filled up with condos or mini-mansions."

"No argument here. But more importantly, let's see how Mr. Kranowski feels about it."

They walked around the house again and up the porch steps. Suzanne rang the bell, and the door flew open instantly. Farmer Kranowski had obviously seen the car and had been waiting for them.

Suzanne quickly introduced herself and Lucy in a surprisingly professional tone.

"Come on in, ladies. I was wondering what you were doing out there all that time. It's hard for me to be on my feet. I got the gout real bad," he explained, leaning on a metal walker.

He was a big man, Lucy noticed, quite tall with wide

shoulders that looked like he once could have balanced a piano on them. But now his back was stooped and rounded, his head jutting out an odd angle. Large gnarled hands held the edges of the walker as he led them from the dark foyer into a small cluttered front parlor—or what had once been a parlor, Lucy guessed, now hidden under piles of newspapers and miscellaneous trash.

"Sit anywhere. Make yourselves comfortable," he invited them as he more or less fell into a huge recliner that was covered with several afghans. Like a crocheted sultan's chair, Lucy thought.

The women quickly cleared piles of magazines and old newspapers off a lumpy plaid couch. The upholstery felt sticky and emitted a strange odor. Lucy was extra careful not to touch anything or even to breathe too deeply. From Suzanne's stiff pose, she guessed her friend felt the same.

Suzanne began the conversation with a few preliminary, warm-up questions. Walter Kranowski responded with his life story.

Potatoes, potatoes, and more potatoes. Sometimes a few cabbages or turnips. But mainly potatoes. He was sick of the mundane, prosaic, ubiquitous tubers, and he wanted out, bad.

His mother had given birth to him in this small house, right on the kitchen table, he reported. Lucy could picture a midwife quickly clearing off a pile of potatoes to make way for his arrival in the world.

He'd lived under this roof his entire life, except for a short stint in the army. More than seventy years now. He had three grown children; two lived in Boston and one in Connecticut.

They'd all left the farm right after high school and never looked back.

No surprise to hear that. Though they could have sent a cleaning service around to visit their father once in a while, Lucy thought.

"I don't blame those kids one bit. They all did the smart thing. I would have, too, if I'd had any choice in the matter," their father said finally.

"So you're interested in putting the property up for sale?" Suzanne eased out of the Kranowski saga into the main reason for the visit.

"I'm thinking of it. You're not the first real-estate gal who's been out here," he added.

And probably not the last, Lucy guessed. She sensed a cagey spark under his potato-ish appearance. He seemed the type who would gleefully pit one agent against the other, negotiating down the commission.

Had he been talking about potatoes so much that he'd skewed her perception? Or did his head really resemble the vegetable? His face was long, his features lumpy, and his skin dark brown from the sun. He had a full head of white hair, buzz-cut, flat on top and short on the sides of his head. A hairstyle that was so far out of fashion it had come back in. Shaggy white eyebrows punctuated his heavy brow and his chin jutted out in a perpetual defensive expression.

The sound of a cell phone jarred Lucy from further study of the farmer.

"Sounds like my telephone. . . . What did I do with that now?" Kranowski sat up and patted his clothing, frisking himself for his phone. When he finally found it in the pocket of his shirt, it flew out of his big hand and rolled under his recliner.

"Oh, blast . . ." He peered over the edge of the chair, like a man in a boat watching his car keys sinking.

"You sit, Mr. Kranowski. I'll get it for you," Suzanne gallantly offered.

Lucy nearly gasped and nearly pulled her friend back before Suzanne jumped up off her seat. But it was too late. She crouched down to look under the chair, and Lucy squinted. She did not want to imagine what might be under there. She was sure Suzanne was motivated by some innate saleswoman code of honor, believing she must go to any length to clinch a deal. But Lucy thought a listing for Buckingham Palace would not be worth a Dumpster dive under that chair.

Seconds later, Suzanne's dark head popped up. "Here you go, sir," she said, handing up the phone to Kranowski. She had a strange smile on her face, Lucy thought, as she poked under the chair with a ballpoint pen, fishing out something else.

"Why look at this. . . . Is that a hand spindle?" Suzanne took a tissue from a box on the coffee table and used it to pick up the hidden treasure.

Lucy had to stifle a gasp when she saw the distinctive stamp on top. It was one of the spindles from Ellie's fair. She quickly looked at the farmer to gauge his reaction. Had Suzanne just uncovered a spare murder weapon?

"Is that what you call it?" He pulled his head back, staring down at the object. He didn't look particularly alarmed, Lucy noticed. But maybe he was just a good actor.

"Do you spin, Mr. Kranowski? Or knit, perhaps?" Suzanne sat down on the couch again, going on in her talk show hostess voice. "I hear many men are taking up that hobby now."

"Me . . . knit?" He laughed at her. More of a snort, Lucy thought. "No way, that's ladies' territory. My daughter must have left that here. She's a knitter. She came out for a visit and went over to that fair, at the llama farm. What a racket. I think people should get permission from their neighbors for that sort of thing. They can't make a carnival ground out of this whole place . . ."

"I know what you mean. But it was their grand opening," Suzanne cut in smoothly. "The Kruegers are trying to start a new business."

"So I heard." He shifted in his chair, wearing a grumpy expression. Lucy couldn't tell if his feet were aching or if he just didn't like being contradicted. By a "real-estate gal," no less.

"Those Kruegers will need all the help they can get," he predicted. "That farm is bad luck for anyone who lives there. No one's ever been able to make a go of it on that land for as long as I can remember."

Lucy had never heard that bit of folklore, and she could tell from Suzanne's expression this was news to her, too.

"Bad luck? How is that?" Suzanne leaned forward in her seat. "Did you know the former owners there?"

"Of course I did. I've lived here forever. Let's see, before the Kruegers there were the Dooleys. Husband had an accident, fell out of the loft, and broke his neck." He made a cracking gesture with his hands, as if breaking a stick in two. Lucy hid a shudder.

Then he leaned back and looked up, thinking. "Before them, there were the Turners. Husband ran off with a waitress.

The wife kept the farm up by herself for a while. But she got up on a ladder one day, to fix the roof or a broken window or some darn thing. Fell into a bunch of wires and electrocuted herself."

Lucy winced at his lethal litany. "That is a bad run of luck."

"Damn right. And I'm not done yet," he said quickly. "Then there were the Hoopers, Joe and Trudy. The wife was a real looker. Only about twenty or so when she married Joe. He was maybe fifteen, twenty years older? That never works out. He drank too much and slapped her around. I thought, Well, here we go again. She's going to run off with the first guy who knocks on the door. Some fellow reading the gas meter is going to get lucky. Turns out, one night, Hooper just walks out on her. Trudy came over here, all banged up. My wife took care of her. She told us they had a big fight. Joe beat up on her and jumped in his car. Like he always used to do. But this time, he never came back. I think they found the car up in Maine somewhere. He drove off a dock, right into a lake. I don't think she ever got the insurance money, though. She couldn't keep up the mortgage. She lost the place pretty quickly after that. Long time ago. I think Jimmy Carter was president."

That was a long time ago, Lucy thought. She and Suzanne could hardly believe these tales of woe. Personally, she didn't need to hear more. Did Ellie and Ben know the history of the farm when they bought it? It seemed almost . . . cursed.

Since they were on the subject of neighbors, Lucy decided to jump right into the deep end. "What about your other neighbor, Justin Ridley? Did you know him?"

"Sure, I knew him. I flat-out hated him. I know it's awful

to say, but I nearly did a tap dance when I heard that news. Not that I can even stand on my feet right now," he clarified, looking at his slipper-covered feet, elevated on the recliner. "I'm not surprised someone crept up on that dude. He was a dirty, thieving scoundrel. A phony, to boot, for all his 'nature boy' talk. What a crock of cheese."

"Was it just his opinions about land use that annoyed you? Or was there something else? Something more personal, I mean. If you don't mind me asking," Suzanne added politely.

Walter Kranowski gave her a wide-eyed stare and shook his big head. "I don't mind one bit. He was a nasty son of a bee. He stole my electricity . . . and my cable TV! Can you beat that?"

The women stared back at him with puzzled expressions. Lucy wondered if Mr. Kranowski was a little senile and prone to imagining things.

He answered with a look that was a mixture of amusement and disgust.

"You girls are naive, aren't you? That low-life scum would sneak around in the middle of the night and fix a hookup to my wires. All hidden in the branches and such so I couldn't see. Until I got wise. All the time acting like he was so self-sufficient with his little windmills and solar panels."

Kranowski started to cough and shook the recliner with such force that a coffee cup dropped off a tiny table attached to the arm rest and rolled on the floor.

Suzanne began to rise to pick it up, but Lucy caught her arm and shook her head. Who knew what else was under there? Suzanne had already done her duty in Lucy's book.

"Don't mind that, I'll get it later." Kranowski waved his

hand, and they felt absolved. Though Lucy wondered what he meant by "later." In a year or so?

"Wow, that's quite a story," Suzanne said finally. "Did you ever get the police involved?"

Kranowski made another frightful face and nearly shouted at her. "What could they do? Make him give me back my electricity? That guy was nuts . . . and he owned guns." He took a breath and calmed himself, realizing that he'd lost his temper. "I didn't need to add that worry to my list every night when I went to bed. Besides, my wife was pretty sick back then. I had more important things to think about. I just let it go."

"Sure, that was the smart thing," Suzanne assured him. "Is that why you say he was a phony? Because of the electricity and cable?"

"That's not even half of it. All this 'saving nature' baloney. Like he's J.C. and Al Gore rolled into one. Those Friends of Farmers are no friend of mine." He'd gotten the name of the group wrong, Lucy noticed, but the revised version fit fine. "I'm sure Mr. Ridley had a sweet deal set up for himself, once they got their way with the zoning. I'm sure they all do." His face turned beet-red, and he was shouting again.

Lucy was glad he was fairly immobile and didn't have any dangerous weapons of his own nearby.

"What kind of deal, Mr. Kranowski? I'm not sure what you mean." Suzanne's calm and curious tone seemed to calm him down a bit, too.

"The county has a big slush fund to buy up land out here and protect it." He let out a raspy breath and stared at the women, as if deciding whether to tell them the rest. His eyes were beady and bloodshot, Lucy noticed. She hoped all this excitement didn't give him a stroke. "I heard Ridley had a deal with someone in the county to sell his land for triple the value, drawn out of this fund. Nice profit . . . even after deducting a few kickbacks to grease the wheels. I think all those Friends are on the inside, waiting to sell back to the county and clean out this fund. Well, most of them anyway." The old farmer shifted in his chair, the conversation making him restless and annoyed. "Take it from me, Ridley was no folk hero. He was just a pig at the trough, him and the rest of them."

Suzanne sat back against the couch cushions, her binder balanced on her lap. "That's a pretty serious allegation. Have you told anyone at the village hall that you heard this gossip? The trustees, maybe?"

Kranowski waved his hand, as if batting away an insect. "Who am I going to tell? They've all got their hand out down there. They wouldn't do anything. Besides, what's the difference now?" He shrugged. "Ridley's gone. I think his group is going to lose steam pretty quickly and disappear, too."

It didn't look that way to Lucy, but she didn't bother to contradict him.

"Most problems solve themselves, if you wait long enough." He sat back in the recliner and sighed. "Even a guy like Ridley. There he was, gumming up the works, preventing a lot of honest, hardworking people like me from finally reaping the fruit of our labors." In his case, one might say the potatoes of his labors, Lucy thought, but she didn't interrupt. "What right did he have to do that? Now he's gone. Out of the way. I can't say I shed any tears to hear that news."

Lucy nodded. But the problem had not really solved itself. Someone had deliberately stepped out of the darkness that fateful night and forcefully removed Justin Ridley from the picture.

Had it been Walter Kranowski? His ailments appeared real enough. But couldn't immobility from gout and arthritis easily be faked, Lucy speculated. If the old farmer could get out of that chair, he would be a force to be reckoned with. Even if it had not been Kranowski, maybe Ridley had met with some other hardworking farmer like him?

"You ladies want to see the house? I'm sorry I can't give you the grand tour today." He looked down at his feet regretfully. "Walk around, take your time. Go on outside when you're done in here. I have a copy of the property lines for you, out on the kitchen table. My feet are aching something awful. Do you mind?"

"That's just fine. We can find our way around. Don't you worry." Suzanne rose and patted his shoulder.

"Let's go upstairs first, Lucy." She tilted her head to the side, and Lucy followed.

"So . . . what do you think?" Lucy whispered once they had reached the top of the stairs.

The smell on the second floor was even worse than in the parlor, and Lucy held her hand over face and tried to hold her breath. Suzanne was much hardier, used to these situations, no doubt, though she did have a sour expression.

"It's a knock-down. No question," she whispered back. "I'll just take a few pictures so I won't insult him."

"I don't mean that," Lucy whispered back hoarsely. "I mean, about him and Ridley."

Suzanne glanced down the stairs and put her finger to her

lips. Lucy caught her meaning. Walter Kranowski was sharper than he looked and could very well be listening.

Suzanne quickly peeked into the bedrooms and pushed open the bathroom door with her pen. She made a few notes on her pad, while Lucy waited in the hallway.

They walked down a back staircase and emerged in the kitchen—another disaster area, Lucy thought. Suzanne found the surveyor's map of the property on a small wooden table and led Lucy out the back door.

Lucy gratefully breathed in the fresh air, then followed Suzanne to the barn. One of the big doors was ajar, and Suzanne pushed it the rest of the way open. A few chickens sat in a wire coop or scratched around the dirt. A skinny tabby cat ran out from the shadows and startled them.

The property did not boast any cute, gingerbread-trimmed cottages, studios, or country shops like the out buildings found on Ellie's pretty farm. It was all very drab and utilitarian, Lucy thought.

Except for the glorious acres of fields that stretched out behind the barn. The two women stood along a rail fence and gazed out to the horizon.

"He's got land. It's better than gold, and he knows it. They ain't making any more of it," Suzanne said simply.

Lucy couldn't argue with that.

They gazed out at the fields a few minutes more. When Lucy turned and looked back at the house, she thought she saw a curtain stir at one of the back windows, but it quickly snapped into place again. Was Mr. Kranowski spying on them? It wouldn't have surprised her, though he portrayed himself as practically immobile. It all happened so quickly, she didn't even bother alerting Suzanne.

When they came back inside, Mr. Kranowski appeared to be dozing in his recliner. He roused with a start and then looked up at them as if they were burglars. Lucy wondered if he really had been napping all this time, or was just play acting. Had she just imagined someone at the window before? That seemed possible now, too.

"It's just me, Suzanne Cavanaugh. From the real-estate office?" Suzanne reminded him.

"Oh, yeah, Susan . . . right." He'd gotten her name wrong but nodded to himself. "You're still here? What time is it?" He stretched out his arm and squinted hard at his watch.

"About noon. Can we get you anything before we go?" Suzanne asked him.

A very kind and brave offer, considering the state of the kitchen.

"Me? I'm fine. Football game is on TV today. . . . So, what do you think of the place. Nice, right?" he asked, perking up a little.

"You have a fine piece of land, Mr. Kranowski. Prestige Properties would be proud to represent this listing. I'm going to work up some figures and call you next week with the details."

"For selling as a subdivision, right? I'm waiting on that vote about the zoning. If they vote to keep the laws intact, I know a group out here willing to sue the village," he confided. "I hope it doesn't come to that," he added. "Lawsuits take time and I'm not getting any younger. My kids want me to sell, and my hands are tied until this zoning business is settled. But it doesn't hurt to have your ducks in a row, right?"

Or your potatoes, Lucy added silently.

This was the first Lucy had heard of a group ready to sue the village if the vote didn't go their way. But it made sense. If the open space laws remained intact within village limits, residents like Kranowski, who were itching to sell, were bound to protest. And the Friends of Farmland would probably go to court if the laws were lifted.

The issue could take years and a lot of legal fees to figure out. There were a lot of moving parts here, Lucy realized, and a lot of money at stake and passionate feelings in play.

Suzanne chatted with Walter Kranowski a few minutes more about business matters, took a few more photos of the front parlor, and left him her card.

As soon as they got into the front seat of Suzanne's SUV and had closed the doors, Suzanne whipped out a big bottle of hand sanitizer. She quickly poured a puddle in her palm and passed it to Lucy.

"Ewwwww!" they said in unison as they briskly rubbed their hands together.

Lucy finally glanced at Suzanne, while still madly rubbing her hands. "I'm sure you've seen some messy houses, but that one could be in a special episode of *Hoarders: 'Buried Alive.'*"

Suzanne shook her head, her big earrings jingling as she started up the SUV. "I don't judge 'em, I just try to sell 'em, so let's not even go there. I'd like to enjoy some lunch before I head back to the office."

"Fine with me. There's plenty more to talk about. Like how much he hated Justin Ridley."

"'Truly, madly, deeply' I think covers it," Suzanne replied.

"And he just happens to have the same spindle that was used as the murder weapon lying around in that indoor garbage dump. I know a lot of people took those spindles. But I doubt any of them hated Ridley as much as Kranowski claims to."

"Detective Walsh probably wouldn't believe us if we told him."

"True. But seeing is believing, Lucy. While I was taking photos for the appraisal, I just happened to get a nice shot of the spindle . . . which I left in a convenient spot on the coffee table."

Lucy turned and stared at her friend in admiration. "Wow, you are good. No question."

"Thanks. . . . An inspired moment, I have to say. I'll tell you something else, that gout story? I'm not buying it. My father-in-law has a touch, and a person can be immobile one day and feel perfectly fine the next."

"Ready to tap-dance with glee if he hears good news?" Lucy couldn't help recall Farmer Kranowski's own words about his reaction to Ridley's death.

"Exactly. Maybe he tap-danced over to the woods that night, too."

"Who knows if he even has gout . . . or even needs the walker. That could all be an act. While we were outside behind the house, I thought I saw someone watching us from behind a curtain. The window was pretty far from the living room where we had left him, too. But when we came in again, there he was, sound asleep in his recliner," Lucy added. "Do you think the police checked all this stuff out or just took Kranowski's word?"

Suzanne didn't answer right away. She kept her gaze fixed on the road as they left the farm and turned onto the main road.

"Hard to say. I guess Dana could find out. But I will get that photo of the spindle to the police. One way or the other. Maybe that will help Walsh start thinking outside of the box."

"Do you really think Ridley had an inside deal? I've never even heard of a special land protection fund."

"Oh, that part is true. I didn't even think of it," Suzanne admitted. "But there *are* county funds set up to buy back land at market price, or below, for the purpose of conservation. It would be a very clever real-estate scheme to exploit that system. A real reversal of the typical trickery, which is called flipping," she explained.

"Run that by me again. . . . I'm a little slow with this stuff," Lucy admitted.

"People flip properties all the time, just to make a profit. They buy something run down, fix it up, and sell it quickly. But there's another kind of flipping that's more like insider trading. For instance, when you buy land that isn't zoned for development—but you have inside knowledge that it *will* be. So you get in early for the sole purpose of selling to the highest bidder once the laws change."

"That's what Ridley accused Ellie and Ben of doing," Lucy recalled. "He kept calling them flippers and squatters."

"Exactly. But Kranowski was saying that Ridley was trying to do something very much the same under the guise of preserving the land. He wanted to buy up land in this area with the purpose of making a killing by selling back to the county at an inflated price. One he was fixing with a county official willing to make a secret deal."

"Maybe that's why he was so intent to buy Ellie and Ben's farm. And so angry when they beat him out of it."

"Exactly." Suzanne nodded. "I'm sure this type of scam has been pulled before, somewhere. Wherever the government leaves a substantial pile of money sitting around, there are people up nights, figuring out how to get their hands on it. But it does take a certain kind of contrary genius to think of such a convoluted scheme," Suzanne added.

"Ridley was a contrary man, if nothing else. If we believe his passion to save the environment was just an act, then I think he would have definitely been capable of it. Ridley was a cipher. Everyone who knew him has a different idea of his character. But now we know something we didn't know before."

"We know a *few* more things," Suzanne said. "It was well worth the ride out here. Even though Farmer K. is just jerking me around about that listing. He'll never give it to me." Suzanne turned to Lucy a moment and smiled. "I'll put out some feelers about Ridley and the Friends of Farmland trying to scam the county. Maybe somebody in my office or around town heard the rumor, too."

"If it's true, that would be a real game changer. And a new direction for the investigation. One that leads away from Ben," Lucy added.

That was the most important thing right now. To steer the police away from Ellie and Ben and onto some new suspects.

Chapter Ten

When they arrived in town, Suzanne called her office to say she was picking up some lunch and would be back soon. She forgot to tell her boss that she planned on eating with her friends, at Maggie's store.

Lucy and Suzanne walked into the shop with their bags of takeout just as one of Maggie's classes had ended and a wave of women was leaving. Lucy did a quick side step to avoid bumping into some very pregnant moms-to-be.

She leaned over and whispered to Suzanne, "Looks like we just missed Bibs, Booties, and Beyond."

"But not the boobs and bellies," Suzanne whispered back.

Lucy walked back to the worktable, which was now deserted, and put her bag down.

"What are you two giggling about? You sound like two middle schoolers." Maggie stood at the table, sorting out the supplies from the class. She swept a few bits of yarn off the table with her hand. "Come on, share the mirth."

"Nothing important." Suzanne put her lunch down and took a seat across from Maggie. "We do have loads to report from our visit to the potato farm. Walter Kranowski was a talker. He did not hold back."

But before Suzanne could say more, they heard Dana's voice from the front of the shop. "Wait for me. . . . I want to hear this, too."

Dana scurried back to the table and took a seat next to Lucy. She was dressed for yoga, with a denim jacket on top. Her blond hair was swept up in a ponytail, and little blond wisps were plastered on her forehead. She took a large paper cup out of a paper bag and stuck a straw in the lid.

"Okay, shoot."

Suzanne gave her a look, then quickly related their conversation with the potato farmer, his allegations about Ridley, and the incriminating spindle she'd spotted under his favorite sitting chair.

"She should get a medal for sticking her hand under there and fishing it out," Lucy added. "You have no idea what that house was like."

"I mostly used the tip of a pen. Didn't want to smear any fingerprints," Suzanne explained.

"Or catch any antibiotic-resistant germs," Lucy noted.

"A spindle from the fair? That could be significant. Too bad you couldn't take it with you," Maggie said.

"I didn't want to arouse his suspicion. It was there all right. Here's the picture I took." Suzanne held out her phone for everyone to see.

The spindle, identical to the murder weapon, sat on a

tissue among a random assortment of odds and ends on Walter Kranowski's parlor coffee table.

Maggie put on her reading glasses for a better look. "Yes, I see the imprint from the farm very clearly."

"And it's not even blown up." Dana was also leaning over to the photo and now leaned back with an expression of awe. "Bravo, Suzanne."

Suzanne bowed her head slightly and smiled. "Finding it was just dumb luck. Sneaking the photo while I appraised the house . . . now that was an inspiration.

"After his tirade about Ridley, it gave me the creeps to see it just sitting there while we talked," Lucy admitted. "He hated Ridley. He made no pretense or apology for it. He said he would have done a tap dance when he heard Ridley had died . . . except for his gout."

"His gout? Was that his alibi?" Maggie asked curiously.

"I suppose he was telling us that," Suzanne replied. "He needed a walker to get around and kept complaining about the pain. But that could all be an act. Lucy thinks she saw him spying at us from a window on the other side of the house when we were outside. But he was back in the living room when we came inside again. That would have been an Olympic dash on a walker. How do we even know if the police checked that gout story?"

"He's a big man, and looks like he's still strong to me," Lucy added. "I wouldn't want to run into him one night in the woods, with or without his walker."

Dana had been sipping from the straw in her big cup—a frothy, dark green concoction that was healthy for her, Lucy had no doubt. She paused and looked up at Suzanne again. "Did you ask why he had the spindle?"

"He said his daughter came to visit and went down to see the fair. He didn't say much about Ellie and Ben. Only that he felt sorry for them and the farm is jinxed or something."

When Maggie frowned with disbelief, Lucy rushed in to convince her. "He's lived there his whole life. He's seen families come and go from that property. He rattled off a long list of former owners and their sad histories."

"Someone being killed on the back pasture isn't even the worst thing that's happened over there," Suzanne added. "Though it's fairly high on the list of unfortunate events."

"I don't think the police give a fig about local folklore and jinxed property. But they might be interested in this photo," Maggie mused. "Though they'll be annoyed with us for snooping. Maybe there's some discreet way to do it."

"If we go straight to Walsh, he'll go ballistic. It might even make things worse for Ellie and Ben, once he knows we're all friends," Dana speculated. "Jack probably knows someone we can call who won't get all bent out of shape. I mean, we're basically just a few concerned citizens who want to see justice done."

"How nicely you put that," Maggie commended. "I think she's the one for the job," she told the others.

"I second the motion," Lucy said between spoonfuls of chicken soup.

"Take it away, Dana. I never get very far with the police. I can't even talk a fine down on a parking ticket." Suzanne shrugged and, with a few taps, sent the photo to Dana's cell phone.

"I'll have to wait until tomorrow night to ask him. He's

away tonight on a little golf trip. I couldn't deny him, with the colder weather moving in." Dana adjusted the straw and returned to sipping her drink.

"I'm not even going to ask you what you're eating." Suzanne was eating a turkey-and-Swiss on rye with lettuce and tomato, and coleslaw. She had flung off the top piece of bread and bunched the rest up onto one exploding slice.

"Same here," Dana replied, looking askance at the sloppy mess in Suzanne's hand. "That reminds me, Maggie: What are you doing tonight? Want to join me for dinner and a movie?"

Maggie smiled over at her. "I'd like to say I already have a date . . . but that sounds good to me. It's been so slow here today—everyone must be in their backyards, raking leaves. I was thinking of closing a little early anyway."

"Let's see what's playing." Dana took out her iPhone and tapped a few times on the screen.

The phone rang, and Dana checked the number. "Hi, Ellie. How are you?" Dana said cheerfully.

Lucy watched her expression quickly change from a relaxed smile to somber concern.

"They did? When did that happen?" She paused, listening, and then said, "Gee, that's too bad . . ." She stood up and walked away from the table—to have some privacy, Lucy assumed.

She talked with Ellie for a few more minutes. She seemed to be listening mostly and using a comforting tone when she did speak.

Dana returned to the group at the table before hanging up. "Why don't you come into town and hang out with me and

Maggie? We were going to go out to dinner and a movie. You can even stay over—Jack is away," Lucy heard her say.

She paused, waiting for Ellie's answer, then said, "Let me ask her and I'll call you right back."

Dana ended the call and turned to Maggie. "Ellie and Ben had a big fight. They're under so much stress. I'm not surprised. I asked her to come into town, but she can't leave the farm. Dot has to go to her other job tonight and won't be back until tomorrow. I'm sorry to change the plan, but she sounds so upset. I really don't want to leave her alone."

Maggie also looked concerned after hearing the story. "It's fine with me. I don't mind visiting Ellie. We can bring some takeout and a DVD. Cheer her up a bit. . . . But won't Ben be coming back? It might be awkward," Maggie added.

Dana shook her head. "I don't think so. Ellie said he packed a bag. She thinks he went to visit his mother, in New Haven."

"Uh-oh. Whenever luggage is involved in a marital spat, it is not a good thing." Suzanne shook her head as she gathered up her trash and tossed it into a basket.

"It does sound like more than the usual disagreement," Dana agreed quietly. "Ben is emotional. He has a temper. They've been under a lot of stress, and it seems the police have been digging into his past and uncovered some unsavory information. It doesn't prove anything about the murder, one way or the other," she quickly pointed out. "But it puts him in a bad light."

"How bad?" Lucy asked. "Was he ever arrested?"

"Ellie didn't go into the specifics. She did say that he'd told her about some of this dirty laundry before they got married. Obviously, not everything."

She glanced over at Maggie and then at the rest of her friends. "I guess we'll hear the rest when we get there."

Suzanne had taken out a compact and was freshening her lipstick. "I'd make some corny joke about the guy having skeletons in his closet . . . but I don't even want to go there."

Maggie shook her head. "Good move. Please don't."

On the drive over to the Krueger farm, Maggie and Dana did not speculate about Ben's unsavory past. There would be plenty of time to talk about that tonight, Maggie thought as Dana's Volvo cruised up the gravel drive in front of the farmhouse. They'd picked up some dinner and wine. Ellie said she had dessert and not to bother with that.

As they walked toward the house they met Dot, who had just come out the back door.

"Oh, hello. You're Ellie's friends, from the knitting shop, right? Nice to see you again. I'm glad you came out here tonight. I hate to leave Ellie alone. She seems so upset. But I have to go to my other job now, in town."

Dot had lowered her voice a notch and spoken with concern. Maggie realized Dot had to be aware of the tension between Ellie and Ben, and maybe even had overheard their argument. It was practically unavoidable when they lived in such close proximity. But Ellie's helper did seem genuinely concerned and glad to see Ellie would have company.

"Oh, we'll cheer her up," Dana promised. "We have a load of sushi, a good movie—"

"And we brought our knitting," Maggie added.

"Sounds like a real party. Sorry I can't stay," Dot replied

with a grin. "But Mrs. Foley needs me. That's the woman I work for. She's having a rough time right now," she said sadly. "The llamas should be fine through the night. Ellie has my number if anything comes up."

"We'll take good care of Ellie and the llamas, too. Don't worry," Maggie told her.

The women said good night and Dot headed toward her cottage. Dana and Maggie walked up to the farmhouse, where Ellie was now waiting for them, framed by the doorway, in a welcoming, golden light.

A short time later, they were all seated around the table in Ellie's kitchen, picking and choosing pieces of sushi from the big platter that Ellie had arranged for them.

"I think I'm so nimble with chopsticks from all these years of knitting," Maggie remarked as she slipped a bit of marinated ginger on her dish.

"Ben loves sushi. He's probably eating some right now." Ellie sighed and dipped a piece of sashimi in a tiny bowl of soy sauce. "That's one thing he didn't really like about moving here. Nobody delivers this far out. It was a big change from the city, where we could just step out the door and find anything we wanted."

Maggie glanced at Dana. So far, they'd just passed the time with small talk, but this seemed like a good moment to initiate some big talk—to ask what the police had uncovered about Ben.

Dana seemed to feel the same, or had picked up some subtle cue from Maggie, but she started on a more positive note.

"We have some good news for you. Suzanne and Lucy talked to one of your neighbors today, Mr. Kranowski. He had a lot to say about his relationship with Ridley. None of it good," Dana added.

"He did? How did they manage to get him talking?"

Maggie helped herself to another bite of Out-of-Control Roll. A bit rich, but what the heck, it was Saturday night.

"Suzanne got an appointment there to appraise his property," Dana continued. "They said he seemed lonely and had no qualms about speaking his mind."

Ellie didn't look surprised. "I know he hated Ridley. With a passion. Much more than Ben did. I can't understand why the police never suspected him but jumped all over Ben."

"After talking to him awhile, Suzanne and Lucy wondered the same thing. They even found a spindle under a chair. It could have just rolled under there . . . or been hidden. It's one of the spindles you gave away at the fair," Dana added.

Ellie was lifting a bite of food to her mouth but suddenly put it back down. "They did? Did they tell the police about it?"

"Suzanne took a photo, and Jack will help me put it in the right hands," Dana replied. "Mr. Kranowski has a pretty good alibi, though. He suffers from gout and uses a walker. He must have told the police that on the night of the murder, he was home, incapacitated."

"Gout can be very painful," Maggie added. "A person really couldn't sneak through the woods and kill someone in that condition."

"He also has a story about how he obtained the spindle. But it does show the police that there was more than one person close by with motive, opportunity . . . and maybe even the means, if Kranowski is lying about his gout," Dana quickly added.

"I see what you mean. It does help Ben." Ellie let out a long breath and closed her eyes a moment. When she opened them again, she said, "I wish I could tell him. This would definitely make him feel better."

"Has Ben been in touch at all since he left?" Dana's tone was light but sympathetic.

Ellie looked down at her dish. "No, he hasn't. I sent him a text, but he didn't answer. I guess I could call and leave a message. But he should be calling me. And apologizing," she added in an angrier voice.

"Are you worried about him?" Maggie asked her.

Ellie shrugged. "He's a grown man. He can take care of himself. I just hope he doesn't rack up too many bills on the credit cards." It sounded to Maggie as if Ben had pulled this disappearing act before. But she didn't feel comfortable asking.

"How did the fight start?" Dana chose two more pieces of sushi and put them on her plate. "You said it was about something the police found out about him? Something he never told you?"

Ellie nodded and sighed. "Ben is an independent type. He never liked having a boss and has always been in business for himself. I've always known that about him. It was a quality I found attractive, when we met."

Maggie could understand that. After opening her shop, she doubted she could ever go back to a normal job again, answering to someone else's rules.

"But?" Dana prodded her.

"But he hasn't always been successful. He's had some business failures and bad investments. And left some partners on bad terms. It isn't as if he never told me but . . . he did leave out a few details."

Dana and Maggie waited for Ellie to continue. When she didn't, Dana prodded her. "Such as?"

"Let's see . . . where should I start? He lost his Massachusetts license as a CPA. I didn't know that. I thought he was still certified and could jump back into the field anytime. He also has some sort of judgment from a lawsuit pending in Florida. That had to do with a business breaking up. I think his partners are still trying to sue him for money they say he owes. The police say he's been known under several other names . . . I can't even remember them," she confessed. "I was so upset, I just blanked out at that part. And he'd always told me that this was his second marriage. But it's actually his third," she added.

She sighed again and sat back in her chair, fiddling with her wineglass. Maggie sensed that revealing Ben's dirty laundry was embarrassing for Ellie. She could understand that, but she thought her friend really needn't feel that way.

"That is a lot to take in at once. And you had no idea of any of this?" Dana asked.

Ellie shook her head. "No, I didn't. I felt so . . . betrayed. As if I married a stranger. Especially when I heard about the fake names. I felt as if I were some sort of colossal dummy or just hopelessly gullible. It's so embarrassing."

Ellie's eyes were getting teary. Maggie didn't want to see her cry but knew that there was no way to change the topic of conversation. Now that they had waded into this river, they had to swim through it.

Dana reached over and touched her hand. "Don't blame

208 / Anne Canadeo

yourself, Ellie. You did nothing wrong. He should have been honest with you. Did he deny these things were true?"

"No, he didn't. He tried to explain things to me. But I was too angry to listen. I felt like I couldn't believe anything he told me. It made me doubt myself, my own judgment in marrying him. Maybe we didn't know each other long enough. Maybe I was just too eager to get married again. I think he knew that and knew how to say all the right things to win me over."

Maggie's heart went out to her. Ellie felt betrayed by the person closest to her in the whole world. No wonder she had trouble hearing out his explanations.

"How long did you know Ben before you got married? I don't think you ever told me," Dana said.

"About six months. That's not very long, I know. But we told ourselves that we were mature, at a certain stage in life, and we knew what we wanted. We didn't have to wait."

Maggie could understand that. If she met someone and fell in love at this point in her life, she would feel the same way. "How did you meet?" Maggie asked.

Ellie glanced at her. She hesitated before answering. "An Internet dating site. HappilyEverAfter.com. They claim to have made the most matches that result in marriage." She rolled her eyes. "I guess their questionnaire didn't have a section for Ben to describe the shady side of his past."

"I guess he could blame it on that," Maggie said. "Did he explain why he hid all that from you?"

They were done with their dinner, and Ellie picked up the dishes and brought them to the sink. "He said he was afraid that he'd lose me. He thought I was so successful with my business without taking any shortcuts. He didn't want me to think that he wasn't at my level."

Dana cocked her head to the side. "That sounds plausible."

Maggie agreed. "It's something a man might say."

"He claims that he's changed completely and he didn't want me to judge him from his old, bad habits. He thought when we married it would be a fresh start for him and I would be a good role model."

"What do you think now?" Dana asked quietly.

Ellie walked back to the table and wiped it off. "I think he was just trying to talk his way out of it by flattering me . . ." She sighed and hung her head a moment. "Honestly, I don't know what to think. Obviously, he's not the most forthright man in the world. He's walked a fine line but never really broken the law. Even if he wasn't the most scrupulous businessman, it still doesn't mean he killed Justin Ridley. I think the police are just trying to scare him by throwing all this up in his face."

Maggie could tell from her tone that she was mad at her husband and had even lost trust in him. But she still loved him and believed he was innocent. And that's what really counted after all, wasn't it?

Dana nodded thoughtfully. "I think you're right. They can't use any of this in court. They obviously don't have any concrete evidence linking Ben to Ridley's murder, or you would have heard about it by now."

Dana's reply was not entirely reassuring. Maggie almost heard the words she'd left out: ". . . or they would have arrested him by now."

Ellie must have heard the words, too. "This can't go to

court, Dana. I don't think I could stand it. I don't think our marriage could hold up under that pressure."

Ellie started crying and covered her face with her hands. Maggie felt so bad for her. She didn't know what to say.

Dana stood up and put her arm around Ellie's shoulder. "Ellie, please don't cry. You're under so much stress right now. It's hard to keep things in perspective."

"I know but . . . it wasn't smart of Ben to just take off like that. The police told him not to leave town without telling them. What if he's so scared that he does something stupid, like drive up to Canada and cross the border? He may never be able to come back," she said, launching into a fresh bout of sobs.

"Did he tell you that he might do that?" Dana was trying hard to hide the note of alarm in her voice, Maggie thought, but she was not entirely successful.

Ellie nodded sadly. "He did, when we were arguing. He was angry and tired of being questioned and accused. It was just an offhand remark. Almost a threat, I thought. Now I'm really worried."

Maggie didn't blame her. A desperate act like that was practically an admission of guilt. The police would think so, anyway.

Dana spoke quietly and tried to catch Ellie's glance. "He was probably just blowing off steam. Let's hope he has more sense than that."

Ellie nodded. She wiped her eyes, took a deep breath, and seemed a bit calmer. "I have a nice pie for dessert. Let me get it." She walked over to the sideboard and carried a very pretty pie with a golden lattice crust back to the table.

"Dot made this pie," Ellie said as she set it on the table.

"She brought it over this afternoon. After Ben left. She said she'd found a few apples hiding out in the branches, trying not to get picked. These were the really clever ones." The description made Ellie smile—for maybe the first time that evening, Maggie realized. "I promised to save her a piece. She won't be back until tomorrow morning. Anyone want coffee or tea?"

Maggie and Dana both wanted tea, and Ellie went over to the sink to fill a kettle.

"We saw Dot when we got here," Dana said. "She's a home health aide someplace?"

"She works for a woman who lives nearby, Elizabeth Foley. She's an invalid, with multiple sclerosis. A few other aides come and go. Dot isn't her only help, but she seems to be Mrs. Foley's favorite. Dot works there about ten or twelve hours a week. It depends on Mrs. Foley's condition and how much she needs her."

Ellie set the kettle on the stove and turned on the gas burner, then opened a cupboard and took out three dishes and mugs.

"Dot has a lot of energy for a woman her age, doesn't she?" Dana said.

"Oh, she's remarkable. I don't know what we would have done without her. When we bought the place, we ran an ad to rent the cottage, but we also needed some help with the animals and running the orchard. Especially during the picking season. Dot couldn't really afford the rent we were asking, but she's lived on farms her whole life, so it all fell into place."

"That was lucky," Maggie remarked.

"She's been a good friend. In her quiet way," Ellie said. "I know she's aware of all the tension between me and Ben. But she doesn't judge. She's been very sympathetic, a real support." Ellie sighed. "I'm sure she's wondering if we're going to really stay here, after all. But she hasn't asked yet."

"If you're going to stay?" Dana looked up at Ellie. Maggie felt surprised by the comment, too. "Are you and Ben talking about selling the farm?"

Ellie took a creamer and sugar bowl out of the cupboard. She glanced at Dana, then focused back on her task. "That was part of the argument, too. I hate to say it, but in the last few days, it seems as if all this hard work, all the time and money we've spent trying to get this business going . . . it's all been for nothing. A colossal waste of time. Ben is so unhappy. He says this whole situation has soured him on this place, on the farm . . . on everything."

Maggie felt very bad hearing that, though in a way, she was not surprised. "I'm sure he feels that way now," she said to Ellie. "But he might feel differently when the police find Ridley's murderer and his name is cleared."

Ellie seemed lost in thought for a moment, then looked over at her friends again. "I don't think so. He sounds very definite. He says the people around here just don't want to accept us. We're just not welcome and they'll always make life difficult for us, one way or the other."

Maggie didn't know what to say to that. Dana didn't seem to, either. Maggie thought Ben was right, in a way. Some circles of Plum Harbor, like this farming community, were made up of tightly knit families who had lived here for generations, closed to outsiders. After ten or even fifteen years, the Kruegers might still be considered "newcomers."

On top of that were all the rumors and gossip about Ridley's death. That was a potent combination that could drive even the most committed newcomer into retreat.

Maggie knew from firsthand experience that once you were smeared with such serious accusations—even if you were totally innocent—it was hard to shake it off and move on. It was hard to live it down.

Finally Dana spoke. "Even with Ridley gone, he still thinks you'll be bothered?"

Ellie nodded bleakly. "He's convinced now it wasn't just Ridley. He thinks the rest of that group will keep bothering us until we go. Unless the police can catch them, I guess. But they're so busy trying to prove a case against Ben, I don't think they've followed up at all on our complaints."

The teakettle whistled shrilly, and Ellie stepped back over to the stove. Maggie was about to say something when suddenly they heard another shrill alarm. Coming from outdoors, somewhere behind the house.

Ellie quickly shut off the burner and ran to the window over the sink, which faced the barn and the pasture.

"It's one of the alarms out back. Either the corral or the barn. I have to go check." She turned to them, her skin white as paper. "Will you come with me?"

Maggie jumped up from her chair, and so did Dana.

"Of course we will," Dana said quickly. They followed Ellie to the mudroom and grabbed their jackets off the coat hooks. There was a boot bench below and a shelf above, with cubbyholes that were jammed with needful things for farm life—garden gloves and cans of insect repellent.

214 / Anne Canadeo

"We'd better grab some flashlights. Do you have any handy?" Dana asked.

"I have a bunch in one of these baskets . . ." Ellie reached around to find the flashlights.

And not a moment too soon. The light in the mudroom flickered and suddenly went out.

The lights had gone out all over the house, Maggie realized, and outside, too.

"Gee . . . looks like we've lost power." Dana's voice sounded a little shaky in the dark, stating the obvious. As if she was struggling to remain calm.

And Ellie still hadn't found the flashlights. "Here's one . . . no batteries, darn it." Maggie heard a dull clicking sound, but Ellie didn't sound worried. "The power goes off a lot. The wiring is a mess. We had it upgraded, but it's still very iffy. The generators should come on soon."

Maggie felt a notch better. At least the screaming security alarms outside had gone silent.

But now she heard another sound. A different kind of screaming. Not quite as loud, but very unnerving.

"What in the world is that?" she asked.

"The llamas. They're crying. They're scared of something . . ." Ellie sounded panicked now. "I can't find a flashlight. . . . Let's just go out there."

Maggie was closest to the door. She turned to open it and peered through the windowpanes first. It was pitch-black outside. She couldn't see a thing.

Then another pair of eyes stared back at her.

Chapter Eleven

aggie screamed and jumped back, bumping into her friends, who stood behind her. They had all seen the eyes, too.

Ellie pushed passed her and pulled the door open. "It's one of the llamas. She got loose . . ."

Ellie was fast, but the llama was faster. It quickly trotted across the patch of grass and flower beds behind the farmhouse. Ellie chased it to a clump of trees, then gave up.

She turned to Dana and Maggie. "The llamas are loose. That's why we heard the alarm on the gate. Someone opened it and let them out."

Then she took off, running out to the dirt road that stretched between the farmhouse and the meadow. Dana and Maggie followed, just a few yards behind. Maggie was glad she had on flat shoes. But they weren't sneakers and weren't made for farm work, either.

"Look, there's one . . . and another over there." Dana

slowed her pace and pointed to the large, slow-moving shadows that lingered near the Country Store. And another that stepped out from behind a tree.

"Yes, I see them now. . . . They're all over the place," Maggie answered.

It was a clear night, and a half-moon cast the grounds in a shimmery light. Enough to see the animals if you knew they were there. Not enough to chase them around the farm on the uneven ground without breaking your neck, Maggie feared.

Never mind worrying about how they'd gotten loose in the first place—and who else might be out here.

Suddenly, bright lights shone from within the barn doorway. Maggie saw Ellie inside, and she soon came running out, carrying big yellow flashlights and leather leads for the llamas.

"At least the generator in the barn is working. Here, take these lights. When you find one of the llamas, just hook the tether to its head halter. They should follow you without too much trouble. We have to get them all back in the pasture. I'm afraid they might wander out to the road or get hurt in the woods."

"We'll get them, Ellie. Don't worry." Dana switched on her flashlight and turned to Maggie. "Let's split up. I'll go back toward the house and the field near the road. Why don't you look around here and then back in the orchard? Ellie can take the area closest to the pasture and help us put them back behind the gate."

"Good plan . . ." Maggie trotted off with her flashlight and llama leash. She actually had hoped to patrol the area near the pasture. The orchard was the darkest corner of the property.

She didn't want to seem like a wimp, but she did feel around in her pocket for her big key ring.

She'd often read that a fistful of keys made an effective weapon. While she thought that might be true, she sorely wished she had her knitting bag handy. A thick, number-nineteen needle or her top-quality, Swiss shears would have given her even more courage.

Maggie soon spotted two of the escapees, both hiding behind Dot's little cottage. Their long graceful necks were bent toward the ground as they nibbled on nubs of dewy grass in the moonlight.

Maggie paused to admire the surreal, dream-like picture.

Then sprang into action.

"Come here, you rascals . . ." She moved slowly and spoke quietly, mindful that they scared easily. The llamas lifted their heads, staring at her with heavy-lidded eyes. But they didn't make a run for it—luckily, she thought.

Finally, she stood close, face to face. One llama was brown; the other had a light-tan coat. The brown one seemed to be squinting at her, then curled back its lips and spit.

Maggie felt the llama drool hit her face and saw green slime run down her good wool jacket. She started to brush it off with her hand, then got the creeps at the thought of touching it.

"How do I get myself into these things?"

She took a deep steadying breath, put down the light, and stepped quickly to the offender, who pulled its head back away from her hand, looking ready to bolt.

"Not so fast, pal." Maggie grabbed the animal's halter and clipped on the lead. "Gotcha."

The llama squirmed a moment, then bowed its big head, acknowledging her victory.

"Now what about your friend? That's the question."

The other llama had been watching this capture but was still too interested in the sweet grass to take a cue and get on the move. Or perhaps it was tired of wandering and wanted to go back to sleep in its own pasture. Or do whatever llamas do at night, Maggie thought.

She considered the problem for a moment, then pulled off her scarf and tied one end to the tan llama's halter. With both animals secure, she led them out from behind the cottage, back toward the pasture.

She was relieved to see that they followed without much fuss. Ellie had mentioned that all of her llamas were trained, but Maggie had not understood what that meant. Being led on tether by a human had clearly been one lesson. It was a little like walking two large dogs, and Maggie spoke to them quietly as they made their way back to the fenced section of the meadow. As much to calm their nerves as her own.

"Good girls. Very good. We're almost there. Just a little farther to go."

There was one more llama left in her section, back in the orchard, she'd noticed. She'd have to go back to nab that one, too. She certainly couldn't leave a man behind on the battle-field.

"Oh, great . . . Siri and Natasha." Ellie ran up to them, recognizing Maggie's charges immediately. "I'll put them behind the gate. We're only missing three more." She sounded breath-less but far less panicked than before.

"Here comes Dana with two." Maggie pointed with her light. "And there's one more in the orchard. I'll go back and get her."

"Great, I'll take these girls from you." Ellie took hold of the lead and the scarf attached to the second animal, then gave Maggie another lead that was slung around her neck.

Maggie waved her light at Dana as they passed each other in the open space between the house and barn.

Dana waved back. "And we thought this was going to be a dull night. Dinner and a movie," she called over.

Maggie just laughed. The orchard still looked dark and spooky, but she forced herself to focus on the llama, which she had captured in a beam of light.

The long-necked beast wandered between the rows of apple trees, moving with a surprisingly deft step. The trees were planted very close together, bare now of leaves, the thick low branches clawing at the night sky.

The ground felt soft and bumpy under her shoes, and her head filled with the sickly sweet scent of rotting apples. She felt them underfoot, spongy and mushy as she walked along. They were all around on the ground, in various states of decomposition, and more than once, her feet nearly slipped out from under her.

Maggie began to pick up her pace, casting her light on the ground instead of at the llama so she wouldn't slip. She came to the end of a row of trees and spotted her prey behind another fence, the temporary type that gardeners put up to keep deer and rabbits out of the vegetable patch: thin metal stakes in the ground, with cheap wire fencing wrapped around.

A section had been pulled loose and the area opened far

enough to allow the llama to wander in. Maggie wandered in, too, her gaze now fixed on the llama.

There were some shovels on the ground and piles of dirt. She carefully stepped over them. She saw saplings, newly planted, the edges of burlap bags showing where the trunks met mounds of fresh ground. It looked as if she'd wandered into a new section of the orchard, one that was just being planted.

The fenced-in space was not very large, and Maggie was determined to catch her prey before the llama could go full circle and escape through the opening again.

"Maggie . . . where are you?"

She heard Dana calling and glanced over her shoulder to see a beam of light, waving around in the apple trees.

"Over here . . . at the end of the row," Maggie called. She waved her light and hoped she had not startled the llama.

The llama suddenly stood stone still. Perhaps it was scared but didn't know what to do. Time to make my move, Maggie thought. No guts, no glory.

She leaped over a mound of dirt and made a grab for the llama's halter. Too late—the llama jerked away and jumped over the fence. Maggie watched in shock for a moment, then took a step forward.

She suddenly felt herself falling, through thin air. She screamed as the flashlight flew from her hands, and she landed face-first in a pile of wet, gritty dirt.

She lay facedown for a moment, in total shock, then managed to turn her head to the side and moan. She felt dirt in her mouth and in her eyes. She ached all over and could barely lift herself up on her arms.

A light flashed down on her. "Maggie! Are you all right?"

She slowly turned and saw Dana, a few feet above her. Dana crouched down and stared at her, looking shocked and alarmed. "Are you all right? Did you break anything?"

"I don't think so," Maggie mumbled, brushing more dirt from her mouth.

"At least you didn't hit your head. . . . At least you're conscious."

"Just barely." Maggie groaned. She sighed and rolled over in the dirt so she could at least sit up.

"You poor thing. Let me help you." Dana extended her hand, but it didn't reach quite far enough. "Wait, I'll use a shovel . . ." She ran over to the shovels and pointed the handle down at Maggie. "Just grab on and I'll pull you up."

"All right. Just give me a minute to get my bearings."

Maggie could see now that the ditch she'd fallen into wasn't all that deep. Only about four feet or slightly more. Just deep enough to rattle every bone in her body.

She grabbed the end of the shovel, and Dana pulled while Maggie pushed herself to her feet. Dana leaned over and helped her climb up and out.

Maggie slowly came to her feet. She tried to brush the dirt off herself, but it was no use. She took a tissue from her pocket and got some grit out of her mouth before she tried to speak again.

Dana reached down and picked up the flashlights, then handed one back to Maggie. "Guess you didn't see that hole."

"Obviously not. I was so focused on my quarry. Llama Most Wanted. That must be why the fence is here. So no one has an accident." She sighed and shook her head. "Did you see that sucker take off on me? She jumped right over the fencing. I thought llamas were a cousin of the camel. I didn't know they were part kangaroo."

They had left the fenced area and walked down the row of apple trees again. Dana put a comforting arm around Maggie's shoulder.

"Ellie says they can jump very high but are trained not to. I guess the llama felt cornered—not that I'm blaming you, of course," she quickly added.

"Thanks. I tried my best. Just not cut out to be a llama wrangler."

"Me, either," Dana agreed. "This won't be my retirement dream when Jack and I are ready, I'll tell you that much," she confided.

Maggie just nodded. Unfortunately, it wasn't turning out to be Ellie and Ben's, either. More like their worst nightmare.

Dana flashed her light around the apple trees, searching for the missing llama. They soon spotted her, staring back from behind one of the trees.

"Give me the tether, I'll get her," Dana volunteered.

"I think this is a two-woman job. You circle around that way. I'll come in the opposite direction. We'll meet in the middle and nab her."

"Good plan," Dana whispered back.

With slow, steady moves, they soon had the leaping llama securely tethered and headed for the pasture. Maggie began to feel all the aches and bruises from her fall.

But she didn't want to complain. This night had been quite

an adventure. She hoped it would soon be over, though, so she could go home, take a nice hot shower, and put antibiotic cream on her scratches and ice bags on the rest of her body.

Ellie was in the pasture and quickly opened the gate for them. She led the last llama to the flock and unhooked the leather lead from the halter. "Bad girl, Lola. You nearly got away from us."

Lola tossed her head back and hissed at Ellie—but didn't spit, Maggie noticed. She had been the only one to get that special treatment.

"I'm just going to count them again. I'm so . . . rattled by all this," Ellie said, flashing her light around the pasture.

The llamas stared back, most clustered together in small groups that dotted the field. The three-sided shed in the back of the pasture also held a few llamas, and Ellie counted those, as well.

She walked toward the gate to meet Dana and Maggie. "They're all here. I counted twice. They all seemed fine, too. No injuries or anything."

"Could the gate have been loose and blown open somehow?" Dana asked. "Maybe this wasn't another case of trespassing and criminal mischief."

Ellie thought a moment. "No, that's not possible. We had a buzzer installed that makes a sound when the gate is opened and closed securely. The sensor is part of the security system. If the gate had been left ajar, the alarm wouldn't have been set, so it wouldn't have gone off before," she concluded. "No, the gate was closed. Someone was out here and opened it."

Maggie had had a brief moment of thinking this was just a false alarm. Apparently not.

"Is anything else disturbed?" Dana asked. "Anything in the barn?"

"I didn't really check. I just ran in to get the flashlights and the leads. It is odd that the door was open, though." She turned toward the barn and started walking in that direction. "I could have sworn that when Dot left, it was closed . . ."

They followed Ellie to the barn, the three beams of light bouncing around in the dirt yard. The big red building loomed up in the darkness. A bird flew out of the hayloft, the flapping sound making Maggie jump back. But she caught herself before making a startled sound.

Ellie stepped forward and pulled the barn door closed. Maggie and Dana held out their lights for her. Then just stared.

A message had been painted on the white doors in huge red letters. The words oozed down the wooden planks, like dripping blood.

MURDERERS! YOU STAY, YOU PAY!

Ellie backed away, her hand over her mouth. "Dear Lord . . . I was afraid of this. I can't take it anymore. I really can't."

She'd been very calm and levelheaded so far, Maggie thought, but now burst out crying. She covered her face with her hands and sobbed freely.

"Where is Ben? Where is he when I need him? He should be here . . . helping me with all this . . ."

Dana sighed and rubbed her shoulder. "It's only words, Ellie. Don't let it get to you. Don't let them win. The person who did this was a total coward."

"She's right. They're just trying to unnerve you," Maggie agreed. "At least the llamas are all safe and sound. It could have been much worse," she added.

Finally Ellie stopped crying and lifted her head. "Yes, this is hardly the worst of it. Though it is wearing on me." She sighed. "I don't know what to do. . . . Should I call the police again?"

Ellie turned and looked at Dana. "Yes, of course you should. This could be connected to Ridley's murder."

Maggie knew that meant she and Dana would have to stay here and be questioned by the police, too. But it was unavoidable.

Ellie's lips drew together in a tight line. "What about Ben? What will I say? They'll definitely ask me why he's not here."

Whoops. That was a problem. Maggie had forgotten all about that sticky wicket.

Dana rested her hands on Ellie's shoulders and looked her in the eye. "You just have to tell the truth, Ellie. You and Ben had a fight, and he left the house. That was his own decision. Besides, the police can ask someone to stay in town, but it's just a request. They have no right to restrict his movements. He hasn't obstructed or hindered the investigation by driving around for a few hours. But they could accuse you of that if you don't report this right away."

Ellie listened to Dana's advice and seemed to be considering it. Maggie could sense her weighing the safety of her husband against what she knew was the right decision here, to call the police and report this latest incident.

Ellie's phone sounded. She pulled it out of her pocket. "It's Ben. He finally answered my text . . ." She fumbled a moment, then read the note on the phone screen. "He says he's sorry he ran off and wants to talk. 'I know you're mad at me. Can I come home? Can we talk this out?'" she read aloud.

Ellie looked up at her friends. "I'm going to call him. He needs to know someone has gotten onto our property again. Then I'll call the police," she promised.

Dana nodded, then looked over at Maggie. Maggie could guess what Dana was wondering. Would Ben try to talk Ellie out of calling the police? Would Ellie be persuaded?

There was a chance of that happening. Ellie didn't seem to have much defense against her husband's powers of persuasion, despite his lies to her and her disappointment in him.

This was her life, her call. Maggie was sure Ellie knew what her friends thought she should do.

"I'm heading back to the house. I really need to wash up," Maggie said.

"Oh, poor Maggie. I'm in such a dither. Of course you do. The big bathroom is at the top of the stairs. Use anything you want in there. The first door to the right is a guest room. There are some sweatshirts and things in the closet. Borrow whatever you need."

Maggie nodded and forced a smile. She could still feel grit between her teeth and could only imagine what she looked like. As if she'd been trampled by a herd of llamas.

"I'll walk back with you," Dana said, quickly catching up. Once she was alongside Maggie, she whispered, "We should give them some privacy. They have a lot of issues to work through."

"That's putting it lightly. But I guess we need to stay until the police come. They'll want our statements."

"If the police come. I hope she decides to report this right away. They could get into even more trouble if they don't. This has to be connected with Ridley's murder."

Maggie coughed up a bit of dirt into her hand. "It could be. But not necessarily. That message could have been left by someone who's just still trying to scare Ben and Ellie off the farm. Or someone who truly believes Ben is guilty. Or someone just trying to promote that idea," Maggie mused. "Maybe even by the person who really murdered Ridley," she added.

"I came up with the same possibilities," Dana agreed.

Maggie felt a chill realizing that Ridley's murderer may have just visited the farm. May have even still been out there, while they were chasing the llamas. But she didn't want to dwell on those thoughts too long. She did hope Ellie would call the police and they would arrive soon.

The power was still off in the house, but Maggie and Dana found their way with the aid of flashlights. While Maggie cleaned up in the bathroom, Dana waited in a nearby guest room. Maggie heard a loud humming sound, and the power suddenly came on again.

Then they heard Ellie call from the bottom of the staircase. "Guess what? I went down to the basement and the generator was shut off. Dumb, right? I would have checked right away, but I got distracted by the animals."

Maggie heard Dana answer from the top of the stairs. "Understandable. First things first."

"Ben is on his way back," Ellie continued. "He's not far. He was just sitting in a restaurant up in Newburyport."

"That's good," Maggie heard Dana say. "What did you decide about the police?"

Good for you, Dana. Cleaning up here is fine for now, but I really want a shower in my own bathroom, the sooner the better.

"I just called them. They didn't have a patrol car nearby, but one should arrive in a little while to take our report. I guess you and Maggie need to stay. Ben and I are going to tell the police the truth when they ask where he was. We'll tell them we had a fight and he wasn't here when the llamas got loose."

Dana answered quickly. "That's the best thing to do. They shouldn't give him any problem about that. We'll be done in a few minutes. Maggie's still changing."

"Take your time. I just made some tea, and we can finally have that pie."

Well, that was some consolation, Maggie thought. The pie had looked good. She leaned over the sink and picked a bit of dirt out of her hair. Yes, she would eat her pie and even some ice cream on the side with impunity after this ordeal.

The women had finished their dessert but were still talking over the wild events of the night when they saw the lights from a car drive up and park at the back of the house.

Ellie peeked through the curtain. "It's Ben," she said, then sat down again. She took a breath and suddenly looked tense again.

They heard the back door open, and then he called to her from the mudroom. "I'm back, Ellie."

He sounded tired . . . and somewhat chastened, Maggie thought.

"Yes, Ben. I saw your car." She rose from the table and left the kitchen to meet him.

Maggie and Dana retreated into the front parlor, to give them privacy, though they could hear just about every word of the conversation. Ellie was tearful and Ben very apologetic.

"I think they'll work through this," Dana whispered.

Maggie nodded. She'd taken out her knitting and was stitching away when the police finally arrived.

Two officers came to the front door. Ellie and Ben showed them in. Ellie explained the events of the night and introduced the police officers to Dana and Maggie.

"Officer Hanson and Officer Stahl have been here before. When Daphne was attacked," Ellie explained to her friends.

"I can see everyone is tired. I'm just going to take your statements and you can go home," the older police officer told them. He already had a notepad out and began asking them questions.

Meanwhile, Ellie and Ben were talking with the other officer, a bulky, dark-haired young man who Maggie guessed was less experienced than Hanson. He bounced on the balls of his feet as he listened to their replies to his questions. The Kruegers took him outside to see the gate that had been opened and the hate message that had been painted on the barn doors.

They came back in just as Maggie and Dana were finishing their interview with Officer Hanson.

"I think that's everything." Officer Hanson looked over his notepad, then flipped it closed. "The detectives on this case will be in touch if they need any more information."

Maggie was relieved to hear that they could go. She imagined Dana was, too. It was already past midnight.

Officer Hanson was now intent on catching up with what the Kruegers had to report. Ellie broke away briefly and gave Dana and Maggie a hug good-bye at the front door.

"Thank you both so much. I don't know what I would have done if I'd been here all alone. I would have lost my mind." She sounded as if she was either about to laugh or cry. Her nerves were frayed to the breaking point, Maggie thought.

"You would have managed, Ellie." Dana hugged her back. "You led the charge. We were just foot soldiers. You're very strong and brave."

"It was an adventure," Maggie said wryly. "Now I can tell everyone I've taken part in a llama roundup. Hang in there. This will be over soon. I just have a feeling."

"I hope you're right, Maggie." Ellie gazed at her a moment, then stepped back. "Get home safe. I'll call when I get a chance."

"Yes, please do. Call me soon," Dana said.

Maggie and Dana didn't talk much on the ride back. They were both exhausted, Maggie thought, and crashing after the rush of adrenaline they'd felt while chasing the llamas.

The road back to the village was dark and empty. They passed few cars or trucks, just the rolling, silent landscape, fields and woods, the occasional house or barn bathed in silvery moonlight. Maggie stared out the window drowsily until Dana's voice roused her.

"I know this has been an ordeal for Ellie and Ben, and a strain on their marriage. But I hope they don't give up and leave. I think they should wait a while before they make such a big decision. At least until this investigation is over."

"I do, too. But I can understand why Ben wants to go.

Nothing has turned out as they'd hoped or planned. Not even their marriage, from Ellie's perspective."

"That was a blow," Dana agreed. "But Ellie's hanging in there. Maybe they'll talk things through and end up feeling even closer."

"I hope so." Maggie thought that was an optimistic prediction, all things considered. But who was she to say? "It was scary out there in the dark. But no harm done to the animals, luckily."

"Yes, no harm done." Dana nodded, her gaze fixed on the dark road. "But I wonder what the police think now. Obviously Ridley did not come back from the grave and paint that message on the barn."

"I think we can rule that out. Either he wasn't the one harassing them, as his daughter claims," Maggie recalled. "Or he wasn't the only one. And it could be entirely unconnected to the other incidents," she added, reminding Dana of their earlier conversation.

"It's hard to say. Either way, I'm not sure this latest incident does anything to support Ben's innocence one way or the other."

"Unfortunately not," Maggie agreed. She turned and stared out the window again. "It doesn't help us figure out who killed Ridley, either," she added. "I'm starting to think someone is trying to frame Ben. But I can't figure out who or why."

"I know what you mean. The pieces are all there . . . but it's very frustrating." Dana turned to her. "The pot is still simmering, Maggie. But it hasn't boiled down yet."

"Not yet. But it's getting there," Maggie predicted.

She could almost taste it, in the damp, earthy scent that clung to her hair and clothes. And the sour-sweet smell of rotten apples.

Chapter Twelve

Maggie started off Monday with two Advil, swallowed down with a gulp of coffee. She still ached all over but went on about her business, getting dressed, going into town, and unlocking the shop at twenty to nine. She wasn't the type to stay home and baby herself.

This is the way it is when you take a fall in middle age, she told herself. It feels even worse a day or two later. She'd taken it easy on Sunday, read the newspapers and knitted a bit . . . and ignored the thick layers of leaves that covered her lawn.

She hadn't even made much effort to get in touch with Lucy or Suzanne to relate her wild night with Dana on the llama farm. She'd simply sent out a short e-mail and expected Lucy be the first to rise to the bait.

Maggie was back in the storeroom when she heard someone come in the shop before the official opening time.

"I'll be right out. I'm just making some coffee," she called out, expecting her early visitor to be Lucy.

"Mrs. Messina? It's Detective Walsh . . . and I've already had my coffee."

Maggie didn't like hearing that. She didn't like Detective Walsh. Never would. And with good reason. He'd practically arrested her for murder—and had never apologized, she always remembered. She knew he had only been trying to do his job. But in her humble opinion, he did it very badly.

She took her time fixing her own mug of coffee, put on her shopkeeper's face, and walked out to meet him.

He had walked to the back of the shop. Maggie found him standing near the worktable and guessed that he'd probably been debating whether or not to hunt her down in the storeroom.

Detective Walsh looked much the same, she noticed. A tall man with a long, typically unsmiling face, dark eyes that looked as if they'd seen a lot of sad situations. Not too much could surprise him, or move him, anymore.

"Hello, Detective. How can I help you?" Maggie greeted him.

"I understand that you were at the Kruegers' farm Saturday night, Mrs. Messina. Visiting Ellie Krueger."

"Yes, I was. With a friend of mine, Dana Haeger."

He nodded quickly. He knew who Dana was. He probably knew her husband, Jack, at least by name and also knew that Jack still had a lot of friends in the police department. More friends than Walsh did, Maggie would wager.

"We got there about six, for dinner, and had planned to watch a movie and do some knitting. Then ended up helping her round up the llamas," Maggie explained.

Maggie had told Officer Hanson the same, in just about

the same words, too. She wondered why she rated this special visit from the head of the investigation.

"I understand that another friend of yours . . . Suzanne Cavanaugh," he read off the pad again, "has some sort of photograph she wants to give us."

Maggie nodded. "She was doing an appraisal Saturday at a property right next door to the Ridley farm, and she saw the same sort of spindle that was used to kill Mr. Ridley, on the floor, in the front parlor." Well . . . under a chair, more precisely. But that was a long story and not worth going into, Maggie decided. "And this neighbor, Walter Kranowksi, disliked Justin Ridley. He went on and on about it."

Detective Walsh didn't answer right away. He tilted his head, staring at her. "I had a feeling I was going to run into you on this case, Mrs. Messina. Your name and the names of your friends are all over the reports of these incidents."

"We all know the Kruegers and happened to be at the festival or visiting the farm when these strange events occurred."

He smiled slightly and shook his head. "It is uncanny how that always happens to your group, isn't it?" He forced a thin smile. Maggie found it menacing but had a feeling it was an effort on his part to be friendly. "I'm only going to warn you once. If you meddle in this investigation in any way, you will all be charged with obstruction. I'm serious this time."

Maggie nodded quickly. "I understand you, Detective. Believe me."

He didn't look truly satisfied by her answer. Maggie wondered if more threats were coming. But finally he said, "You do your job, Mrs. Messina, and I'll do mine."

"As it should be," Maggie said agreeably. She tried to look contrite and properly scolded. It was hard, but she tried.

He stood back, and she could tell he was ready to go. She was relieved he didn't ramble on with more warnings.

There were a lot of questions she wished she could ask him about the case. But even if he did take the time to hear her out, she was sure he wouldn't answer them. He probably didn't know the answers to most of them anyway, she decided.

His phone sounded, and he pulled it out and checked the number. Then he looked back up at her. "That's all I came to say. As long as we understand each other."

Maggie nodded again, feeling as if she'd been dismissed. Even though it was her own shop and it should have been the other way around.

"Good-bye, Detective. Have a good day."

He nodded, seeming unaware of her sarcasm. Then he turned and left without noticing her sly smile.

When the shop was empty again, Maggie felt mildly infuriated and totally invaded, though she wasn't sure why. She used the nervous energy to rearrange the stock, emptying a few baskets that still held summer colors and fibers and refilling them with enticing fall and winter choices.

She hardly noticed when Lucy strolled in. "Aren't you the little whirlwind today. Looks like you're pulling the store apart."

"It needed to be done," she said shortly. "I just had a visit from Detective Walsh, and that always raises my blood pressure. I'm just working off some steam."

"Uh-oh. What did he want?" Lucy flopped on an armchair and stretched out her long legs.

"Oh, just the usual macho beating-his-chest routine about any of us—particularly me—screwing up his investigation."

"Oh . . . the irony." Lucy smiled and looked at the ceiling.

"Exactly," Maggie agreed. If they hadn't asked a few questions around town and put things together when Amanda Goran was murdered and when their friend Gloria drowned last summer, both of those investigations would have gone nowhere.

Maggie sighed and clamped her yarn swift to the table.

"Why even go there?" she said finally. "I did want to ask him if the police had ever checked out Kranowski's story about his gout and so many other questionable points. But, of course, I couldn't say a word about it. He would have found some reason to lead me out of here in handcuffs."

"Oh, Maggie. I know he's a twit, but now you're exaggerating. Besides there's a big difference between meddling in police business and just . . . well, living your life."

Maggie wasn't sure where this was going. But Lucy had piqued her interest. "You mean like all of us just happened to be at the festival when the llamas were attacked?"

"Right . . . or, for instance, I can't help it that Matt found a home for Ridley's spaniels, and now Janine Ridley wants someone to go out to her father's house and pick up all their doggie belongings." Lucy turned and smiled at her. "See what I mean?"

Maggie smiled back. "So you're going to see Janine Ridley today?"

"I am. And maybe I'll talk to her a little about her father and if she's selling his property . . . and get some idea if Justin

Ridley really had an inside deal going with the county. The way Walter Kranowski claimed."

Maggie had fastened the skein to the swift and began winding up a ball of yarn. "Do you really think she'd admit that? She sounded very loyal to her father's memory. No question."

"I know you said that. I was just going to ask if she had some plan to sell the property herself and mention the rumor that her father was going to sell it back to the county. I won't say that the rest of the rumor is that he'd made an inside deal for an inflated price. That would be a little too much."

"It would be," Maggie cut in. "I'm wondering if this whole outing is too much."

"I have to go anyway. I promised Matt. I won't be pushy, don't worry. She might say something that gives us a hint, one way or the other."

"As you're just going about your everyday life?"

"Exactly." Lucy shrugged and stood up. "Want to go about my everyday life with me?"

"To Ridley's farm? How can I?" she answered without looking up from the swift. "I'm working all day. Shouldn't you be?"

"I don't mean right now. Later, around four or five. I can pick you up here." Lucy paused and looked over at her. "Just a little drive in the country. You've already met Janine Ridley. Sounds like you got pretty chummy. I'm sure you can get her talking again."

Maggie had a feeling she could, too. She did feel a niggling little tug from the promise she'd just made to Detective Walsh.

But easily managed to shake it off.

"Okay, I'll come." Maggie glanced at her watch. It was

getting late. "I'll save the details about Saturday night for the ride out."

"Oh, right . . . rats. That's why I came here in the first place. I guess I'll have to wait on that story." Lucy stood up and headed toward the door.

Phoebe had just come downstairs from her apartment. She hadn't heard the full story, either, just the high points from Maggie's e-mail. "Too bad that llama roundup will never make it to YouTube. Somebody should have taken a video. It sounds like a record breaker."

Maggie had finished rolling the ball of yarn, and the end of the strand flew off. "That was dumb of us. I'll try to think of it next time."

Lucy was laughing as she left the shop to retrieve her dogs. Maggie spotted two customers on the front porch, petting them. She was thankful for the momentary delay and quickly put the yarn swift away.

"It was all very odd. I felt as if I was running around in a dream or a surrealist painting," Maggie summed up.

That was the way Lucy had been picturing it. Maggie had begun describing the strange events of Saturday night shortly after they'd left the village. As they rounded the last turn to Ridley's farm, they talked over the high points.

Lucy glanced over at her. "You're lucky you didn't break anything when you fell in that ditch."

"I was lucky the fencing was there. I never would have caught up to that last llama otherwise. They've been planting some new trees in that part of the orchard. Ellie told us later that Ridley's dogs were getting in there and digging everything up, so they put up some temporary posts and wire fencing."

"Another bone of contention between the Kruegers and Justin Ridley," Lucy noted.

"Not that they needed any more on the list. But yes, you have to add that one, too. But since this event happened after Ridley's death, it undermines Ben's claim that Ridley was behind all the mischief."

Lucy had thought of that, too. "What about the message that was painted on the barn? I wonder if a handwriting analyst could compare all the harassing notes that were sent to the Kruegers to the graffiti from Saturday night to figure out if it's the same person. I wonder if they could match any of the notes to Justin Ridley's handwriting."

Maggie hadn't thought of that. But it made sense. "If someone has a certain style of writing on paper, maybe it does carry over if they're painting graffiti. But I don't even know if the Kruegers saved the notes. Ellie said the first few times they were bothered, they didn't want to report it to the police. Maybe they just threw any notes away."

Lucy had forgotten about that. "Oh, right. Too bad."

She recognized the stretch of road—she'd been out here so often lately—and knew they had only a few more miles to go before they came to Ridley's farm and the Kruegers.

The days were getting shorter now, and dusk was already settling across the land. Lucy slowed down so she wouldn't miss the entrance. A few moments later she saw an old green mailbox leaning to one side on the shoulder of the road, displaying the house number.

Lucy steered her Jeep through a narrow space chopped out from the trees and overgrown shrubs on either side of the rough dirt drive that led up to the house. Set on a small hill, the house was three stories high with a sharply peaked roof, rough dark brown shingles, dark green trim, and a porch in front, enclosed with screens.

Tall trees surrounded them as they emerged from the car into dark, cool shadows, though just a moment ago, out on the road, the fields and farms had been cast in golden light.

Some distance back, Lucy saw a big gray weather-beaten barn. An old car sat nearby with its wheels and engine hood missing and a tree sapling sat nearby, growing up through the engine block. The space between the house and barn was mostly high, thick weeds, and there were no tractors or farm machinery or even livestock to be seen.

But Lucy did see some solar panels set in a row, in a clearing between the house and barn.

A giant wooden pinwheel stood to one side of the barn, just about as tall as the house. The paddle-shaped blades of the wheel turned slowly in the breeze, and at first she thought it was a grain mill of some kind.

Then she realized it was a wind-powered generator, one that had allowed Ridley to stay off the grid. But she'd also heard from Farmer Kranowski that Ridley snuck back on occasionally, if he could. Lucy didn't know what to believe.

Only one thing could be said for sure: It was a very gloomy, severe-looking place, just the way she imagined Justin Ridley's personality.

"Looks like he didn't even own a chicken," she whispered to Maggie as they walked to the front door.

"Maybe the chickens flew the coop. Or committed poultry suicide. This place is so depressing," she whispered back.

They started up the porch steps, Lucy in the lead, when the front door opened. Janine Ridley appeared. Lucy had told her that Maggie was coming along to help move the dog crates, so she didn't have to explain her friend's appearance.

"Good, you're right on time. I have everything out on the porch. I can help you bring it down to your car," Janine offered.

Lucy smiled. "Thanks. I think we can handle it."

Rats. She really had been hoping to get a peek inside. Jack had heard a rumor that the police had found Ridley's command center in an upstairs room—the walls covered with articles clipped from newspapers and magazines, all about the battle between land preservation advocates and development companies. He'd posted a big map of Essex County with Xs to mark the spots where his battle would be waged. And faces of the biggest offenders—like the Kruegers or Kranowski?—hung up in "Most Wanted" mug shots.

Dana wasn't sure whether the story was true, but it seemed to fit Ridley's legendary persona. Even if there had been such a psycho command center, Lucy knew the police would have taken it all down by now and brought it in as evidence. There would be nothing left to see, she consoled herself.

Lucy grabbed the two dog beds and headed back to the car. She heard Maggie greet Janine and strike up a conversation.

"How are things going, Janine? Did you finish that sweater?"

Janine smiled. "Not quite, but I'm getting there. I'm almost too tired at night to knit now that I've started cleaning out this house."

Maggie nodded sympathetically. "You have a lot to do here, don't you? Sorting through all of your father's belongings."

"He was a pack rat. No question. I'm giving most of it away to charities. They're willing to come all the way out here and take furniture, clothes. Whatever."

Lucy came back up to the porch and picked up a carton filled with dog bowls. "Are you going to put the property up for sale now?" Lucy asked boldly.

"Of course not. That was the last thing my father wanted." Janine looked at Lucy as if she were either crazy or simple-minded. Lucy just smiled. With her blondish hair and easygoing manner, a lot of people assumed she wasn't that bright.

She didn't know what to say now and shifted the box to her other arm. It was heavier than she had expected.

"I think Lucy means sell it to the county as part of the protected land out here. There's a rumor in town that your father was planning to do that," Maggie added smoothly.

"That's what I meant," Lucy jumped in. "I knew he'd never sell to anyone who wouldn't preserve it."

"He wasn't going to sell it. He bequeathed this land to the county in his will, with a stipulation that it never be resold or developed."

Lucy and Maggie stared at her. Lucy felt like a deflated balloon. There went the real-estate scam theory. Suzanne would not be happy to hear that. The emptiness of the rumor showed Kranowski in a poor light and undermined the credibility of all the tales he'd spun. Lucy wondered now if he had just been trying to throw them off the track by tossing out that juicy but patently false tidbit.

Maggie was the first to respond. "How generous of him. He really was dedicated to the land, wasn't he?"

"That is very noble. The town should put up some kind of plaque or something," Lucy elaborated.

"He was noble and dedicated. He was all those things." Janine met their gaze with cool dark eyes. She really did look like her father, Lucy thought again, the photo of him when he was a young man, in uniform.

"I could have used that money," she said frankly. "But I knew about his plan, and I approved of it. I admire my father for doing this. He stood for something. Which is more than a lot of people can ever say."

"That's true," Lucy said sincerely.

"He may have seemed odd and a loner. Even unstable," Janine Ridley added. "Deep inside, he was a better person, more moral and thoughtful, than a lot of people around here. A much better man than Ben Krueger. That's for sure."

Maggie frowned. "I can understand why you might think that. But—"

"Look, I know you're friends with Ellie Krueger," Janine cut in. "I feel sorry for her. Honestly. She's probably a good person. But like many women, she's been totally duped by her husband."

Lucy glanced at Maggie. There was some truth in that accusation, they both knew. Ben had kept certain unsavory facts about his past hidden from Ellie, and who knew what else there was to uncover back there? But Lucy wondered if Janine even meant that. She wondered if she meant something else.

"Are saying that you think Ben Krueger killed your father? I think the police are trying hard to determine that," Maggie countered in a calm, even tone. "I really don't think it's right to accuse anyone of such a serious offense without any real evidence."

"I don't think so. I know so," Janine stated flatly. "The police know, too. They're just waiting to find more evidence, more inconsistencies in his story. . . . I shouldn't tell you this, but you'll hear it soon anyway. I think they have found something that will stick. That will finally put him behind bars."

Lucy felt her pulse go from normal to overdrive in ten seconds flat. She stared at Janine. Maggie did, too.

"What kind of evidence?" Lucy asked. "What did they find?"

Janine looked down and shook her head. "Sorry . . . I can't say. I shouldn't have even given away that much. You'll have to wait and see. It won't be long before the police take action on it," she added.

"Really?" Maggie's voice rose on a note of alarm. Janine nodded.

Then she looked down at the boxes and the metal dog crates that had been taken apart and laid in pieces.

"I have someone else coming over soon. I'll help you move these things to your car." She looked eager to see them go and a bit embarrassed, Lucy realized, as if she had just realized she'd said too much.

"Of course . . . thanks." Lucy turned and led the way to her car, carrying a box. Maggie took a bag in each hand, and Janine followed with sections of the wire crates.

A few minutes later, the porch was cleared. Maggie and Lucy got back into her Jeep, and Lucy turned the vehicle around to face the narrow drive. She saw Janine in her rear-view mirror, watching from the top of the wooden steps, her arms folded against the cool night air.

Lucy felt chilled, too, but for a different reason entirely.

Before she could say a word to Maggie, a pair of headlights faced them, coming up the drive. She squinted and hit her brakes.

"Busy spot for such an out-of-the-way place," Maggie said drily. She glanced out her window and watched the shiny black SUV pass by and turn to park in front of the house. As Lucy started down to the road again, she saw a woman emerge from the SUV, wearing jeans and a black poncho. A long braid swung from side to side as she hopped up the steps.

"Angelica Rossi," Maggie said. "I'd know that alpaca cape any-where. She's quite proud of it. I'm surprised it doesn't have some advertisement for Sweet Meadow yarns stitched into the pattern."

"It's logical Angelica would befriend Janine. She was close to her father."

"And they both want to get rid of the Kruegers . . . for dif-ferent reasons, of course," Maggie remarked.

The Jeep had slowly rolled down the dark drive, and Lucy turned onto the road. But she didn't hit the gas and make a beeline for town, even though it was getting late.

"What should we do? Should we tell Ellie and Ben what Janine just said? It may have been a lot of wishful thinking on her part," Lucy realized. "But maybe we should warn them, just in case."

"I think you're right. Let's just stop there right now. It's hardly out of our way."

Lucy pulled a quick U-turn on the deserted road and headed for the Kruegers' place.

Minutes later, she turned at the familiar sign. But her stomach lurched when she spotted two white police cruisers and a dark blue sedan parked in front of the farmhouse. The lights on top of the cruisers were turning in slow circles, casting the scene in an eerie blue glow.

She turned to Maggie. "The police. . . . I wonder if they're here to arrest Ben."

"Let's hope not. Maybe something else happened . . . though I hate to wish for that, either," Maggie added.

Lucy brought her Jeep to a stop a short distance from the police cars. "Should we get out? Detective Walsh will be mad if he sees us here. And Ellie might feel we're intruding."

Maggie thought a moment. "I think Ellie will be happy to see some friendly faces . . . and I can take the heat from Walsh if you can. We're just doing errands in the neighborhood, living our lives, right?"

Lucy nodded, glad that Maggie had reminded them of that. "We have every right. . . . Let's go."

They jumped out of the Jeep and walked up to the front door. Just as they approached, it opened. A police officer in a blue uniform walked out first, followed by Ben, who was followed by another officer and, finally, Detective Walsh.

When he saw the two women waiting at the bottom of the porch, his mouth hung open a moment. "What are you two doing here? Do you have a police radio hidden in your knitting bag?" he asked Maggie.

Lucy had to laugh at the idea, though he sounded perfectly serious. And angry.

"No, I don't . . . but that is an idea," Maggie countered.

"Whatever you're here for . . . you're too late." Walsh prodded the parade along and came down to face them. But before he could say more, Ben stopped in his tracks and looked over at Lucy and Maggie.

"I'll be out in a few hours. Just make sure Ellie calls my lawyer and stay with her, will you? I don't need her at the station. She gets too upset."

"Yes, Ben. We can do that," Maggie promised.

"Move along," Walsh said to the officers and Ben. Then he brushed past Maggie and Lucy and headed for his car.

Ellie was in the doorway, watching everything. Her eyes were red-rimmed from crying, her face pale and drawn. "Oh, thank goodness you're here. Did Dana call you?"

Lucy was confused but then realized Ellie must have just called Dana and asked her to come out to the farm.

"We'll explain everything inside, Ellie," Maggie promised. "What are they charging Ben with?" she added as they walked inside. Lucy could tell she didn't want to say the word "murder" if she didn't have to.

Ellie sighed and closed the door behind them. "It's not even about Justin Ridley," she began, her voice sounding shaky. "They say . . . Ben has been doing all those things . . . all the vandalism, the threatening notes. The police say they have proof that he came back to the farm Saturday night and let the llamas loose . . . and painted that message on the barn."

Lucy felt as if someone had just socked her in the stomach. She knew she was standing there with her eyes bugging out and her mouth hanging open, but she was simply dumbstruck and couldn't speak.

Maggie stared wide-eyed at Ellie for a moment and pressed her hand to her forehead. "How in the world do they know that?"

Ellie shrugged, a hopeless, defeated gesture. "I'm not sure. Ben's attorney will find out. The police have to tell him. They're charging him with criminal mischief and filing a false police report."

That's why Ben had been so reluctant to go to the police when these incidents occurred, Lucy realized. He knew that once the police started to investigate, they'd be bound to trace the harassment back to him, sooner or later. No matter how clever he was about covering his tracks.

But Lucy didn't want to say that out loud. She wasn't sure if Ellie still believed Ben was innocent, and it didn't seem right to talk about him as if he was definitely guilty.

"Have you called his attorney yet, Ellie?" Maggie asked.

"Yes, I did that first thing, while the police were still here. Then I called Dana. Did she call you? How did you get here so quickly?"

"We were just down the road, at Ridley's farm. Lucy had to pick something up there. . . . It doesn't matter," Maggie said quickly. "Janine Ridley told us that the police had found some new evidence against Ben. She didn't tell us what it was, though."

"We were coming to warn you," Lucy explained.

"Oh . . . I see." Ellie nodded. She seemed a bit in shock, Lucy thought. She sensed that Maggie had noticed this, too.

Maggie gently took Ellie's arm. "Sit down, Ellie. Why don't I get you something? How about a shot of brandy?"

"Do I look that bad?" Ellie forced a smile, but her mouth trembled. "Oh, I suppose it couldn't hurt. That's what they give people in the movies, isn't it?"

They had walked into the parlor and Maggie led Ellie to a chintz love seat. "Yes, it is, and for good reason," she added. She walked over to a small antique chest that held a silver tray of liquor bottles and glasses, then poured some liquor from a crystal decanter and handed it to Ellie.

Lucy watched her sip from the delicate glass, staring blankly into space.

All of this pretty furniture and the antiques purchased with such care and enthusiasm to make this house look just right, a stage set really, of a cozy country home. It suddenly seemed so sad. All of Ellie's hopes and dreams had come to such an empty, sordid end.

Ellie sipped her brandy and shook her head. "Our own farm? Ben has been the one all along? . . . I can't believe it," she murmured.

"Do you think he really did this, Ellie?" Maggie asked gently. "Did you ever suspect anything?"

Ellie shook her head. "Never. . . . I can't understand it. He always seemed so angry and surprised. He kept insisting that no one was going to chase us off the farm or make us give up the property. Even when I would have doubts and say, Maybe we made a mistake. Maybe we should sell the place and go back to the city . . ." Ellie shook her head, as if trying to recall pieces of a dream.

"What would he say then?" Lucy asked, leaning forward in her seat.

"He'd tell me not to worry, that it would all blow over. Except lately, he was pushing for us to leave. But I could understand that. I finally agreed with him," she admitted. "This morning I thought, Enough is enough. I love this place, but it isn't worth losing my marriage. So I told Ben I thought that if we could sell it, we should. That seemed to make him happy . . . until the police came."

They heard a sharp knock on the front door. "It's Dana," Ellie said, glancing out the window.

"I'll get it." Lucy rose and went to the foyer. She opened the front door and let Dana in.

"How is she?" Dana asked, slipping her coat off.

"Not good. She seemed to be in shock. Maggie gave her a shot of brandy."

"That sounds about right." Dana sighed, her expression serious. "Jack got in touch with some of his friends at the station. It doesn't look good for Ben. They have him red-handed, on camera."

"But how? Who took the video?"

Dana left her coat and bag on a chair in the entrance hall. "Let's go inside. I'll tell you all at once."

Ellie was glad to see Dana and rose to give her a hug.

"Has Ben's lawyer been in touch yet?" Dana asked. She sat next to Ellie on the love seat.

"Not yet. He said it would take a while for Ben to be processed and he would call in a few hours, when there was some news. Did you speak to Jack?" Ellie asked quickly. "Was he able to reach anyone?"

Dana nodded. She reached over and took Ellie's hand. "It

sounds very serious, Ellie. The police have a video of Ben coming back here on Saturday night. They say the quality is good. He can be clearly recognized."

Ellie took a few short, quick breaths. As if she were having trouble getting air. "How did they get this video? Who took these pictures?"

"You weren't the only one frustrated with the investigation," Dana told her. "Janine Ridley thought the police weren't doing a very good job, either. She hired a private investigator to follow Ben. She feels sure that he killed her father. The PI didn't find any proof of that. Just the criminal mischief. That seems enough for the police for now," Dana added.

"Oh, dear . . . I still can't believe it. I can't believe Ben did all those things. Vandalized our property. Attacked the llamas . . . killed poor Daphne. I've been such an idiot to believe him all this time. All his lies. His deceptions. He's really just . . . just a horrible person. And I let this all happen. I can't forgive myself for that, either . . ." Ellie's words trailed off as she leaned forward and covered her face with her hands.

Dana leaned over and placed her hand on Ellie's back, gently soothing her.

Lucy's heart went out to Ellie. It was going to take a very long time to process and accept the truth about Ben. He was a real Dr. Jekyll and Mr. Hyde type when you thought about it. She had been gullible, but she loved him and believed that they were working together to save the farm. She'd been too close to see the truth, Lucy reasoned and now shared the guilt and responsibility for the way he'd harmed the animals that had been entrusted to their care.

"You can't blame yourself, Ellie. Ben had us all fooled. Myself included," Dana added.

While Dana held back on any formal diagnosis, Lucy had a good guess of what that might be. She'd often heard Dana list the classic characterstics of a psychopath—charming, grandiose, and definitely lacking empathy, and Ben could easily check off all those boxes.

"I know I shouldn't blame myself. But I do," Ellie finally answered. She sat up and dried her eyes on a tissue. "Now that I know, it's all starting to make sense to me. The way he managed to trick me and cover up afterwards. We bought some security cameras online. Ben said he could put them up himself, to save money. But they never seemed to work right. Every time someone vandalized the property, the cameras were either pointed the wrong way or the picture went black and all you could hear was the sound." She looked over at Lucy and Maggie. "Now I can see he must have been fooling around with them."

Dana turned to Ellie. "What happened to the video from the cameras, Ellie? Did the police ask for it?"

She nodded. "Yes, they took some discs the night Daphne was killed and after Ridley's murder. They took the rest of them tonight. It's all on CDs. I guess they'll go through it and look for Ben."

"Did you ever look at it?" Lucy asked curiously.

"A few times. Ben would usually check it and show me. Or tell me the camera didn't catch anything. He'd say he didn't hook it up right, or the vandal was just out of range. Once he even said an animal must have knocked the camera out of place. Now I know why." She sighed and rolled her eyes. "We didn't see anything after Ridley died, either."

Lucy recalled she had already told them that at a knitting meeting. "Do the police have all of that now, or do you have some backup?"

"Good question, Lucy," Dana remarked. Lucy shrugged. "I work on my computer every day. If I didn't back up my projects . . . well, let's just say there were times when I would have jumped out a window if I didn't have a backup file."

"I think there's a backup set," Ellie said after a moment. "Our attorney just asked me tonight, and I checked. Do you think something is on there that will help Ben?"

"I don't know," Lucy said, "but it's worth taking a look."

Dana glanced at her watch. "We don't have anything else to do until your lawyer calls back."

Except knit, Lucy realized. Though it didn't seem very polite to mention that right now.

"I don't expect you all to stay with me. That would be asking too much," Ellie told them. "I only called Dana because Dot is away tonight and Jack has such a good in with the police."

"I don't have any place to be," Maggie said.

"Matt was going to the gym tonight. He won't be home until pretty late anyway," Lucy said. "Besides, now I'm curious to see those CDs."

"Oh . . . all right. That's a good idea . . . but the police took our computer." Ellie looked at the other women with a dismal expression.

"Don't worry, I have my laptop in the car," Dana said.

A short time later, Dana had set up her notebook on the kitchen table and begun looking through the CDs that were covered with paper jackets and marked with dates. There were two outdoor cameras, one focused in the direction of the barn and the orchard and another on the pasture.

"Let's look at the night Ridley was murdered," Dana said. "That's the most important time right now."

Lucy agreed. The real question was who killed Justin Ridley. If Ben had some weird reason to vandalize his own property or suffered from split personality disorder . . . well, that was unfortunate but beside the point.

Dana removed the most important CD, the one that filmed the property the night Ridley had died, and slipped it in the computer. The picture came up quickly and they all started watching over her shoulder.

The footage was very boring, just blurry black-and-white pictures of the two perspectives, taken at night. A raccoon or skunk scurried across the barnyard. The llamas out in the pasture walked across the screen from time to time.

"Go forward, Dana. Like to midnight, or something," Lucy said.

"When was Ridley killed? Why don't we just go up to that time frame?" Maggie suggested.

Ellie agreed. "The police say Ridley was killed Saturday morning, between two and four. Ben and I looked at this disc the day after. I was so nervous and upset, I couldn't even see straight."

Dana fast-forwarded until the time stamp showed 2:00. She slowed it down, and they all watched quietly.

"His body was found in the meadow, wasn't it?" Maggie asked.

"Yes, in the meadow, past the big tree back there," Ellie answered. "I don't think the camera reaches that far. Even if it's pointed the right way."

"But maybe we'll see something. Someone walking around where they shouldn't be," Lucy suggested.

"Don't you think the police have looked at all these tapes very carefully by now?" Ellie asked after a few minutes.

Maggie turned to her. "You can look but not see . . . especially if you're looking with certain expectations."

"It's called cognitive dissonance," Dana murmured, her eyes fixed on the screen. "There was a famous experiment where students were asked to count players with white shirts on a basketball court. Most of them never saw a man in a gorilla suit who came on the screen and—"

"I was thinking Detective Walsh," Maggie interrupted. "He has more blind spots than an armored tank."

"Wait, what's that?" Lucy cut into the debate. She pointed at the screen and Dana stopped the tape. They all leaned over and peered at the computer.

Maggie leaned closer. "I don't see anything."

Dana turned to Lucy. "What did you see, Lucy? Someone out in the field?"

"No . . . back here, behind the barn. . . . Go back a little," Lucy told Dana. The video went backward a moment. The screen was split, showing the video from both cameras simultaneously. But Lucy was focused on the footage from the camera that had been pointed at the barn.

"Stop!" Lucy said suddenly. Dana froze the frame. Lucy leaned over and pointed to a blurry figure at the upper left-hand corner of the picture. "Look back there. . . . Someone is in the orchard."

Dana quickly zoomed in on the spot.

"See? It looks like someone digging," Lucy told the others. "There's a shovel . . ." Lucy pointed out the outline with her fingertip. "It's hard to see more through the apple trees."

"It's Dot." Ellie had been leaning over Dana's shoulder with the other women, but now she jerked back as if she'd been struck in the face.

"Are you sure?" Dana asked her.

"I'm positive. That's her coat and the hat she always wears. I just recognize the way she moves. But she wasn't even home that night. . . . She was working at Mrs. Foley's," Ellie insisted.

Everyone was quiet. They didn't know what to say.

"Apparently she got off early," Maggie said quietly.

Ellie shook her head and pressed her hands to her forehead. "This is too much. I'm so confused. What does all this mean?" She stared at Dana and then at Maggie and Lucy.

Dana stood up and turned to face her old college friend. "We don't know yet, Ellie. But there's one way to find out. Let's go ask her."

Good idea, Dana. Why didn't I think of that? Lucy nearly said out loud.

"She's not home. She's working at Mrs. Foley's. Or at least, that's what she told me," Ellie murmured. "She left right before the police arrived. She doesn't know about Ben yet," she added.

"I think we should go over to her cottage." Dana looked at the others to gauge their reactions. "If she's there, we can confront her. If she's not there . . . well, it's your call, Ellie. But we could take a look around. You must have a key; it is your property."

"I don't really have a right. But I do have a key . . . and my husband has just been arrested," she added. "I'd usually never do such a thing. But I don't mind going through her things if it could help Ben. No matter what he's done, I still don't believe he killed Ridley," she added quietly.

Their steps made a crunching sound on the gravel and frost-covered grass as they marched over to Dot's cottage. Lucy's breath made white puffs in the cold night air.

They passed the gate to the orchard, and Lucy noticed the small, fenced-in space where the new trees were planted, where Maggie had fallen in the ditch. "Maybe we should look in the orchard, at the place where she was digging."

"Good idea. But let's look in the cottage first," Dana said. "She might even be there."

"The lights are off, and her car is gone. I'll knock anyway." Ellie knocked twice, waited a minute. "Well, here goes," she said, then took her key ring from her pocket and unlocked the door.

The cottage was dark and silent. "Dot . . . are you here? It's me, Ellie," Ellie called as she walked inside.

When no one answered, Lucy and her friends followed. Ellie turned on a small lamp next to a rocking chair.

The cottage was not large, but clean and neat. You could practically see into all three rooms from the doorway—there was a sitting room, a kitchen behind that, and off to the left of the kitchen a bedroom and bath.

"What are we looking for?" Lucy asked, strolling around.

"I'm not sure. . . . Anything that looks interesting or suspicious," Dana answered.

"Something that might explain why someone would be digging a hole in the middle of the night," Maggie added.

Dot's sitting room furniture was spare: a hook rug, a wooden rocker, a small futon with a brown cover, an end table that held a milk glass lamp, and a standing lamp near the futon. Lucy saw a bag of knitting near the chair, too, and some roving and a hand spindle in a basket on the table.

"Look, a spindle," she said to the others. "It's the kind Ellie gave out at the fair."

Ellie stood nearby, examining the shelves of a bookcase. "Dot likes to knit, and I taught her how to spin. I don't think that means anything."

"Maybe not," Lucy agreed. Everyone in town seemed to have one of these spindles. They had to find something more significant.

In the kitchen, Lucy saw a small round table, with seating for two, pushed against the wall, below a window. The kitchen looked tidy and smelled of sugar and cinnamon, as if Dot had just made a pie. Lucy pulled out a few drawers and opened the cupboards but didn't see anything interesting at all.

Maggie was already in the bedroom, looking through the drawers of the single dresser, which had a wide mirror on top.

There was a white chenille spread on the full-size mattress and a black camp-style trunk at the foot of the bed, trimmed with brass on the edges and on the lock in front.

Dana went into the bathroom and opened the medicine

chest—a typical thing for a doctor to do, Lucy thought. She came out and shrugged. "Nothing unusual in there. She seems to practice good dental hygiene. Lots of floss and plaque rinse."

Maggie glanced at her. "That's a comfort."

Ellie came into the bedroom, too. She suddenly seemed anxious. "What are we doing in here? There's nothing suspicious, nothing out of order. . . . Dot is a friend. I know it seemed odd to see her digging like that in the middle of the night. But maybe there's some explanation?"

Maggie stood in the middle of the bedroom, staring at the camp trunk. "That very well may be. But I think we should open that trunk up before we go. It's big enough to hold a body," she said casually. Lucy sucked in a breath. "Only joking, Lucy. Don't look so weak in the knees."

"In that case, you open it," Lucy challenged her.

"You called it, Maggie," Dana prodded her. "Need some help?"

"I'm fine. I've seen a few of these in my day. It's the kind you pack for kids, when you send them away for the summer." She had crouched down and was working on the latch. "I hope it's not locked. That would be annoying," she murmured.

Lucy suddenly hoped it was.

But the latch quickly gave way and Maggie lifted the trunk's lid. Lucy squeezed her eyes partly closed. She wasn't sure she wanted to see what was inside.

Maggie leaned over and looked in. "It's just clothes," she said, holding up a sweater. She felt around a bit more. "Winter clothes, looks like. I can smell mothballs . . ."

Maggie stood up. "Well, that was disappointing."

She was about to shut the lid when Dana stepped forward. She knelt down and reached around to the bottom. "Wait a second. I just remembered when we sent Tyler to camp and he wasn't allowed to bring any candy or junk food. He cleverly rigged up a false bottom. It worked, too . . ." She paused and tugged at something in the trunk. "Just like this one," she added, pulling up a piece of cardboard.

She quickly leaned over to see what, if anything, was hidden beneath it. Lucy and her friends drew closer.

"Look . . . I think I found something . . ."

Chapter Thirteen

*A*ll eyes were on Dana. She held up an old black photo album, then set it on the bed and opened it. "Look at these photos. Looks like they were taken around here," she said. "This one could be your farm, Ellie. See the barn . . . and that tree in the middle of the meadow?"

Ellie quickly stepped over to take a look. "It does look like this place."

"Let's see. . . . There are some people on this page, a man and a woman," Dana continued. "Looks like these were taken at least twenty years ago . . . maybe longer." She slipped a photo out of the plastic holder and checked the back. "The good old days, when people had to take film someplace to be processed and the date was stamped on the back."

Maggie looked over Dana's shoulder. "What's the date, does it say?"

"'June 1977. Trudy.'" Dana turned the picture over and Lucy looked at it, too.

A young woman, in her early twenties, leaned against an apple tree. She had a lovely round face, full cheeks, and bright eyes. Long golden hair with a natural wave dipped over her eyes. She had a nice figure, too, displayed to advantage in a cotton sundress.

"Trudy's a looker," Dana decided.

"She is," Lucy agreed. "Or was. . . . Wait a minute. There was a woman who lived on this farm named Trudy Hooper. Walter Kranowski talked about her when Suzanne and I visited him." Lucy paused, remembering the rest of the stories he had told them. "He said that everyone who has ever lived on this farm has had bad luck." Lucy avoided Ellie's gaze for a moment. "He told us what happened to all the families that have lived here, going back almost to the time he was growing up. He said there was a family named Hooper. Trudy and Joe. Joe was a lot older, and Trudy was in her twenties. . . . 'A real looker'—that's what Kranowski called her."

"Great. . . . This must be her then." Dana stood up, holding the album. "Let's look for Joe," she said, turning the page.

"You might find him in there, but in real life, he disappeared," Lucy told them. "Kranowski said he abused Trudy, drank a lot, and one night, after a big argument, he got in his car and disappeared. I think they found the car someplace in Maine. He'd driven off a deserted dock, into a lake. Trudy lost the farm to the bank and moved away."

"Sad story," Ellie said, coming closer. She stared down at the picture, too. "Oh, dear . . . that looks a lot like Dot, don't you think? Look at the eyes . . ."

It did look like Dot. Lucy had only seen her once or twice. But there was definitely a resemblance.

"But if Dot was twenty-something in 1977, she'd be in her late fifties now. She looks older," Lucy said.

"She does," Dana agreed. "But maybe she's aged badly . . . or is making herself look older on purpose. So that no one around here recognizes her? Let's see what else is in here . . ." She flipped through the pages quickly. Lucy saw the usual family photos: a Christmas tree . . . a new car . . . a child running through a sprinkler . . . a birthday cake.

"Wait . . . what's this?" Dana pulled out a folded piece of paper. The paper was yellow on the edges. She opened it up and put it down on the bedspread. "It's a map of the orchard. Look, all the rows of trees are labeled: Macoun, Braeburn, Pink Lady, Granny Smith, Fuji."

Lucy loved the names of apples. She loved hearing the list read out loud, though this was no time for that pleasant distraction.

"Look at the map. Someone's marked it with Xs. There's one right on the spot where she was digging, too." Maggie pointed with her finger. She glanced over at Lucy. "What did you say happened to Joe Hooper? He drowned in a lake up in Maine?"

Lucy nodded. "That's what Kranowski told us. Hooper drove off a dock. The car was found in a lake, he said. But Trudy never got any insurance benefit and lost the farm to the bank." She paused a moment, thinking. "He never said why she didn't get an insurance claim. But probably because they couldn't find his body in the lake and she couldn't prove he was dead?"

"Because he wasn't in the car when it went off the dock," Dana said.

Maggie picked up the map and looked over at the other women. "I don't think poor Joe ever made it off the farm. That's why the police never found his body up in Maine."

"Do you really think so? . . . You mean . . . she's been digging up his bones?" Ellie almost sounded hysterical. "I can't think about it. It's just too . . . gruesome."

Maggie took a deep breath. "Tell me about it. I'm the one who fell in that hole the other night."

Lucy felt a horrible chill. She looked at Dana, who had closed the photo album and set it on the bed alongside the map of the orchard.

"What should we do now? Is this enough proof to show the police . . . and what are we going to tell them anyway?" Lucy continued. "That Dot killed her husband about thirty years ago and buried him in the orchard?"

"What does that have to do with Ridley?" Ellie asked. She sat on the bed and stared up at them.

"Well . . . maybe Ridley saw her and figured it out, too," Maggie speculated. "You said that he was out a lot at night, hunting. Dot probably couldn't . . . excavate anything important in the daylight, even if she could disguise her search as work in the orchard. Didn't you say that his dogs were digging in that spot and that's why she put up the fence?"

"That's right. Dot found the dogs. She was very angry and upset. She said they were going to damage the new trees she'd been planting and needed to fence them out . . ." Ellie swallowed hard. "That wasn't it at all, was it? They must have dug something up . . ."

"Enough. . . . I've got the idea," Lucy interrupted.

"And we know she had access to the spindles," Dana said. "Lucy just saw one in the parlor. Maybe she had one in her pocket."

"Maybe Ridley confronted her, and she stabbed him impulsively. Or he may have been trying to blackmail her. Or maybe she knew he was starting to figure her out, so she snuck up on him in the woods one night," Maggie guessed.

"With all the animosity between Ben and Ridley, and the vandalism going on, it was easy to frame Ben. Maybe that part wasn't even intentional but it worked out well for her," Dana added.

"I think we need to go to the police with all this," Lucy said. "Dot could come back any minute, to get back to work in the orchard," she quipped. "If she sees the lights on in here, she'll know something is up."

"Lucy's right. Let's get out of here. Leave everything the way we found it," Dana said quickly. She folded back the edges of the trunk's false bottom and carefully replaced it.

Maggie straightened out the clothes, put them back inside, and closed the trunk again, just the way they'd found it. Dana took the album and the map and smoothed off the bed.

They checked the other rooms quickly for signs of their entry, then shut off the lamp and went back to Ellie's house.

Back in Ellie's kitchen they took a few minutes to strategize.

"I guess we can just go down to the police station with all this and see if Walsh will hear us out," Lucy suggested.

Maggie sighed. "Do you have a backup plan?"

"We need to bring it to Ben's lawyer," Dana told the others.

"He has to work this out with Walsh and, if necessary, force him to look at this evidence. I think we should do it right away. Dot—Trudy—whatever you want to call her—might get nervous and take off. That would be very bad for Ben."

Dana was right. They had to bring this story to light immediately. Detective Walsh wouldn't pay much attention to them. But he would have to listen to Ben's lawyer or some other legal authority.

Ellie had taken her jacket off but quickly put it on again. "I'll bring it down to the police station right now. I'm very angry at Ben, but . . . I have to help him. He has no one else. I can't turn my back on him now."

"I'll go with you, Ellie," Dana offered. "I'll call Jack and have him meet us there. He can find some way to help you, I'm sure."

Lucy felt relieved. Detective Walsh might even try to blow off Ben's attorney with this wild twist in the case. But Jack would find someone in authority to make Walsh listen.

Ellie and Dana gathered up the evidence—the CD from the surveillance camera, the photo album and the map from Dot's trunk. Then Ellie locked the house and they left for the village. Ellie and Dana drove off in Dana's car, headed for the police station. Lucy and Maggie left in the Jeep. It was late, and they were both eager to get home.

"Do you think they'll be able to get the police interested in all this? Or will it take a lot of nagging? Dot might figure out something is up and disappear," Lucy realized.

"It depends on getting the right person to listen to the story, I guess. I hope Jack can go over Walsh's head somehow. That seems to be key here."

Lucy thought so, too. "Ben will still be responsible for the criminal mischief and false police reports, but maybe he won't be accused of Ridley's murder now. That's really why the police were after him, I think."

"Yes, I think the police were pressing him on the charges they could prove and hoping Ben broke and came forward with the rest. But I never thought he killed Ridley. I just don't think he's that forceful a person. He's more . . . manipulative."

Lucy thought that was true. Her gaze was fixed on the tail-lights of Dana's car just ahead on the otherwise empty road. Stars were scattered in the blue-black sky, showing through bare branches.

"So that leaves Dot," Lucy said finally. "She is a forceful person, and probably knew how to distract Ridley's dogs."

"I think she did it. But it might be hard to prove unless she confesses. I think she killed her husband and came back for his remains. I wonder why she risked it, though, after all this time."

"I wondered about that, too. She must have noticed the news about the open space laws expiring and the debate over development here. If the farm was sold to a builder, they'd bulldoze that orchard and find Mr. Hooper pretty quickly," Lucy pointed out.

"True. That must have been worrying her. She thought she'd seen the last of him." Maggie had been staring out the window on the passenger side and now turned to look at Lucy. "I wonder what she's been doing with the remains she's found so far. Burying them someplace else?"

Speculation on that question gave Lucy a queasy feeling. "Let's leave that for the police to figure out."

Maggie laughed. "I never realized you were so squeamish, Lucy. It's sort of cute."

Lucy made a face in the dark. "Thanks . . . I think."

Lucy got up the next morning almost an hour later than usual. The sleuthing adventure at the farm had worn her out, and she'd been wide-awake after telling Matt about it. She was roused from bed by the buzzing sound of her cell phone vibrating on the dresser top, signaling a text message.

She got up and checked the text. It was from Dana:

Just want to let you all know what happened last night at the police station. Big news. Meet me at Maggie's shop around 9–9:30? Up all night and getting a slow start to my day.

Lucy had a feeling they were all having a slow start today. She quickly texted back that she would be there. When she went downstairs, Matt was still in the kitchen, putting his breakfast dishes in the sink. He kissed her cheek and handed her a much-needed cup of coffee.

"Thanks, pal," she said, settling on a kitchen chair. "Hard to wake up this morning."

He didn't look as if he'd woken up on the right side of the bed, either. He had not been happy to hear that she and her friends were mixed up in another police investigation and was still wearing that grumpy, worried face.

"I just want to say one more thing about this Dot woman and what happened last night. You promised that you wouldn't get involved, remember? When the llama was stabbed over there? What if Dot had come back while you were in her cottage? If she's really as violent as you all think . . . I don't want to think of what could have happened."

"It wasn't smart, I know. But there were four of us. Safety in numbers?"

"Safety in dumbness, I think." He shook his head and kissed her good-bye. "See you later. Try to stay out of any more murder investigations today, okay?"

"Yes, dear. Whatever you say." Lucy mimicked a simpering wifely tone and gave him a matching smile. "By the way, all that stuff for Ridley's dogs is in the back of my car. I'll drop it at your office later."

"After you stop in at Maggie's shop?" he teased.

She looked down into her coffee cup. "That's right. I need some yarn for my knitting."

And I can't wait to hear what happened at the police station last night.

Dana had sent out an all-points bulletin, and Lucy found all her friends at the shop when she arrived a few minutes after nine. Maggie ushered her inside and flipped the sign on the door to "Sorry, We're Not Here . . . Resting Our Needles."

"Good thing there's no class here this morning. I want to hear all of this, without any pesky customers hanging around." Maggie led the way to the back of the shop, where Suzanne, Dana, and Phoebe were sitting at the worktable.

"I can't believe I wasn't with you guys last night," Suzanne said to Lucy as she sat down. "I miss all the fun stuff."

"I'm glad I wasn't there." Phoebe shivered under her black

tie-front sweater. "Someone digging up bones . . . that is so totally creepy."

Maggie took a seat at the head of the table. She already had her knitting out and started stitching away—fueled by caffeine and nervous energy, Lucy thought. "Okay, we're all present and accounted for. Start from the beginning, Dana. We want to hear exactly what happened at the police station last night."

"You'll read about it in the newspaper, I'm sure. But here's the inside story," Dana began.

She and Ellie met Jack at the station, showed Ben's lawyer the evidence about Dot, and related their theory that she was Ridley's killer.

As they had all guessed, Detective Walsh brushed them off, claiming it was some desperate maneuver to distract from Ben's role as the murderer.

"Which he was still unable to prove in any way," Dana clarified. "But Jack found a police captain still on duty who was willing to hear them out. Ellie and Ben gave permission for the orchard to be searched, so the police didn't need a warrant, which definitely saved time. A forensics team went there very early this morning to look for Hooper's remains. They also found Dot in her cottage, dressed and wide-awake. Wearing her gardening clothes, let us say," Dana added, glancing at Lucy. "She was just about to load some trash bags into her trunk, too . . . with more of good old Joe."

"Thanks . . . we get the picture," Lucy cut in. "So they arrested her for that murder, at least?"

"They took her into custody, and she just gave a full

confession to Hooper's death, which she claims was an accident during one of their fights. She was an abused wife. There are reports on file about domestic violence," Dana quickly added. "She also confessed to killing Ridley."

Dana turned to Maggie. "It was pretty much the way we guessed. Ridley was wandering around one night and saw her digging. His dogs got away from him and found one of Hooper's bones. He recognized her and figured out what she was doing. Instead of going to the police with his suspicions—who Ridley hated and maybe even feared—he went out one night and confronted her. She said that jabbing him with the spindle was very impulsive. But she did admit that since she actually does have some health aide training, she knew landing a blow in his neck could be fatal. She also had some meat in her pocket, to distract the dogs, so I'm not sure about that part of her story."

"Look at my skin. . . . I'm covered in gooseflesh!" Suzanne held out her arms for everyone to see.

"I have my own gooseflesh. I don't need to look at yours, thank you very much," Maggie said.

"That is like a scene from a Harry Potter movie or something," Phoebe decided. "Those two ghouls, meeting in the woods. Battling in the middle of the night."

Lucy agreed. "We already figured that Dot must have come back when she heard the whole area would be open to development. How did she disguise herself so well? Wasn't she afraid people would recognize her?"

"She took a chance, I guess. But she's been gone about thirty years. You saw her old pictures. She looks much different now and even dyed her hair white, to age herself more. She always wore baggy men's clothing to hide her figure," Dana added. "She was worried that when the open space laws expired, the farm might be sold for development. But she had even more reason to fear being found out. When she left Plum Harbor and moved to Vermont, she remarried and had a son. Her married name is Pendleton, and her son, Eric Pendleton, is in public office and running for Congress. She was terrified that the discovery of her first husband's remains would ruin his life and his career."

"So she was trying to protect her son. That's why she took such a big risk. That's interesting," Maggie said. "And it makes sense, too."

"Why did it take her so long to find those bones, if you'll excuse me for asking? I mean, you said she had a map and everything," Suzanne cut in.

"The police asked her that, too. She was pretty annoyed by that herself. She thought it would be a quick job. Everything seemed to fall into place for her so easily when she came down from Vermont. The Kruegers were just moving onto the farm and had the cottage for rent. They needed help with the orchard. It was apple-picking season, and they knew next to nothing about running that part of their farm. Dot knew it all, of course. She knew that orchard like the back of her hand. But in thirty years the topography had changed. Her map didn't match the orchard that well, or she hadn't marked the spot clearly. She just couldn't find the site of Joe's remains as easily as she expected."

"Could you imagine making a map of your husband's

bones and carrying it around for thirty years?" Suzanne stared around at the others, wide-eyed. "I think I saved the movie ticket stubs from my first date with Kevin . . . but I don't even know where they are now."

"It does seem very ghoulish," Maggie agreed, "but practical. Dot is clearly a very realistic, pragmatic person and I suppose she wanted to be prepared in case she needed to return and retrieve Joe's remains someday. Maybe she only meant to bury them there temporarily but didn't have a chance to dig them all up when she was forced off the farm."

They were all quiet for a moment, considering Maggie's explanation. Suzanne had brought some muffins from the bakery, but only Phoebe had appetite enough to eat one.

Maggie was the first to speak and turned to Dana. "One more question, if I may. What did she do with the bones once she found them? Did she say?"

Lucy felt her coffee catch in her throat and gulped it down. She glanced at Dana, not really wanting to hear the answer but unable to resist.

"That is a good question, Maggie. Remember her patient, Mrs. Foley?"

"The invalid with MS?" Maggie replied quickly.

"The same. Turns out that Elizabeth Foley is an invalid and does have MS. But she's also Dot's sister. She helped Dot make Joe Hooper disappear years ago by driving his car up to Maine that night and letting it roll off an old dock. She was helping Dot again, providing another cover story and, let us just say, storage for her former brother-in-law's remains . . . until other arrangements could be made."

"That's like a Hitchcock movie or something," Phoebe said. "We just saw *Rear Window* in my film studies class. Raymond Burr was carrying his wife around in a suitcase. There was even a dog digging up her bones in the garden."

"Now you have a real-life example to cite in your term paper," Maggie pointed out. "Speaking of old movies, that reminds me. Remember when Ben told us he'd gone to see *Arsenic and Old Lace* at the Newburyport Cinema Arts Center? That movie wasn't showing. It was, fittingly enough, *Gaslight*, another classic."

"Good old Ben. It seems that he was rarely any place that he said he was," Dana replied. "The private investigator that Janine Ridley hired told the police Ben had not been catching up on old movies but meeting with representatives of different development companies, trying to negotiate the best deal for the farm. He planned to have a good deal in place by the time he persuaded Ellie to sell. He also admitted that he never wanted to run the farm and pretty much despised the whole operation—the spinning, the llamas, the works. But he knew the land would be valuable once the open space laws expired, so it was a fantastic investment. He knew they'd be set for life if they lived there a short time and flipped it. But first he had to sour the whole situation for Ellie. That's why he started vandalizing the place and acting as if their neighbors wanted them out."

"So he had only bought the place to resell it. Just what Ridley had accused him of doing," Lucy realized.

"Exactly. Ridley saw right through him. Ben was a squatter, exploiting the land preservation issue for his own gain. Ellie was innocent and totally used by him."

"Poor Ellie. How is she holding up? I forgot to ask about her." Suzanne sounded a bit guilty, and Lucy felt the same. She had been the pawn in both scenarios, tricked and betrayed by both Dot and her husband.

"Ellie is very shocked and sad. She won't even speak to Ben right now. But she was relieved that he didn't murder Ridley. He'd hidden so much from her, she told me last night, she'd honestly been afraid that he was guilty," Dana confided.

"I guess they'll separate," Suzanne said quietly. "Do you think Ellie will leave the farm? It might be hard for her to stay there, after all these weird events."

"I don't know. I didn't ask her about that. It's too soon for her to decide," Dana replied. "She did say she was glad that she had at least made some good friends here, and is so grateful that we all stepped up to help her these past few weeks."

"I hope she doesn't go," Phoebe said suddenly. "I really like Ellie, and I love that farm. Maybe I could move out there and be her assistant now . . . and live in that little cottage." Phoebe darted a playful glance in Maggie's direction.

"You already have a good job, Phoebe, and a nice apartment. And a very nice boss, too," Maggie patiently reminded her. "And there's no llama herding or mucking out barns involved. The grass is always greener, you know?"

"Especially over a dead husband," Suzanne piped up.

"Suzanne . . . please. It's nothing to laugh about," Lucy scolded her, though she couldn't help laughing as hard as anyone. Queasy stomach and all.

Epilogue

hat a beautiful pie. Did you make that, Dana?" Maggie and her friends sat around the worktable at the back of her shop. All eyes were on Dana as she came out of the storeroom with their dessert.

"Yes, I did," Dana replied with an air of subdued pride. "I'm not a big baker, as you all know. But Ellie gave me an easy recipe for the crust."

Maggie wondered if the recipe had come from Ellie's former farmhand, Dot . . . also known as Trudy Hooper. But she decided not to ask. Why ruin everyone's appetite? She'd warmed the pie in the oven, and the sugary, cinnamon smell was a sweet perfume, especially on such a chilly night.

"Too bad Ellie couldn't come tonight," Lucy said as Dana sliced into the pie. "I was hoping to see her."

"She's been very busy on the farm, getting ready for the winter. But she actually had to go into Boston today to meet with a divorce attorney. It will take a while for everything to be finalized. But Ben has signed a separation agreement, so it shouldn't drag out too long."

"That's the least he could do for her, all things considered," Maggie said tartly.

Suzanne had already taken a bite of pie but couldn't help responding. "What a big fat zero that guy turned out to be. She is so well rid of him."

Dana nodded. "I think she knows that, rationally. But she did love him, and she married him. She has a lot to work out before she gets past this. It's not just signing a document. Though that will help," she added.

"I'm glad she decided to stay on the farm and run it herself. At least she didn't let him take that dream away from her, too," Suzanne said.

"I was happy to hear that, too." Maggie took a bite of the pie, savoring the sweet and tart flavors. "I think in time she'll find that this whole, difficult ordeal has made her a stronger person. And a wiser one."

"She's sad now . . . and tired," Dana admitted. "But she does seem more centered somehow. And even more determined to make the farm a success. I'm glad she has that to focus on."

Suzanne had finished her pie and taken up her knitting again. "She'll need some help, I guess, with Dot out of the picture."

"She does need help but is going to wait until the spring to hire someone full-time. She's already rented out the cottage to a young couple," Dana added. "That reminds me, there was some news about Dot in the paper today. Did anyone see it? She worked out a deal with the district attorney for a reduced sentence to Ridley's murder. The state has decided to forgo a trial for Joe Hooper's murder since she was on record as a battered wife and claims it was self-defense."

"I was wondering about that. I'd been picturing Walter Kranowski called to the witness stand," Lucy told the others. "For some reason, every time I imagined the courtroom, there was this big, ugly recliner next to the judge instead of a witness chair."

Everyone laughed—except for Suzanne, Maggie noticed. "That is so weird. I pictured it the same way," Suzanne confessed. "We may see Farmer Kranowski in court sooner or later anyway. I bet he wanted to run someone over with his tractor when he heard the way the town council voted on the open space law proposition."

"The Friends of Farmland had a victory party," Lucy added. "Angelica Rossi was on TV the other night. Did you guys see her?"

"No, thank goodness. That woman gets on my last nerve," Suzanne said bluntly. "Not just because I'm in real estate and she has single-handedly ruined our college tuition fund." She laughed at her own joke. "Seriously, I'm glad the town decided to keep the open space laws around here. But like Kranowski said, this isn't the last of it. There are going to be a lot of lawsuits, back and forth, for years."

"Just like there was a lot of debate for years about keeping the laws, or letting them expire," Dana noted. "Despite the way I feel about Angelica, I've already donated to the Friends of Farmland legal fund. They have a website now if anyone is interested."

"I am," Lucy replied, as she took out her knitting. "But speaking of worthy causes, how are we doing with our llama fund? Is anyone keeping track of our progress?"

Maggie glanced at Phoebe, who was quietly eating her second slice of pie and ice cream. She'd hardly touched Maggie's hearty vegetarian chili, so at least she was eating something, Maggie thought. Apples were healthy. Ice cream had calcium, didn't it?

"Don't worry, guys. I've got it all figured out. I think we're pretty close." She scooped up a last mouthful, then wiped her hands on a napkin before reaching into the shiny plastic Hello Kitty tote bag she used for her knitting.

She drew out a sheaf of papers, fastened together with a big pink paper clip. "Wait . . . I need to borrow these a minute." She picked up Maggie's glasses and slipped the beaded chain around her neck, then sat up straight, assuming a much more dignified air and attitude.

"Phoebe . . . is that necessary?" Maggie turned to her, feeling a bit miffed but still amused by the imitation.

"I'm not dissing you, Mag. Just getting into the mind-set," Phoebe said innocently.

Maggie sighed. "All right. Just get on with it."

"Well, ladies, I've been looking over the numbers and we're doing very well, actually. We're very close to our goal, and there are six weeks left until Christmas."

Phoebe's imitation of Maggie made the rest of the group laugh out loud.

"Thanks for the good news, Maggie—I mean Phoebe," Suzanne countered. "So what's the bottom line? I remember we needed about four hundred and fifty dollars to donate three llamas. How close are we?"

"We've collected three hundred and forty seven dollars," Phoebe reported, reading off the top sheet. "We have twenty-two items out for sale at this shop, The Country Store at Ellie's farm, the Schooner diner, and Suzanne's office. If we sell all of those things by Christmas—which is highly likely," she added, slipping into her Maggie voice again, "we will surpass our goal . . . and can probably donate something more, a few chickens or maybe a pair of rabbits?"

"Thank you for that encouraging report, Phoebe. Good work, everyone," Maggie added, glancing around at her friends.

"What great news. We are awesome, aren't we? I'd vote for the bunnies. But it's great that we can donate even more than we thought." Suzanne smiled at her friends, looking pleased and proud.

"I'm willing to keep going," Lucy replied, taking up her needles again. "Let's look at the Heifer catalog later and see what else we can get."

"Wait . . . I found this cool quote for you guys . . ." Phoebe flipped a few pages and began to read aloud again. "The anthropologist Margaret Mead said, 'Never doubt that a small group of thoughtful, committed people can change the world. Indeed, it is the only thing that ever has.'" She looked up at her friends and smiled.

Maggie had heard that bit of wisdom before and definitely agreed. "I think that goes double when the committed people are wielding knitting needles. But I suppose I am biased on that subject."